W9-CCC-883

BEDSIDE MATTERS

A NOVEL

RICHARD ALTHER

Rare Bird Books
Los Angeles, Calif.

THIS IS A GENUINE RARE BIRD BOOK

Rare Bird Books
453 South Spring Street, Suite 302
Los Angeles, CA 90013
rarebirdlit.com

FIRST HARDCOVER EDITION

Set in Minion
Printed in the United States

Jacket cover photograph by Izabelle Acheson

10 9 8 7 6 5 4 3 2 1

Library of Congress Cataloging-in-Publication Data

Names: Alther, Richard, author.
Title: Bedside matters / Richard Alther.
Description: First hardcover edition. | Los Angeles : Rare Bird Books, 2021.
Identifiers: LCCN 2020045295 (print) | LCCN 2020045296 (ebook) | ISBN 9781644281635 (hardback) | ISBN 9781644281970 (epub)
Subjects: LCSH: Older men—Fiction. | Death—Fiction. | Spiritual life—Fiction.
Classification: LCC PS3601.L826 B44 2021 (print) | LCC PS3601.L826 (ebook) | DDC 813/.6—dc23

LC record available at https://lccn.loc.gov/2020045295
LC ebook record available at https://lccn.loc.gov/2020045296

for
Sara Alther Bostwick

My soul is from elsewhere, I'm sure of that,
and I intend to end up there.

—Jalaluddin Rumi,
thirteenth-century Persian poet

Of all mortals, some dying men are the most tyrannical;
and certainly, since they will shortly trouble us so little evermore
the poor fellows ought to be indulged.

—Herman Melville, *Moby Dick*

Chapter 1

As the saying goes, the pot drips what is in it.
—Rumi

"YOU'RE JUST DYING, WALTER," Irma, his caretaker, has said. "We all do."

A poor boy who made good, now flat on his back and slack as a bean bag, Walter does not feel sorry for himself. Luck of the draw, his disease. But he does not apologize for his foul cast of mind. That has not changed nor will it likely. *I was prickly way before this business*, he acknowledges, *and if ever I've earned my right to grouse…How else could I have ended up with my widget empire if not for pushing, shoving, plotting, nothing ever good enough, needled by my cantankerous, hell-bent ambition?*

Irma is looming over his bed, shrinking his newfound picayune place in the universe all the more.

"How goes it today, Walter?" To him she's Gulliver as seen by the tiny people. Hungarian by birth, broad-shouldered, her big bones overwhelming any trace of tenderness, which, of course, is there: she's a caretaker. She runs the household of which he has become, as far as he's concerned, a bit player, the spare tire, an afterthought, considering the beehive of activity that propels his estate. She moves about the bed fussing here and there with ballerina grace despite her girth. Walter both worships and demonizes Irma upon whom he is now totally dependent.

"I used to be in charge, Irma. This is the hardest part."

"I know, Walter. The mighty hath fallen. But look: now you get to drink in all the beauty of your splendid home and surroundings. Forced to sit still and count your blessings. Here, take this pink pill."

He swallows. "I'm not complaining. I'm just stating the reality, because it's still difficult for me to believe. There's just so much amusement staring out that window. I am goddamn sick and tired of Gomer Pyle reruns."

"Try Andy Griffith." She flattens her apron. On a svelte woman it could pass for a dirndl, but not on Irma. "All right, Jackie Gleason, more sophisticated." She pinches his exposed big toe and cracks a smile. "Seriously, there are all these books Paula has brought."

"Another thing," he hurls to the side. "Would you please have the pats of butter room temperature? How can I spread them when they're like bricks?"

Pathetic. It's reduced to this, a command about butter hard or soft? *Well, dammit, I'm still the boss, albeit of a handful instead of hundreds.*

Irma waltzes about, stretching wide the curtains astride the large picture window, refilling his water glass, straightening the sheets. She's ignored the snippet about butter.

He fixes her with his gaze. He was a slight man to begin with, mostly bald, about as undistinguished as is possible for an early-ish elder. Irma rests her wide bottom at the base of the bed, to Walter more like a souped-up La-Z-Boy rocker with all the bells and whistles, emphatically not a hospital device. Not yet. She can tell he has more to say, apart from their initial joust of the day, smooth large hands now folded in her lap.

"I'm fine with dying, Irma. I'd just like to know when."

She gently shakes her head, not to the point of whipping about the thick, blond braid that forever strikes Walter like a military guard with a rifle strapped to his back. Softly, she says: "It could be months. Years."

"My whole life has been a schedule. Up at dawn, desk at seven-forty-five before the troops traipse in. Home at seven. Listen to the wife. Listen to the kids."

"You mean, you sat there, stone-faced like now? In one ear and out the other."

"It was family time."

"Be curious what Polly would have to say."

Christ, his caretaker is sounding as smug as his ex-wife at her battle-readiness. He slumps and stares off.

"Oh, I admit. Guilty of my age, my generation. I'm the breadwinner. Bushwhacked by the time I got home. All hell breaking loose there. I'm about to add to the mayhem, the shouting match, or worse, the silence, the kids and Polly seething? Best to shut up, I always thought." He takes a slug of water. Sick of water, too, the incessant intake of which Irma enforces, bad as an enema.

"I realize this is misery for you, Walter. An itch like you with me in charge."

"Thank God for that." Instantly, he regrets the praise.

"You've got ahold of God, finally?" She stands, apparently deciding enough of such an exchange, her upper hand reconfirmed, thus needling him all the more.

"God? Hell, no. I haven't gotten that far in this affair."

~

WALTER MISSES POLLY, HANDFUL that she was. She crashes the party whenever it suits her, no matter his present fog. She's a shortcut to his past, which he cannot black out and so must tolerate her insistent, electric breath into his still-surging bellows. He let her dominate center stage. And yet, much as he tries to replay the merriment, their early years, Walter can be swamped by the pain of losing her. It's as if his mind keeps touching a live wire when he's supposed to be in repose. In some benign sense, he reflects, he's already lost his mind given the recent regimen of drugs.

Oh, Walt, do shut up, she would say. *I'll be in charge of this business too between us*, she pronounced even before they were married, as she placed two of his fingers onto her upper labia ever so gently and instructed him on the rotations and confounded intimacies of women's plumbing about which he hadn't a clue, true to this day. *You just keep that pointed Puritan nose to the grindstone and raking it in.* She didn't really say that, but that's how it seems to him their marriage meshed when it did.

Without intending, his mind blessedly taking a break, Walter is gazing dreamily out the window, hoping that hummingbird would come buzzing out of nowhere and insert its beak into the tiniest nodule of the blooming lilac. How the devil do they do it? But this conjecture fritters away as do all others, leaving him a blank slate for whatever mental assault or visual distraction might next dash across his muddled playing field.

Sometimes things come and go in a desultory fashion, like seagulls weaving slow circles in search of a cast-off fish. Other times it's like the fifty-yard dash, if the drug stupor is momentarily lifted from its smothering layers.

Good man, you're getting a lighter touch with the nipple, and kissing with parted lips. Oh, her again. His own damn fault, always letting her take the lead.

I'll admit, the clitoris can have a mind of its own, she said, forever teasing him. *Still, it's more persistent and less fickle than your beloved penis.* And here she nibbled an earlobe, nuzzled his neck. Of course, he adored her to pieces. *Did I ever adore, let alone enjoy, anything else, ever?* thinks Walter.

Jolted back to the moment, he can picture as they predict in a month or a year not being able to move his toes, lift his head, command his bladder. Despite some shaking, the hands are fully functional, for now. Adjustable bed at his disposal. The checkbooks, credit cards, laptop, cell phone right by his side, as if nothing has changed. *I can drive! And not to the office but for the heck of it.*

I can walk wherever. I'm just in bed all day because I've become lazy, not immobile.

And frustrated as hell.

There's a commotion in the kitchen. Walter is installed in the former dining room, adjacent, footsteps from Irma, just as she likes it. A young girl holding something squirming comes abruptly through the door, Irma at her side with a devilish grin.

"Walter, you have a visitor. Well, two. It's June, a high schooler, with something special."

Beaming, the girl comes to Walter's bedside and places the wriggling, fuzzy, golden puppy on his lap. He sits upright, horrified, abhorring pets. "What the he—" but cuts himself off.

"I'm from the Shut-In Squad!" young June announces proudly, still holding the puppy but gradually releasing it onto Walter's chest.

Walter strains to thrust his back into the elevated bed, forcing himself to touch the eager creature, the petting drawing upon his very last straw for a tad of civility.

The agony lasts a god-awful ten minutes, Walter attempting not to shudder—did it pee?—the puppy's slick drool coating the back of his hand. Irma makes small talk with June, compensating for the sourpuss. June gets distracted by Irma's earth-motherly warmth, the puppy suddenly charges up Walter's chest with him practically prone in retreat at this point, and slobbers his neck, cheek, reaches his lower lip.

"All right," croons Irma. "This's been delightful for us. June, you're a doll to do this, isn't she, Walter?" And Irma escorts the guests out. She promptly returns to the master of the house.

Walter can tell his face is aflame, probably crimson.

She gets right to the point. "Well. What about a cat?"

"No, damn it. No cat."

"It wouldn't cuddle. They're aloof. Just quiet company."

"I don't need company!"

"What do you call me, dallying with you all day? You're more effort than the kitchen, Walter. I could just cook and deal with the staff. You could rot, I mean rest, peacefully by yourself."

Walter laughs. "You got me there. Just like Polly. What would I have done without her running the show? Like you, now?"

Stop abdicating to the foxy bitches! Being prone you can still be a foil.

Irma goes to fix his lunch, leaving him to his own bedeviled thoughts. He closes his eyes, the better to bring closure at least to the Shut-In Squad.

~

He is shoveling the sidewalk. The snow is impossibly heavy and wet from an early spring storm. He struggles with all his ten-year-old might, taking a full scoop, defying his aching limbs, eager to finish Mrs. Russling's, collect his dollar, and get on to Auntie Cable, the widow lady who presses two whole dollars into his hand each time. He thinks Auntie Cable might be crying with utter pleasure, squeezing his hand best she can, being severely crippled. His own aunt said the elderly soul has runny eyes, not tears, but still he's thrilled by her generosity. Auntie, not his real aunt who's raising him, is a fixture in the high-end neighborhood several blocks from his own home. She reeks to Walter of a violet perfume that almost stinks. She has shoulder pads of doilies pinned in place with diamond and sapphire broaches. He knows she is wealthy, the biggest house on the street, but that doesn't mean she would pay him double. He knows he brings joy into her parlor, darkened and deadened by huge, heavy drapes. She is a true shut-in. After church every Sunday he delivers to her that week's bulletin from the service—who were the ushers, the title of the sermon, who gave the flowers—but he understands deep-down he is courting her because she is rich. She will not let Walter leave, him practically pacing in place to get to Hubschmidt's, his next customer, without Auntie foisting upon him a large bottle of Hire's root beer, she knows his favorite. If he drinks it all she could chatter on, adjust her beautiful curls of silver hair piled atop her gently shaking, palsied head, smile, and come alive as if she was a young girl again. She vibrates with palpable cheer like a roly-poly Santa. But by the time he finishes his soda, answers her questions about his school—she avoiding discussing his father—stuffs his pockets from the candy dish she has thrust at him, he is reluctant to leave. He hates to disappoint her, to see her cheeks overly pink with rouge abruptly collapse into their usual folds, layer upon layer, an abandoned rag doll gone limp. But he forgets her the minute he gets to his next job.

Walter is startled by the brush of a lilac branch against the picture window. Must have dozed off.

Someday soon he will have to roll off and pee into an elevated chamber pot, so he's been told. For now, he can shuffle to the bathroom night and day. He suppresses an incipient urge to relieve himself and lies still. This state has become almost bearable, Walter muses, after the Sturm und Drang of his life. He should appreciate this "final resting place." What will he ever know of a grave, ashes, memorial service, or a wake? This is it. *All the stuff of my life,* Walter thinks, *has been crammed into one of those Cuisinarts and pulsed into puree. I'm blended in, no more me. No more strained silence with those kids, no more attempting to make sense of surly Paula and sour Gavin—mumbling incoherently if I did speak up. Even after Polly was gone, she the family CEO, no quibbles there, she had a way of presiding in absentia. As visitors, Paula and Gavin, long since adults on their own, plus others, come and go. I wish that were so with all my lingering confounded judgments, disgust over Gavin, bossy invective from Paula—why can't all that just go up in smoke?*

~

Irma squats on the armrest of the big upholstered chair while Walter sucks at his beef broth with limp noodles. He pauses.

"All these blasted memories, Irma. Like I'm facing a firing squad. The family..."

"Not to worry, Walter. With so much time on your hands. Go on, give 'em hell, at least in your own mind. Get it out of your system. You'll feel better."

"Regurgitating all the crap. Who needs it?"

"You do. Trust me, you do."

He nods. Once again, the lady knows best.

~

Walter became an orphan, sort of, when he was six. His mother and older sister, his only sibling, were killed in a car crash, breezing through a red light. A flask was on the seat between them, the backseat littered with bottles and beer cans, easier for her, Walter figures in retrospect, than dealing with their flat already crammed to the hilt with junk. His father supposedly worked on construction crews, but spent every night at some casino. Horses, Walter was told by his aunt who was really a foster parent; there was no regular family for him like the kids in school. But Aunt Peg had more than her share of work dealing with three foster babies—she was paid for doing this—and four druggie teenagers apparently long before authorities kept a close tab on this stuff. The teens ignored him, so Walter, by nine and ten, found plenty of action at odd jobs after school. Little time or interest in having fun. One thing, though, was the newfangled television, which shut everybody up, enthralled. The rag-tag household would gather in front of the four-inch-thick plastic bubble rigged over the miniscule screen to enlarge the image to a full foot wide. They all howled with tears over deadpan Groucho Marx, outrageous Milton Berle, side-splitting Sid Caesar and Imogene Coca. But it was dashing, icy-cool Steve Allen and his luscious wife, Jayne Meadows, that implanted seeds into the marrow of Walter's grammar school bones. Thanks to the suave Steve Allens, belly laughs aside, there was laid out the serious and beckoning path from which Walter was never to waver.

It's been over a year since Walter was told he would have another year, maybe two or three, no way of knowing. Like Parkinson's, but not in fact. Like MSA—Multiple Systems Atrophy—but he was not entirely following that course either, other than the very gradual and inevitable deterioration of his nerves, muscles, organs—everything will go but his brain. There is no cure, came the simple statement. He was satisfied with the initial neurologist but Paula demanded second and third opinions. He gave it his best shot for a while, despite his total lack of interest, doing leg lifts, calf raises, arm curls to stimulate his low blood pressure, to maintain a modicum of strength. Bullied by medical types let alone his daughter, he lacked the gumption to resist. But this is not me, Walter concluded. He never exercised. He did watch what he ate. Seven almonds, he counted them out, instead of a fistful. Small portions, he is not a big man. Sip his expensive wines, knowing what they cost. Never swill! His extensive wine cellar, well, it was primarily an investment. This he relates to. After Polly, there were never any friends in his scene. Mostly, the wines accumulated, like his money.

For ages before it became official, he would drop an iron skillet. *At least it missed my foot. Some aches and pains. Hell, who doesn't have them at my age?* Forgetting if he'd already seen that episode of *Murder, She Wrote. Probably forgettable. More likely, I'm losing it there, too.* Tripping and falling backward. Yet again. He simply did not want to be bothered, going to a doctor. And so it went for many a moon. Until now, sequestered, quiet, no decisions, no one to bug him except Irma, whom in truth he empowers to be sergeant-at-arms. *Fine with me*, thinks Walter, nodding off in mid-afternoon, no pain, no worries, and napping guilt-free.

Hello, Walt. Will here. Walter opens his eyes. Clouds the color of ash are obscuring his bay-window view.

Who invited you? Okay. We were equal partners, Will and Walt, until…

Until you saw otherwise, Walt.

It wasn't me. It was your drink. Your all-consuming divorce. Whatever. Let sleeping dogs…I am a sleeping dog, Will, in case you bother to notice.

I was the brains of the business, Walt. You were the rock, never your hand left the wheel.

Ever presiding at meetings, ready to commence ten minutes prior. Terrorized everybody into following suit.

I was the co-owner, my turn at the helm. Yes, it was your wild imagination, Will, your ideas for the products in the first place. I made it happen. We each did our thing, until…

Yes, Walt. We all know. I gave Sandra everything to get rid of her. I ran debts up the yin-yang. Bought myself a mansion, too, squandered whatever was left on the kids…

…until you were no longer functioning as an equal partner, let alone a major employee.

No, Walt. That's your face-saving scenario. I say, until you struck like a stealthy snake and instigated the series of loans, boxing me deeper into debt when the only outcome, the only logical option left for me—logical is your middle name—was for you to buy me out and…

…let me sail solo and hardly coast but magnify all the inherent opportunity…

…to capitalize on my brainpower, my God-given marketing savvy…

…the formula that worked, Will, and simply needed elbow room, without your bullheaded interference for the enterprise to really flourish…

…and make your killing, la-de-da, without so much as a dollar of restitution when you sold…

…you weren't speaking to me. I offered…

…lip service…

…you were so drunk and beyond hope at this point…

…you never touched a drop, Walt. Never lost control.

Somebody had to be.

Well, my dropping dead a few years later left you free and clear.

Walter leaves a pause. *Fuck off, Will. You did your thing, then you threw in the towel.*

You grabbed the stocks. All those shifty legal shenanigans. Behind my back.

You'd always begged me to handle all those boring details.

It's too late. You left me nothing.

We were equal partners at the start. It was never in my power to ruin your life.

Really? Equal? I came to you with multiple talents. You had one. Dead ringer for a manager. Dime a dozen.

Yes, Will. You were the extraordinary salesman, dreamer, infectious personality, mechanical engineer, power player, negotiator, blessed with unbridled energy, womanizer, party boy. I was nothing but a dolt.

At least give me credit for that—my latching on to an even keel.

~

THE BED LINENS HAVE been changed. The next dosage of drugs is at the ready. Who did this? Paula? Is she still here or am I making that up? The dopamine, aptly named, is not working—the latest attempt to restore coordination. They said drugs have never been effective for this, but worth a try. More chemicals at the ready. Don't I already have enough, my bloody switchboard gone berserk…Has Irma wanted to fix lunch but been hesitant to wake me? Irma, forever hovering, damnable much of the time.

Walter adjusts to being contained in only one room now, first floor of course, formerly the beautiful dining room with its soporific, becalming evergreen walls punctuated by handsome ivory crown moldings and chair rails. Did he pay attention to the Williamsburg-inspired layout and filigree of this impeccably crafted neocolonial as they evolved? Apparently not. The two hundred and twenty acres, yes, of those he was acutely aware. He took pride, briefly, paying cash and acknowledging he was, as is said, officially lord of a manor. At this instance he is entranced by a sudden streak of sunlight igniting a shock of lilac in full bloom. However many shades of purple might there be? Violet to inky blue and back again. Is this what painters are all about? When they plunge into their palette do they have a particular, borderline bluish-violet in mind, or is it just a stroke of their genius, another of the million pokes before and after each particular one? Something he's certainly never thought about. The sunshine hides and snaps shut this line of reflection, shifting Walter to the bedside stack of checkbooks. Now here's some food for thought. What to make of it all. He has no debt, of course. The will and legal things are long since in order. And yet, and yet, this mountain of cash…

With Paula he damn well better remain sharp as a sword.

~

WALTER HAD ACED JUNIOR college working full-time in the school cafeteria, and got a full scholarship for his last two years at the state university. He recalls having to work part-time in the loud, grubby printing office—he'd never not worked, it was no big deal. He almost felt sorry for the preppies and kids from the right side of the tracks. It was as if they didn't have a clue of what makes the world go around. As for making a killing? They were way too nice.

Irma hesitates before removing his dinner tray. She closes the curtain, readies the bed-stand pitcher with a clean glass. Amazing, Walter considers, Irma practically pirouetting about the spacious room as if she's really happy, as if she's doing a little dance.

"You're an unusual woman, Irma. All you've ever told me is you left Hungary in your late teens and connected with relatives in Wisconsin. You must have so much history before you landed here."

"I just work, for others. That's enough for me. I love to cook. Knowing all you've been through, Walter, I feel a lucky woman. My life is simple. You're a mess. Just tending you here and now is a full-time job. Steady income, I don't have to think about myself. I think I've got it easy."

"I should reduce your pay."

With a straight face she responds: "No longer your business. If anybody, your daughter Paula's my boss. But frankly, it's me who tells her what's going on, the latest from the doctors and nurses. She's got enough on her plate—her company, divorce, the kids. She keeps wanting to give me a raise as you decline and need more help. I've told her that's not necessary. I already live here, in the lap of luxury. I'm sorry you can't seem to enjoy it anymore." She halts.

"I'm glad you feel that way. I know I can be miserable—like a perpetual adolescent."

"You said it, Walter, not me." Her arms, which have been akimbo, flop now to her sides. End of therapy session. "That self-assessment will keep you out of trouble for the time being, mulling that one over. Perpetual adolescent. I get a kick out of you, Walter. I never raised a kid of my own. You're the closest thing."

"That's good. Because I'll never grow up. Have run out of time for that."

Irma bustles off. Suddenly Walter resents these niceties. What about replacing her with a manservant, humorless, perfunctory, Walter considers. One less dominatrix to deal with, given his fragile state…

Yes indeed, Walter. Your pockets are bulging today! exclaims the lovely red-headed lady cashier at the local bank—an easy, ten-minute bike ride. She is Irish, like his foster-mother Aunt Peg, but this woman has the biggest smile, at least when he is next in line. He unearths his latest treasure, two whole wads of bills. *I'd have even more*, he says, *since Auntie Cable and Dr. Altmann and Mrs. Haas paid me extra for raking the leaves before mowing. Boy, oh boy, this account of yours is really coming along!* she gushes and winks, exaggerating her dimples. As she does her desk work, Walter is bursting head to toes with that amazing sensation, like pins-and-needles but as a thrill. He loves the ever-creeping-upward total amount, nesting safely in the booklet no one in his house knows anything about. The cashier hands him the booklet with another huge smile. He fits it into a front pocket of his dungarees, roomy those days, before hopping onto his bike. He furiously peddles home, even faster than the trip downtown, even though the road back home is all uphill.

Chapter 2

The loose hair strands of a beautiful woman
don't have to be combed.

WALTER HAS STARTED TO keep track of the indeterminate variety of birds fluttering outside his window. Irma gave him a guide "to occupy you in a more positive way than grumbling about your kids. Who are no longer kids, I have to remind you." He refused the offer of installing a bird feeder. "Ruckus, I don't need," he told her flat-out, a rare occasion of his presiding. Normally it was easier to do what he was told, especially by a bossy woman with whom he somehow lacked her language, which left him stumped for a cogent rebuttal. More and more he gazes stupefied out the window, maybe to avoid her, him in the cell, mute and cowering, determined not to provoke his jailer. He recollects the recent flowering shrubs of spring—lilac, forsythia, even some peonies along the edge. But for the most part, the slice of yard he can view is overly groomed lawn, foundation plants, some larger material—American high-bush cranberry, he thinks if he's not mistaken, which he likely is, addled with meds. All this formal stuff is now a big green blur. Irma suggested planting a summer flower garden that he could see, but Walter emphatically declined, and she dropped the subject. "Too fussy," he had snapped. He was turned off by the carnival of colors he thought would shout for him to notice when his preference was becoming for everything to be simpler, and serene. He remembers the off-putting spiky red salvia once bordering the driveway, favored by Polly. Fire-engine red like her lipstick. Drove him nuts, the salvia, not her lipstick. After she was gone, he told Bruce, the head yardman, he thought the salvia "too noisy," and had it replaced with the groundcover pachysandra, much easier on the eye. Little things like this could be irritants, unlike at the business he ran seamless as a fine Swiss watch. At the domestic arts, as he understands them to be called, except for the odd item like getting rid of the screaming salvia, he was deaf and dumb. And now, cast adrift with unpredictable memories, often aggravating as canker sores, he'd rather stare at the gently tumbling clouds, nothing to command an actual focus, as in adjusting binoculars to a razor-sharp line. In fact, his eyes now droop, a harbinger of sleep. How grand, midday snoozing. Like playing hooky as a kid. Of course, given his being the class brownnose, such truancy never crossed his mind.

Walter wriggles in his daytime ensemble—sweatpants, sweatshirt, slipper-socks. There's a misnomer. *Whenever did I sweat?* he wonders. He'd be just as satisfied to stay in pajamas and bathrobe. But it seems even though he's the patient, this particular agenda item falls under Irma's domain, which implies that a certain decorum must be maintained. Day and night in sleepwear could heighten her watchful but often peevish intrusions. Important to fake his continuing independence even though he is feeling weaker and less mobile day by day.

Gradually he sits up. If he's too abrupt, his low blood pressure triggers dizziness. Standing, like now, that too must be as if in a slow-motion film. *Dammit, I am not ready for the walker let alone a cane Irma's pressed upon me for practice. For when. Not if. It will be all too soon.* He takes a deep breath, the better to attempt standing tall. *Walk,* Walter directs himself. *Your exercise for the day. To and from the john doesn't count.* Brushing his teeth? *Listen, while the hands are still good, that's something to celebrate.* He shuffles around the large room, decides on a stroll into the great room, the parlor, the library, what the heck, pace the hall while he's at it. Brownie points for Irma to report at least he got out of bed. *Look at this house, it's so ridiculous, the fireplace big enough to roast a pig, the dark, imposing woodwork, the high ceilings cozy as a cathedral. It's an ersatz Colonial, posing à la Williamsburg but unapologetically a showplace for the nouveau riche. Get me back to my nest flooded with light from the picture window, can't argue with that as a shot of optimism.* And he settles again onto the elevated bed, semi-pleased for his brief spin out and about, so he's not totally dissolute slouched here twenty-four seven.

Ah, he moans with relief, like a bear curled up and hibernating all winter, the rest of his life in his case. Sealed off from the madly spinning world, eyes rested along with his ever-slower breath, grudgingly thankful for the tranquility he's been granted, to collect whatever thoughts, give them their say, and then shove them aside.

~

Having dozed off, Walter is startled to confront a dozen or so gawky teenagers assembling alongside his bed, the scuffling he first interpreting as wind rattling windows. As usual with Irma and her imposing self, he is speechless.

"It's the high school a cappella group, Walter, for a private recital!" announces Irma, clasping hands to her broad bosom. "It's to thank you for your generous donation."

"I gave to the school?" he blurts out, conveying more resentment than wonder.

"Indirectly. These talented young people contribute to Elderly Services that gets funded by United Way. You're their Platinum Placard donor."

A tall, thin girl in the center starts humming, striking a note; the youngsters suddenly stop squirming, more fully erect and on stage. "Our first piece is 'God Shall Wipe Away All Tears from the Armed Man: A Mass for Peace.'"

"A mass? Jesus," Walter at least mumbles under his breath.

The performance begins and carries on, two, three more songs, Walter having to admit the music with its tightly woven threads is so unearthly sublime, so far removed from anything he's ever heard, that it excludes him, the children and especially Irma so intently focused he is invisible and all the better for that.

"Psalm Forty-Two by Palestrina."

Could have skipped the damn graveside title on that one. Is Irma sneaking in ideas for a memorial service against my will? Oh, well. I won't be here, what the hell, if that's what she wants. The kids will be relieved that Irma's still calling the shots.

"Our concluding piece," Walter hears and emits an audible sigh, "is perhaps the most popular a cappella work in the repertory. Pachelbel's 'Canon.'" The lass beams, unable to conceal her pride at the group's perfection, for which she appears principally responsible.

"That was very—sweet," Walter says to Irma after the choristers have left. He says this for Irma's benefit since, like Pavlov's dog, he knows where his bread is buttered.

She heaves a breath, as if in lieu of remarking on his damning with faint praise. "There is more to medicine, Walter, than all these pills." She purses her lips, lifts her blond eyebrows, and saunters off to the next task, content as usual to having the last word.

So, I'm losing that battle. Minor league compared to breathing and eventually not.

~

"PAULA! GOOD GRIEF. YOU'RE still here?"

She squeezes a big toe, runs a hand up his shin. "No, Dad. I just arrived. The flight was an hour late, but it's only early afternoon."

What a strange name, Paula; Polly insisted naming their daughter after her dad Paul. "Did you resent being an afterthought, instead of a name in your own right?" Walter remarks out of the blue. "Today, aren't the girls so much more than Susan or Jane? Sheldon, Brooks, Sydney—so significant they sound like state capitals."

She laughs and perches on, not sits in, the cushy armchair. "My name's never been a concern. Remember you all said 'Paulie'? Littler Paul." She tosses her head and yanks a curtain of long, straight brown hair behind one ear, as if calling the meeting to order, enough of the small talk, so alien anyway for her father and certainly for her. She also has a career, as was her dad's, of issues, crises, deadlines. But lately he finds himself oddly repelled by her coarseness, which he'd always admired.

Paula suddenly pauses, her shoulders drop, eyes holding steady to his and with lowered lids. This is not like her, at ease as opposed to on guard. "You don't seem any worse," she says, resting a hand on his knee. "But no better, of course. You all right with just Irma and the visiting nurse now and then?"

She is wearing dark slacks, not jeans, he notices, and a simple white blouse. No jewelry, makeup, never. "Oh, yes," Walter finally answers. "End in sight but still a way to go. I can handle most all of the basics."

"Thank heaven for Irma. She's fixing you softer foods. And Ana, of course, goes beyond housecleaning."

On the surface Paula seems caring but, from his vantage point of studying all the motion from his stillness, he sees her as reciting not inhabiting the script.

"I'm just in here and the powder room mostly," says Walter. "Good ole Bruce installed bathroom clutch bars but I don't need them. Yet."

"I'm paying him extra, Dad. He's terrific as ever with the garden and lawn crews. He's pleased about the additional income."

"Thank you, Paula. Doing it all and from Philadelphia and your business and the kids." He says this on rote, a mirror image of her own mouthing the pat and predictable. Not that her brassy resolve from the get-go has ever needed reinforcement. She is one person who is self-propelled. Walter is suddenly weary of his dictating daughter and of himself on the receiving end. He'd rather be monitoring

Chuck, a special chipmunk, on display out the picture window. It is ever more out there, and not the world as he's known it, that slips him deeper into a no-man's-land of not caring a whit about much of anything or anyone, especially himself.

Paula is now poking about the room, checking the supply of pills plus nappies should he need them. She examines the upkeep of the bathroom and performance of the staff who, no matter how loyal, she has said, is capable of slacking off, basically unsupervised. "Dad, you should know—the eagle-eye on employees. You did that for a lifetime."

Paula sits and reengages with her father, idle talk fine up to now but again she is upright in the chair. He knows there is something on her mind.

"So, how's Gavin? Anything new?" she asks.

Walter lets his facial shrug be his response. "I know you guys never talk. It's okay, Paula. His die was cast early on, I gather."

"Maybe just as well you're not all riled about him, as usual. Take care of yourself. I'm so glad you can read."

They natter on. She has brought him more books, further emphasis on Eastern religions and sanctimonious uplift. Again, he regards this gesture as just one more on the checklist she should attend.

"More of that poetry crap? Please," he says, but she shrugs, typical naysaying from her father, forever a skeptic at first.

Paula is petite like her mother. But also like Polly her convictions make up for her size, like a rat terrier compensating with its outsize bark. Of course, in Polly's case, in her day, it took commandeering the PTA, fundraising for special candidates, single-handedly orchestrating museum events, ballet recitals, forestalling demolition of historic sites. And here is her daughter cut from the same cloth, with Paula as self-employed gardener cum landscape designer cum old house remodeler with her own construction company now in the leafy suburbs employing fifty-some, not counting the temp hires of structural engineers, architects, forklifts and cranes, where does it end? Walter is exhausted just beholding her, dipping now into his finances with her tightened jaw. She'll be here for a few days, but with his lapses that could register as minutes or weeks. He is straining to follow her emphatic discourse but keeps seeing flashes of himself in the halcyon days of his business. But that, for years, was half Will. He gathers she is doing it all. He knows, silently nodding at Polly all those years, his wife having broadened the scope of mother to amateur psychologist, that he is projecting onto Paula aspects of himself he would rather not claim. She's chips off his as well as Polly's blocks. But he was not just a workaholic. He took on responsibility for hundreds of paychecks. Let it all go, he tells himself, but let it rest in peace. That's another thing her damn self-help books preach.

"Dad, we're expanding."

I knew it! This lights a fuse. Hasn't he loaned her sizable chunks—with no interest!—every now and then over the years? Without telling Gavin. Steeling himself apart from his son's disasters and not brainstorming some ways, just one single project, for which he could offer Gavin resources, a solid investment, a fresh start. But no. It is always Paula. Her playbook is his.

"…a sort of barn/warehouse both for equipment and lumber storage plus temporary housing for custom craftsmen…"

Walter, in a weakened state, is once again bulldozed by her bravura. He's heard she's hired lots of women who hammer nails with the best of them and take no gruff. And she throws barbecues for her team, and they all worship her as do her millionaire customers who swear by her every word. Paulie. Paulie who did all the yardwork at home, at eight years old, without being asked. Without being paid!

"…and you do realize the standard lifetime tax-free gift exemption has been raised by several million?"

Again, he forces himself to concentrate on something so strategic, accounting and tax items he once could recite in his sleep, about which he now draws a blank. Fleetingly in awe of her, he now finds all this boring. Better boring, he continues, than dwelling on the reality of her having become a carbon copy of himself…becoming angry his flesh and blood will live a life as stilted and loveless as his own.

"Actually, you have 3.8 million still available on that score, if they raise the limit," says Paula, settling back into the soft down cushions of the Chesterfield chair, one of how many scores of such with which Polly outfitted their manse? He can tell Paula is relaxed, having broached the subject uppermost on her mind. His well-being is not foremost. This thing, this bedeviled neurological miasma, virtually unknown to modern science, could traipse on for a decade. Fair enough, she, too, is bored stiff with it.

"Whatever you want, sweetheart. Arrange for it. I'll be glad to sign." He's totally drained.

Paula is glowing. She cannot mask her glee. She is a force of nature. *What's it got to do with me?* thinks her father. *I sure don't need the money. What about others? That's not something she could swallow…*

"Actually, we're building this from scratch. I know, Dad, you and Will were devoted to retrofitting deserted buildings."

"Didn't want to overinvest in infrastructure."

"You scrimped and saved. Not my style. I admit, I'm grandiose if anything."

"But look where it's taken you." This remark is devoid of what Walter believes at his core. Debt can be death to an enterprise. Expanding too fast and sacrificing bottom-line can be a never-ending cycle. Paying her this sort of attention is starting to infuriate him. She's interrupting the web of composure he is painstakingly weaving, bit by bit. He pictures a crazed moth bedazzled by shimmering finery and chewing it to threads. Take a breath, he counsels himself. Just because she's fluttering at your side does not mean your boundary has been violated.

Walter inhales. *Breathe*, more of what those get-a-grip-of-yourself manuals lecture. It flashes on him that they assume the same know-it-all tone of Polly. Paula. Irma! But to the books' urging, it is interesting how eliminating others as well as himself from the orb of his consciousness can momentarily unshackle every conceivable chain. He exonerates himself for getting carried away with her. All part of the process of relinquishing control. Perhaps his disease can be seen as a parting gift, a new lease on life. He is rooting for his favorite (fat) chipmunk, Chuck, to devour all the lush array of goodies that he can before the deep freeze. Walter's own role in the world is now no more than a bystander. *It's not Paula's fault treating me like I'm still a player in the game. It's just not the game I'm in. But I'm alert, maybe more than ever.* Thus he is thinking while partially listening to his daughter. She is spouting details to do with the transfer of funds. Next, she is rallying that the present stalemate with his carcass is not a deathbed.

"The hell with any deathbed!" Walter declares. "It's just a damn dress rehearsal."

~

AND WHAT ABOUT GAVIN? Walter addresses himself after his daughter departs, stirred from sleep or another drug-induced dream. Should it be winner-take-all for Paula? Has she ever stuck her neck out for her brother, especially given her avalanche of good fortune? And what have I done, his father? Talk about smashing to smithereens his idyll of repose…

He picks up another of the books Paula has left, selections of her yoga instructor, but still. Even if she thinks she should be doing things like this, he supposes she does mean well. However he sorts it out about this daughter, she will be his legacy. Certainly not his son.

Now you see the nervous greed deep inside plants and animals.
Now you see them constantly giving themselves away.

~

HELLO, WALT. I'D LIKE to visit more frequently, making up for lost time. Polly appears in his dream as in her heyday, not near the end of her tenure. She has uncontainable curly hair. She refused to have it straightened, like black women undertake, Polly oblivious of any fashion of the times. *I did wear my pearls and fun earrings and bright lipstick, unlike our daughter who seems to be making a political statement, avoiding the overly feminine. But my dolling up was superficial. Nothing to do with the real me.*

You made a bold presentation, Walter offers.

I like to think of it as cheerful, upbeat, the right tone to reinforce my message.

You could have been a salesman, Polly. Super-saleswoman. So persuasive. That's what makes the world move from A to B. Will did that for him and me. I hated to speak in public.

So did I. It just became part of the job, a means to an end for some donation or whatever. I was just the intermediary. It was a role I played. She smiles lovingly at him, just as she did in the beginning. This is how he has her fixed in his memory bank, a vault, airless and stationary, hardly the permutations of real life.

I loved you for playing that role, and so effortlessly, he says. *We complemented each other. Two halves of a whole.*

And I did love you, Walt. You were just as driven as I. Just in a totally different direction.

He is admiring her breasts stretching against the otherwise loose, discreet shift. However did a short woman get so endowed, he often wondered, playing with her massive lobes. Her hips and legs were perfect. She was in truth quite plain coming out of the shower, unadorned. But she made herself glamorous through sheer chutzpah or whatever would be the Presbyterian equivalent. Of course those Pilgrims had balls. Paula, far more resembling Polly than her father in every other way, was graced with Walter's height. Paula, too, commands attention, it strikes him, which has nothing to do with outward appearance and everything to do with some natural force that is trajected as through the eyes of a poised and silent feline. Such a person is fully capable of pouncing, their power only magnified by their stillness.

Well, Polly, my dear, you were brazen if anything.

I spoke my mind. When I did to you and to our children, I hoped it was an act of love, respect, honesty. Oh, Walt, at this juncture, looking back, that was merely my hope for the best. I had my share of doubts.

I was dazzled by you, says Walter.

That was part of our problem.

My company grew so fast, so many incredibly talented people, I can see in hindsight I never could clearly define my personal place in it, apart from owning the whole kit and caboodle.

Yes, it was a problem you couldn't gauge your own worth and been a little easier on yourself. But Walt, Polly hastily adds, *your energy and dedication—I was in awe of you, too, darling. You knew exactly what you wanted. Nothing wrong with making a bundle. It's the way of our world, your turn grabbing for the brass ring. What difference in a college prof aiming to be a dean, or for yet another acclaimed work of scholarship? A priest jockeying to a bishop to a pope? A little girl who loves to garden who ends up redoing an old house, finally tackling an estate inside and out?*

I blame Scrooge McDuck squatting on piles of cash, Walter adds for a bit of levity. *It was those stupid comic books I was glued to.*

Polly doesn't smile. Nor does Walter at this interlude. Polly turns her gaze aside, initiating undulations through her curly locks. *We did the best we could,* she sighs. *In spite of Gavin.*

A first marriage, Walter quips. *Isn't it said to be like trainer wheels?*

Polly runs her fingers over the voluptuous Chesterfield armchair, one of her many offsprings, the ribbed, velvet-like fabric in pale golds and cerulean blues, the quintessence of understatement. She did, despite her career of community service, develop a taste for the finer things.

Well, the children were launched by the end of our time together, Walter says, hoping to draw the visit to an affable end. *I'm sorry it's taken me to this point to view us from a broader perspective.*

We forgave each other, says Polly. *I think we knew that in our souls although we could never say it outright at the time.* She is leaning over to kiss his forehead with her lustrous painted lips.

We were a team, whispers Walter. *Kind of like me and Will. Good for a while and then on to the next.*

We're here and then we're gone from each other. I know it's the cruelest thing, adds Polly. She is starting to withdraw.

We are ultimately alone, he says before she's completely disappeared from his daydream.

Certainly for me at this step in the journey. But there's an intriguing line he keeps thinking of in one of those darn books Paula keeps bringing him, another favorite of her yoga teacher's. Irma, the bully, looming bedside, insisted he give it a try. She had flipped through it at random and read: *Try not to be a wave but rather the water.*

Wishful thinking! Pablum in those poems. Walter opens his eyes. *I wrecked our marriage. It was far more my fault. And face it: ultimately, she was the wrong woman. And for her, I was the wrong man.*

Chapter 3

Become the one that when you walk in,
luck shifts to the one who needs it.
If you've not been fed, be bread.

I THOUGHT YOU MIGHT be interested in these, Walter. Found them in a barn storage bin." Irma clutches to her chest several thick, odd-sized books.

"Ledgers? Scrapbooks?" asks Walter.

"Family photo albums. Want a look?" Without hesitating she plops on the edge of his bed. Dutifully he sits up and arranges himself at her side. "They're still pretty dusty, best I could do. I'll keep them on my lap." She begins on one. "Gosh, there's Paula in pigtails!"

He cranes over for a better view. "And Gavin in matching overalls."

Irma flips the page.

Walter places a hand atop hers. "Stop. Please, Irma. They're so innocent." He turns aside.

Irma opens another album, ignoring him. "Look, Walter. You're laughing. Playing ping-pong with Paula."

"I remember beating her. Once. The tournament was her idea, but she was always fierce. I'm sure she wound up winning all the rest after that."

"And here, tossing a football with Gavin. Such a handsome boy."

Next Walter is setting up a trampoline for the kids…on a ladder angling the angel onto the tip of the Christmas tree, Polly smiling wide-eyed, big tits pushing through her frilly holiday apron.

He sighs. "You're right, Irma. I should be reminded of the good times."

"I've already leafed through these, Walter. I thought it might lift your spirits."

Reluctantly he agrees to the parade of old photos, four albums' worth, he and Polly as playful as their kids. He slumps as Irma turns the pages, she again taking the lead at this diversion, knowing what's good for him. He's the patient, she's the doctor, the way of the world, certainly his. The photos picture a life so remote it's unrecognizable, the story of some other family, a fable. Yet there he is, grabbing a laughing Polly by the waist, yanking her off a merry-go-round. There's the beautiful toddler Gavin on his shoulders, little hands clamped over Walter's eyes for support, the boy hollering with glee. The reality is a stooped old man now shoulder-to-shoulder with sturdy Irma, who keeps hiccupping chuckles.

"There were golden years, Irma. Another lifetime. But too much happened. Too long ago."

She twists to face him. "Gavin and all his wreckage, it's in the past. No harm in revisiting when life was jolly. Then let it go. You know how they say, Walter? Today is the first day of the rest of your life."

He hears this as one more platitude, one more dubious drug against the odds of his fatal disease.

~

Dazed, which pill is which, Walter wonders. At times, when busybody Irma isn't looking, he toys with downsizing his dosage. Slip one from each bottle now and then into a spare, for safe keeping. He's amused by that. His keepsake, his arsenal of extra firepower if the pain overwhelms. Who's to notice, who's to care?

Not Gavin, that's for sure. Those damn scrapbooks, all Dick-and-Jane sunny. It was but a flash compared to what followed.

Did Gavin ever pay attention to anyone beyond himself? Did he listen to me or his mother? Of course he did. His entire life was a violent contradiction of mine. Now, Walter. Step back. Remove yourself from the equation. The boy was wired strangely from birth. From inception, according to research Polly insisted Walter read in a scientific magazine. Conscientious Polly wouldn't so much as drink cola or imbibe or inhale any conceivable suspect ingredient during her pregnancies. But twisted Gavin, the article suggested, could result from her stress-induced biochemistry, a toxic brew in the womb. His wife, classic do-gooder, might have been yearning to coast, to collapse, to have fun, be carefree instead of handcuffed to her dullard of a husband. *Polly, like any human creature,* Walter carries on, *is a stewpot of conflicting motivations. It's like fermentation. Will it go beyond sour to downright disgusting?*

Gavin is my polar opposite, Walter floats another trial balloon. *He's been everything I'm not. Free spirit, wild man off the walls. He didn't just break laws; he used them as launch pads to soar into recklessness and mind-obliterating realms. I caused him. Forget fair Polly. He's the product of my being such a stiff, more like a manikin to Gavin during his formative years than the living, breathing thing.*

Walter can go on like this for hours. By the time he's cornered himself into an indictment of his singular culpability for Gavin's impairment, it's canceled by a counterargument. In this case, he regards his single-mindedness at his enterprise as an attribute, he being the stable, consistent parent versus Polly's juggling hither and yon. *What were my conflicts of interest? Drive the business to multiple millions, no questions asked. But poor Polly. She battled brushfires from home to...*He remembers her badgering the school board into reinstating art classes after cajoling local businesses to donate the supplies. And then she was onto the next. Between crafting strategies to cope with their self-sabotaging son. At that, he contributed less than zero.

~

Walter has lost track of the seasons, but he shouldn't. He prefers the lesser demands of staring idly out the window to the ongoing mad rush of his thoughts. He's becoming a mental dust-buster scooping up the last of the crumbs…

At times some new drug can whiplash Walter to hyperalert. Now which of these pills is a downer…If he does decide to hoard, it should be those.

Abruptly, he sits up, seized with apprehension if not downright fear. Irma had said Gavin called and planned to visit. Wonder of wonders. In terms of Gavin, it's best Walter become a pale shell of his ordinary self. No judgment. Just affirm. But isn't that what I'd always done? he asks himself, currently failing to be distracted by chipmunks, the trees, the clouds. Withholding talk and engagement, that was Walter's path of least resistance. Over the course of his life as a father, until now, he had absolved himself from responsibility for the boy, the young man, the adult, a user and abuser at every stage. Walter excelled at steeling himself against heartache.

It's all right, dear, Polly said, excusing him, the man, the husband, the obviously poorer-equipped parent for such dealings, exonerating him her habit. *As long as you permit me to oversee the next program. Dr. Rosenauer thinks if he continues to…*

…and always, as usual, Walter submits to the more pressing concern, the lost time of the factory shutdown or threatened lawsuit from a disgruntled subcontractor. At this point, so long beyond his time as a tycoon, Walter views the workings of his mental apparatus like the US president at a press conference, choosing one frantically raised hand over another. Which one he selects doesn't matter. He's in charge and renders himself immune from ugly assaults.

He grabs the water bottle and sucks at the straw. He fumbles with a new container of pills. This blasted chore was just as confounded prior to his disease and subsequent weakening grip. Whatever does a seriously arthritic, quivering elder do, their making these damn things tamper-proof? Child-proof? But he hates to bug Irma over every single occasion, and there! He opens it. He swallows more pills. His feet, he's been noticing, as they will, can suddenly lose all feeling. But it always comes back and will again. Ideally.

His head along with his whole body now so frequently idle is increasingly cluttered with bombast. Fortunately for others it's boxed within and sealed with a heavy lid. So Polly bore the brunt of Gavin's hell. Well, he did his part in supporting her. Loving her. Doesn't that count? And goodness, now it's water over the dam. Irma knows best! We've all moved on, the final act of my play, a bully pulpit for an audience of one.

~

"WALTER," SINGS IRMA, STRIDING in to retrieve his partially eaten lunch. "So glum. Staring at the floor. Okay now and then, deep reflection, but as a way of life?"

"It wasn't deep, Irma. Beyond shallow. Honestly, there is nothing left."

Too trite to merit a response from Irma. "Here, let's peek into this one." She pulls a chair closer to his bed, grasping one of the books cluttering his stand. "Thich Nhat Hanh, I'm sure I've mispronounced him. But if he's from another universe, all the better, right, Walter? I know you're sick and tired of this other one." She scans various pages, and then reads:

"'*You are lost in your thinking, so you are really not here. For you to truly be here, thinking has to stop*.' Sound familiar?" She pages along. "'*You must find the will to live a new way. We can always start over*.'"

"Irma. Why rub it in? This is guidance for people with potential."

"Oh, hush. '*Enlightenment, awakening*,'" she reads on, "'*is possible for all of us. When we are enlightened…there is no more confusion*.'"

Walter finds balm in Irma's voice if the words, the ideas, are ungraspable.

"Now, this is for you, Walter, daydreaming out the window. Listen: '*Make contact with everything that is beautiful, refreshing, and healing…a gorgeous sunset, a child's smile'*—the photos of your own children as little ones—*'the song of a bird, the company of a friend.'"*

Walter frowns. "Friends," he whispers. "Missed out on that one."

"Me, too," says Irma, her voice no longer lilting. She stands and slowly replaces the book on Walter's stack of bedside companions.

We've been on a seesaw, it occurs: now me, then the other of us, is ascendant. Our simulated tug-of-war, as if we're on an equal playing field. No, my lot in life before and even now is likely a thousand-fold more advantaged than Irma's.

No friends…

~

HE IS REACHING FOR his wallet to retrieve the one credit card he carries. He has plenty of others but, for some crazy reason—probably fearing theft—he only keeps one at hand. And it's missing! He's flabbergasted, cannot possibly recall where he last used it. And left it. *Here, make hundreds, no, thousands of dollars of purchases on me!* he thinks of the open invitation to somebody who claims it. He is sweating. He is sputtering incoherently to the irritated cashier. A hundred and eighty dollars for—he doesn't even know. He only knows it's essential. Must have this! Now! But there is no way to pay. People behind him in line are mumbling then become vocal and angry. Everybody is shouting at him, including the cashier. He wants to hide, to shrink, but he seizes the parcel, whatever it is, tightly to his chest. He is frozen on the spot, suffering abuse, humiliation, despair to a depth he has never known. Fevered and gasping, the white-hot terror abruptly ends. Walter awakes.

~

"DAD. DAD? IRMA SAID it was okay to jostle you. It's Gavin."

Walter cracks the gummy gunk that has glued shut his eyes. He tries to speak but the voice is still not aroused. "Ga-vin," he manages, fumbles for the crank to elevate the bed's upper portion. "Golly. Feels like I've been asleep for forty years."

Gavin stands tall, well over six feet, muscular arms folded onto his chest, biceps stretching the polo shirt armbands. He's wearing that shit-eating grin, self-righteous as an Eagle Scout, as if to say, I made it, I got here, I'm sober. Walter clears his throat, sips water, folds arms over his own ghost of a frame. His son is incredibly handsome, thick shocks of curly dark brown hair like his mother's, goofy as ever, adorable, really—another minefield of explosive consequences for him. And what, forty-something? Maybe more. Walter can no longer pinpoint such a statistic. Finally, Gavin hurtles himself backward into the all-enveloping armchair, slides his rump deeper into the cushions and splays his long legs in the attitude of an adolescent male feigning indifference. That, too, goes part-and-parcel with Gavin's long history as Lothario, as if it's all the girl's doing and far be it from him to turn her down and hurt her feelings. Walter muses on, fighting to listen to his son prattle on about his latest adventure.

"I'm sailing yachts for folks from Florida to their summer places on the Cape, the coast of Maine."

"Surely not alone."

"Trudy's taught me everything. We have her older son from her second marriage. Take on crew here and there."

"Have I met Trudy?"

"Nah. We connected late last summer. After I split with Meg." Again, his arms are crossed, an incarnation of a breastplate for a Medieval warrior, it occurs to Walter.

"Did I meet Meg?" asks Walter, straining to be civil. He believes Meg was the very young one, barely twenty, about whom even he did a double take. Although she was in recovery as had been Gavin—they'd met at a pricey "renewal ashram" in New Mexico—Walter figured it was a step ahead for his son to be so caring of someone else. He supposes it was better than when Gavin kept two women in different towns. Maybe I was a tad jealous, me with my one-and-only Polly ever to be in my bed. Paula had shown her father photos from Facebook postings over which she was outraged, ordinarily incommunicado with her brother.

Gavin has explained how profitable his latest undertaking with the yachts is. "But Trudy, Dad, the fact is she manages okay with the settlement from her first divorce. You know I've never had good sense keeping hold of the cash."

Walter nods, very good, say not a word. Gavin has turned a fraction bashful over this admission while preserving his innocence, like a child admitting to the theft but calculating the confession will outweigh any punishment. Of course, prior financial shenanigans of his son pale in comparison to the far more serious crimes. Although Walter is trying like hell to wean himself from expectations in general, especially ones involving his children, he cannot resist a silent jab slipping through.

"I'm happy you can survive, Gavin, with helping hands here and there. I'm proud of you for not hitting on me. Your mother I know drilled that into you. Money only for serious medical intervention. I'll be gone before you know it, and certainly I'm making provisions for you. No purpose in telling you how much and under what conditions. But for now, as you've been, you're on your own." Walter sinks back into the pillows. Proud? What a falsehood.

Gavin drops the boyish grin. "Thanks, Dad," he says convincingly as a man shuffling to the firing squad. The two men, as adults, have conducted, not embraced, a relationship.

That was a mixed message, thinks Walter—no money now, but soon. I must bite my tongue. Paula asks for money outright and deserves it. But Gavin, stick to what you just said, Walter scolds himself. *He's on his own.*

"You look healthy, Dad. Color in your cheeks." A paltry attempt at flattering? So out of character for Gavin, who relies on his looks as reason enough for his place in the world without extending interest otherwise. Stop judging! Thank him or say something else.

"So you're still all over the map, Gavin. No place of your own. What about Max, is it? The boy you fathered, Jesus, right after high school. He must be all grown by now."

"He's not my son. Never was." Gavin sits erect. "You offered me funds for the girl to terminate. I've never seen or heard from her, from them, since. Mom found out the name, I guess. Ancient history, Dad. Don't hold that over me, the other miseries, sure. Christ, that business was not my finest moment but, hell, I was a kid."

"You'd started college and went at it for a year before you dropped out. You showed potential for getting it together."

Gavin flecks tongue over teeth, as if to audit himself and watch his words. "I'm not here to review my résumé, Dad. I'm not asking you to bail me out. I just wanted to…" He hesitates.

"Check in on your dad."

Gavin hoists his chiseled face and finally looks directly at his father. Softly he says: "You're dying, Dad. The least I can do."

Inexplicitly, Walter melts. He's on the verge of tears. There is his boy, six, seven, eight years old in the full-color photo albums if banished from his memories, beautiful before it all began. And here he is, same curly locks, same irresistible smile. When if not now to dismantle every shred of Walter's intransigence in preserving the moat around his castle? Not dad, not son, not Gavin or Walter. Not old fart, not young stud, not responsible for this but responsible for that. Two flawed souls who happen to be bound by blood, and that from a mere sneeze of the gods that sets these things in motion down a one-way road. We are but two grains of sand on a beach, Walter is now picturing as silence prevails between them. The grains had once, eons before them, served with others as a pebble, before that as part of a rock. Even the original boulder looms lifeless as Walter circles his own insignificance. The image fades. For the few seconds, however, this scenario was soothing.

"I'm pleased you came, Gavin. It's fine you likely won't visit again for a while."

Gavin wrestles his lanky self to standing, lifts aside the throw blanket and fondles his father's feet. He strokes the toes, one at a time. He pinches the pads, tenderly. He is not grinning, his countenance completely neutral. He finishes after a few minutes by pressing his hands together over each foot, a ritual, it occurs to Walter, by way of closure. His son has surely had an assignation or two with practitioners of the many popular bodily arts he's seen documented on TV. Gavin withdraws his hands to his side, perhaps at a loss for words to say goodbye.

"You may not believe this, Gavin, but my feet are positively tingling. A few hours ago, they were numb."

"You should hire a masseuse. I'm not kidding. A woman. They're gentler than men. Do you a world of good."

Walter blinks rapidly. "A young Latin woman comes to do my nails. I could ask her."

"A Latina, all the better." Gavin winks.

Suddenly Walter reaches for a checkbook. "Please, Gavin, please accept something until the next time. Please. This, too, will do me a world of good."

Chapter 4

The news we hear is full of grief for the future,
but the real news inside here
is that there's no news at all.

WALTER STIRS FROM DEEP sleep. He has no idea if it's day or night. It could be just prior to a thunderstorm, the blue-black clouds out his window are that opaque. He adjusts himself, best he is able. When will his immune system simply shut down with nothing left to resuscitate? When did Irma last bring him food, check his water, offer passing observations of the weather? He thinks of Ana recently tending the john, sheepishly answering his inquiry after her granddaughter's confirmation party or whatever. While chatting with her, he maintained his typical detachment, amazed he had the wherewithal to be even marginally sociable, especially given Ana's reticence to be the focus of attention. About none of these things can he muster the vaguest interest. He does not care. He is moving beyond any variation of caring, let alone forming an opinion. He is sliding into a vacuum which dissolves Walter or Walt or whatever vessels those versions of him had been. It's like trying to embrace an armload of autumn leaves but they keep floating away, impossible to grasp. It's been ages since ideas were sufficiently complicated to warrant a conundrum. He's reminded of the life cycle of a plant that has absorbed its fair share of nutrients, sprouted and borne fruit, with leaves now fallen and stem left an afterthought, not rotted but withered, gradually broken down into unidentifiable bits. *This is neither good nor bad,* Walter summons the strength to articulate. *I'm beyond the tedious obligation of "letting go." I'm gone. And for good, with both of those interpretations. Gone is a good state to inhabit. And "for good" tops that with its finality.*

Occasionally Walter speculates—no longer worries—whether future visits with his children, definitely with Paula but Gavin too, and visits real or imagined or recycled with Polly and his business partner Will and any others will occur with him being "present," as they say. It doesn't matter, he's just curious about how this evolution to the finish line will play out, if not for him but for his loved ones. His former loved ones. Love, too, has been shed along the way.

When someone dies, Walter considers, there is a big to-do for those loved ones, especially a spouse, which fortunately is not a factor for him. They grieve and emote, which is healing and good for as long as it takes. For them and everybody else, life goes on, as with a drop of viscous ink dotting a blotter, the patch left to dry and, like the departed, in due course is sucked up and soon an afterthought. Life is for the living. *And I certainly won't care. I'll be dead.*

He comprehends that his mental grasp is deteriorating at a faster pace than his physical self. *Am I willing it?* he ponders. *Or am I just a puppet yanked along for the parade? Everyone crawling through the same tunnel, one after another. Next.*

~

Irma is standing at the base of his bed, slouched, apparently nothing urgent at hand.

"I never should have done it," says Walter.

"Done what?" She has that look of patience down pat, signaling irritation, nonetheless.

"Given Gavin a check like that for no reason. Five grand, I can't remember. I let down my guard."

"Good for you. Making progress. Gavin showed me the check. He was stunned and elated. You're going to bury it all in your mattress, so to speak? He looked healthy and together, even before your unexpected hit of generosity."

"There was no constructive purpose for the money. It must have seemed to him like I'm desperate for his goodwill after years of rebuke, here on my last legs. And just when he appears to be savoring reliable independence from me."

Irma beams broadly. "Walter, forget the dollars and cents. Meaningless to you. Your son came here simply as an act of love. And you returned that with one of your own. Without thinking it through!"

Walter fails to comprehend this. "As always with you Irma, it all sounds so logical."

"You and your logic, lodged in the brain. You know, Walter, the heart, too, has its say."

~

Days and weeks go by. Light, dark, he barely notices. He does observe that the petals of the peonies have scattered to the ground, barely distinguishable from the dirt. He missed their glorious crimson peaks. The daylilies he remembers having been on the verge. Their technicolor theatrics, these too went by while he must have been preoccupied otherwise. In fact, it must be fall. Only the evergreens stand stately, impervious to the fickle flights of the seasons to which humans can only aspire, never achieve.

Apparently, he peed on the floor, and so they've hooked him up temporarily while he's sustaining a urinary infection. Not a catheter, not yet he was told, but more a condom gizmo. He recalls being forever irate over puddles on the floor of a urinal. How could a man possibly miss? Urinals, everywhere, even at the fanciest restaurants, the floor awash, as if in reverse one won by avoiding the bull's eye. Mind-numbing to Walter how a big belly of a bowl could be insufficient to receive the stream of a simple flaccid hose of a penis.

He's dry, tucked in, dealt with for the day. He cannot abide the television. When he finds it on, he turns off the volume. Yes, he knows, the A&E channel, National Geographic, all of it held forth like a butler with a silver tray, waiting to enthrall him from every angle on earth. The incessant news cycles, the talking heads each like a carnival barker, the next exposé more titillating than the naked lady with a beard, the dwarf with twelve toes…

Opinions, pet peeves, he reviews the aspect of his former self prone to trifling irritations. Now, like a classroom blackboard at day's end, all the scribblings and urgent passages are being erased.

He encourages a blank slate, drapes drawn across his mind, and closes his eyes. *I want it to end. It's been enough.* And so he knows he's becoming ever more ready. *I've made peace with myself. There is nothing more to do.* And then he fingers a slim volume from the stack of Paula's books she's brought him. And he reaches for the pen and notebook nearby, jotting down pithy notions mostly to keep his hands from going stiff.

Bardo in Buddhism is the state of existence between death and rebirth. A transitional state.

Thank you very much. However not only can I not embrace your kind offer of reincarnation, but I feel my long life in this embodiment has been more than generous for one being. And why ever perpetrate me of all people? I've had multiple opportunities to become new and improved. I am who I am.

Sufi saying: Allah/God is a hidden treasure that wants to be known and created the world so it could be found.

Now that's a nice idea. It absolves everyone from feeling awful, even him, for never having gotten it quite right. He was meant to give it his best shot even though the game was rigged against him in the first place, imperfect by design.

He pokes on through these funny little books. Homilies, haikus, more serious than himself.

Aspire to meaninglessness. To accept the purpose of The Secret is to tease the conscious mind to higher and lower levels of awareness and insight, which can never be fully achieved but enlighten along the way.

I can live with that, responds Walter. I can die with that, more to the point.

~

MORNING, WALT! HI, WALT. They all hustle in, on time, of course. He's the boss. The senior marketing execs file in to join a half-dozen already placed around the big oval table, poring over notes. He has the table oval so everybody can make eye contact and forge a tighter group. No one left out, each person seen and heard.

After the brief intro by his right-hand man, Alex begins the discussion, the pros and cons of expanding beyond their mostly rural market for yard and garden goods into, for them, untapped cities and suburbs.

The battery-operated mower is perfect for amortizing our proven direct-response TV inquiry techniques into A and B counties, asserts Sylvia, a newly minted Harvard MBA. She's too brilliant for his outfit, but hopefully her time to rule a roost will come.

It's not of interest to our base of a million customers, our best bets for additional sales, snaps a veteran on the team. Put that dame in her place.

We're all about innovation and selling direct without retail presence. The country is ready for this new tool, says another, eager to claim credit for his assertion rather than second Sylvia's motion, which urged the same ideas.

And Walter sits, elbows on the table, preening like a mother hen. As per usual, he keeps his thoughts to himself. For example, those assumptions of sexism are simply his own; his colleagues seem to thoroughly enjoy spirited back and forth. In fact, mentally sticking up for Sylvia is sexist on his part, dated protector of the little woman. Sylvia is full of piss and vinegar, ready to take on the world. His company is all about participation of folks at every level. Even a janitor with a complaint or an idea can pipe up without fear of reprisal. There is no poison in the atmosphere under Walter's roof where he knows the first name of all four hundred employees, addressing them in greeting without guile. He means it. He owns this baby, and is indebted to every single player, however lofty or not the slot that is filled. They are well paid, overpaid some advisers say. But Walter nurtures the profit month in, month out, like a newborn. Is he a slave to it? Frankly, yes, he says in raw appraisal a lifetime later. He is charming and courteous to everyone because, truth be told, the fortune he is amassing precludes all else. Good manners take no toll on him whatsoever.

We can have them built in China for a third the cost and result in a salable price at the local hardware store. Otherwise, manufactured here? No market.

Walter has already decided how to proceed. At the end of the hour meeting, each staffer has had his or her say and next step in place prior to a final resolution on this item. It is only a slice of what each is doing, it doesn't really waste time, it sharpens wits, but bottom line, Walter affects an open process. He needs these people to run his business. Fully empowered, they never quite digest their part in a dictatorship. At least this is how Walter assesses himself near the start of his downward physical spiral, coming face to face with so much of his past. During the course of his career, it didn't seem to him that he was nearly so cold and calculated. Valid at the time, but, in the big picture, it was a contrived configuration he had adapted for himself. Not a very nice guy, despite outward appearances. It just happened to last a lifetime.

So, what say you, Walt? says Alex. *How would you sum this up?*

All eyes turned. Dammit, Alex. Rather the boss than Sylvia having the last word.

~

"ANA, YOU SAID YOUR granddaughter is taking piano lessons. How wonderful." He can't imagine how this is possible, given Ana's daughter is a single mother of four working full-time as a chambermaid at the Holiday Inn.

Ana is startled to be addressed midway in her mopping, let alone on such a personal note. "Oh, Mr. Walt, she sings like an angel and won her class competition. As a prize the school has arranged for piano lessons in the nearby church basement. She's dreamed about playing since she was a tot." Ana leans against the mop, wipes misbehaving hair from her moist forehead.

"Didn't you say you played a church piano yourself at Christmas?"

"Oh, just the carols. I memorized!"

"Look. Ana, you run yourself ragged cleaning up all my mess. What with Irma full-time and the visiting nurse Valerie now, I've got plenty of help."

Ana comes to attention, clearly uncomfortable at this level of informality with Mr. Walt. She is stocky and dark-haired and plain, Walter hates to admit, like every Hispanic matron he's ever met. Must he, in turn, for them appear identical to every other old white man in the world?

"Ana, I want you to take piano lessons, too. Like your granddaughter. Please. Do it for me." And he fetches one of the several checkbooks on his stand. "The same teacher as for your girl. Or ask about another who might be available."

She is blushing, about to stammer. "I work weekends, too, at the hospital cafeteria."

"Then I'll arrange it with Irma so you have one afternoon free each week. No change in your pay."

She is shaking her head. *Is she declining...have I upset her with such an intrusion...admit it, Walter, this is for your benefit more than hers...*

~

Oh, my God, Gavin tried to burn down the house! is near shouted to him on the phone. Polly is stricken as never Walter has beheld her, him rushing home from the office and parking several yards away due to the pile-up of fire trucks and police cars.

Walter clenches his jaw, embraces Polly, gapes at the jets of water raining down on the southside of their earlier house with its roof of blackened herringboned slate. He cannot remember Paula in the picture until later, screaming incoherently at the total destruction of her pretty pink bedroom with its cherished posters, dresses, and dolls. Days later he and Polly with Gavin are sitting like ramrods with the counselor, soon after with the psychiatrist. At eleven Gavin did not have access to heavy drugs or even dope. He had soaked his bedroom from a gasoline can for the lawnmower. He is well beyond playing with matches. Gavin resumes his smiley, cute-boy demeanor. He offers virtually zero by way of explanation although by nine or ten years old it was obvious at least to Polly that Gavin had more than a surly streak. *Speak when you are spoken to, Gavin,* from Polly at the table when he was in junior high school, no longer normal to be tongue-tied. He glances up, all innocent. Befuddled? Not really, even to Walter. There is something recalcitrant in the kid's basic makeup. Polly grows ever more anxious. Walter withdraws, not wanting to interfere in the tender business of childrearing. It will pass, he thinks. A preadolescent rebellion to his sugary-sweet sister. Whatever, Walter figures, dismissing it. I'm not a psychologist. My job, such as I have one in the domicile, is the odd round of ping-pong in the playroom, tossing the football after Sunday dinner, goes his train of thought those years ago. So he "ran away from home" at nine, is easily caught a few blocks away. *Huckleberry Finn,* Walter tries to make light for Polly's benefit, at which she flattens her lips. So Gavin threatens to jump off the roof of their four-story mansion at the time, age ten. Wanting attention, Walter offers. Paula's such a star, now on horseback. Polly disagrees.

And so they carry on as a foursome, their little family perhaps not so storybook perfect. But four independent characters, each forging their separate path, nothing out of the ordinary, really. Nothing over which to fret, far as Walter is concerned.

Until the fire…at age eleven…not even a hormonal, typically angry, obnoxious teen.

As years of havoc alternated with years of renewal and hope, Walter ever more immersed in his business, he could lose track of where things stood with his son. It was like his family was on a stage, anguished and then otherwise, while he gazed on from the audience, front row center, but oddly removed and immobile, with no lines of his own.

Chapter 5

Face to face with a lion,
I grow leonine.

His first orgasm is at the junior-high sock hop. *Remember those, Walter? Orgasms,* he needles himself, *not sock hops.* But one such teen romp was truly memorable. At its conclusion there was the Dead Bulb Dance where the couples could be pressed together and frankly explore. It was only allowed as the final number after interminable twirling and flailing like beheaded chickens doing the Lindy. The more serious couples with the girl wearing the boy's Friendship Ring on a chain preside over the Dead Bulb Dance in the suddenly darkened gym. The wallflowers slink to the sides and dolefully watch the cooler kids. Walter, unpledged and considered a drudge even then, is madly in love with Mary Lou Strauss, but she was claimed by the tall, confident captain of the basketball team. He spots Gloria Berghof milling about near the wall and, astonishing himself, hustles to her side, seizes her hand, and leads her to the floor. Walter doesn't know what loose implies at the time. He only knows that she has winked with a sly grin at him ever since they were ten and played Doctor and Nurse in her treehouse on the next block. He prodded her slit with a popsicle stick, and she measured his hairless prong—diving-board dick, the boys called it—as they wordlessly, solemnly conducted their reciprocal exams. Not that many years later here they are locked together at the Dead Bulb Dance, as Gloria grinds her pelvis into his, rotates round and round, the sides of their damp heads smack together as well so they can carry on without eye contact or inane conversation. The boys in the locker room urged wearing their newly issued jockstraps in case they were lucky enough to dance the last dance but avoid humiliation over their hard-ons. Walter is instantly transported to oblivion, letting Gloria take the lead, whereupon he suddenly near collapses from a geyser released between his legs, flooding his underpants, him thrust into both searing pleasure and utter embarrassment. Gloria continues to grind away, gripping him in a vise. Just before the familiar last notes of "Blue Moon" she arches back her equally sweaty head and sticks her tongue into his ear. Walter can barely stand, is near faint with confusion as they pull apart, the overhead fluorescent lights again flashing on with the glare of a police lineup. Guilty, every one of you. Gloria glances over her shoulder sashaying to the girls' room and shoots him her devastating, rascally grin as he minces to the boys', praying his wet pants don't show.

~

Autumn is advancing without him, but he doesn't mind. He's preoccupied with Polly, as usual. The few but consequential women in his life dominated everything outside of his office. Fair enough. He was the principal there. *But the women,* Walter is thinking, *command an arena far richer, and trickier, to negotiate. It's probably why I don't read novels, but more often biographies and histories and cautionary political tomes. They're straightforward with language I can grasp.* Fiction, when he's dabbled, is fraught with meanings between the lines. Dialogue of characters who say one thing but may mean the very opposite. Poetry, forget it. This one of Rumi's Paula left, for instance. He knows it's supposed to entice one to sidestep literal images and allow resonating with deeper ramifications. Isn't that the same process as confronting a business decision—to advance, recede, or stay put—and juggle, twist about, and finally conclude? It dawns on him that business acumen is as complicated as the psychology that is women's forte. And doesn't men's logic of sequence to resolution serve the admirable goal of sanity? Things get done, human beings survive. But Walter has always felt crippled by feminine guile and their mastery of, to him, the somehow more essential, interpersonal arts.

One of his women reigns above all others: his mother, the first woman to whom every child must be slavishly devoted. After she was abruptly killed, intoxicated, in the car crash when Walter was six, his father, the little he was around and paid any attention, made of her a saint. She was mired in the slums, he claimed. Walter was her dream to gain what she and his father would never achieve. Her mission became his as a boy, all the more ironclad forged by two souls, not one. In death, the little he learned of her mushroomed into myth. Beyond a flawed human being, she embodied a tragic goddess enthroned high above. The devil on earth is drink, his father sermonized, before dashing off to the casino, leaving Walter to fend for himself. Dead drunk is also how her own parents had died, his father forever repeating the saga of the shanty Irish grandparents, as he cursed them, his sweet wife inheriting their weakness. Smoke inhalation from a cigarette tossed aside bellowed into a blaze and did them in.

Gavin attempting to burn the house down is not Walter's first fire. He wonders if the fires perpetrated by his grandparents and his son are connected. He can feel like a pawn in a grand scheme of accidents, like explosions of gasses in the galaxy. A fire here, a fire there. Subterranean infernos just on this planet with no warning, wiping out Pompeii in seconds so that whole bodies are found cast in stone, dashing legs sculpted in flight. Catastrophe can erupt any moment, he muses. My roll of the dice was to be a foot soldier to guard against chaos, a control freak as it's ridiculed by the free spirits. Somebody has to be. A fire scalded his psyche at the start, his father ranting about the dangers of booze that doomed his mother. Gavin torching their home, intentional as it appears, can also be seen as a fickle spasm of his eleven-year-old, still-developing brain. The year before, they were tossed helter-skelter into the January night in their pajamas, the cellar in flames. The kid was caught after the second, more serious fire, both occasions he being first to sound the alarm. It was a pathetic bid to be a hero, authorities later explained. Walter, daydreaming of all these disasters, now regards them as nothing out of the ordinary, it being ordinary to face and try to survive cyclones, earthquakes, tornados, and hurricanes, or the fleeting fragments of a single soul like Gavin as a boy whose fuse suddenly blows and sparks an avalanche, engulfing others.

I've led a perfectly prosaic life, reasons Walter. *My mother, her parents, my son, the human family of crazies, we're all in this together. Like everyone, I've been dodging bullets for a lifetime. Here I sprawl with my creature comforts and damned lucky for that.*

~

"You're still so angry about Gavin," says Irma. She's pulled up a chair to chat, taking a break at Walter's suggestion. "He's on the mend, but toward him you're not."

"I keep thinking of the damage—to himself, his body, his life—and how it's weighed on me for decades."

"You stood by him, as best you could. But, as damaged goods. That's how you label him, Walter, to this day. Perhaps his getting a handle is on the surface for you, but, basically…"

"I know!" he silences her. "I am groping for a new approach before it's too late. I do appreciate your feedback, my dear Irma," he adds, frustrated at being so curt. Exhale. "Paula is easier even though she can be a pain in the ass. But she doesn't bug me like Gavin does."

"Paula is your spitting image. You look at her, the business dynamo, and see yourself. Your narcissist streak!"

"Oh, Christ. This is too heavy," moans Walter.

"You asked for my thoughts, Walter, now with both your children visiting more often. And don't knock narcissism. It can play a healthy if minor part."

"I know you're well-read, Irma, but really."

"Nothing those little books Paula brings don't delve into. I've run through them myself. Your personal censor."

He flexes his left wrist that is definitely becoming more rigid. "Paula and I are always direct with each other. Mostly it's money. I keep wanting to ask her about herself, how she's faring…watching me die. The last time with Gavin was, in a way, more intimate than it ever is with her."

"Now there's an interesting angle. With Gavin you're more concerned with his material welfare. How he could better function in the world, with work and so forth. Not an issue for Paula. With her, you sense an opportunity to nudge her spiritually, reflectively, where she may be undernourished. Keep reading, Walter. I think you're on a roll."

Walter clenches his fists however much he is still able. "What do you know about children, parenting, Irma?" he fires off. "You've never…" Walter bolts upright, gasping at her. "Oh, God, I'm so sorry, so sorry…"

~

OUT THE WINDOW IS smeared a gray-umber morass. No inspiration there. Irma blamed the latest drug for his outburst, letting him off the hook, and he didn't resist. He does fancy, in fact, these little books. He's come to see Rumi's poems are like swallowing flavored acid relief. Kind of a kick at first taste, but then you have no idea what's released into the blood stream, buried in the marrow, trickling on to the simplest of cells hidden beyond recognition.

~

HE IS BESOTTED WITH Alice Remmer his junior and senior years of high school. She teased him unmercifully, "Walter the brownnose" who asked for and did extra assignments in math. She had dark brown hair and was lanky, kind of like Walter himself, a good student, but the resemblance stops there. "I'm calling you Ichabod," she said. "Ichabod Crane because like you he's basically out of it." She is tart-mouthed and sarcastic, which perfectly complements his more often than not being the most gullible of punching bags. Early on he is content to let the women beginning, of course, with his mother and soon after his foster-mother Aunt Peg have the first and last say. So much blather, but it seemed to empower them, exclude or dismiss him, which is fine by Walter, free and unfettered to mind his own business. He aimed at what a man could be good at—numbers, money, steady vision. He holds his own with sassy, bossy Alice. He escorts her to the junior prom, all the dances and make-out parties, then the senior prom. Even at the drive-in, he respects Alice's no-hands-below signals, about which she was adamant. He often fantasizes being one of the cruder boys who were scoring and going all the way, so they said, when parents were on vacation or vacating the house to attend parties of their own. It was happening all over the place. Perhaps he feels safe with Alice, saving him from having to perform. The boy has to be in charge, and what does he know from the locker room rollicking with the braggadocio of virgins like himself? He knows how it is to work mechanically, but he also knows it is more art than science, and with a girl like Alice this is no way to practice. Three girls from their class already had to drop out pregnant.

Right after graduation it is tradition in their town for the more privileged kids to be entertained for a weekend at summer cottages in the country or houses at the shore. This featured iffy levels of chaperoning. Liquor, for sure. Upper-crust Alice, who is semi-popular compared to him with a slide-rule hanging from his belt, gets included in a house party. It only takes a few beers, sips, really, for both of them on the second night, padded rumpus room and lights out, to fall into heavy petting like the rest of the gang. Walter prays his pecker will hold firm, long enough to get a hand job, no way penetrating Alice first time ever at such intimacy and in this setting. He figures she'd probably be happy to get him off with just receiving nipple play for her part. Unlike him, she is hardly the first in her family going to college. Plus, it was understood condoms were for sailors those days, certainly not on display in suburban drugstores. He is roaring hard. Alice is exceptionally agreeable with French kissing, maybe because in this way she can cut loose. Their shirts are off, as is her bra. He is fondling her freely for the first time. The heck with math. He so desperately needs to catch up in this department. She puts fingers on his crotch as he slips a hand between her thighs, jeans but still! He wriggles out of his underwear to let it flop in her lap, finally, but it doesn't even get to land. It's totally awash and wilted once released. Alice backs away. Walter slumps into a sodden heap. She reassembles her outfit, sneaks out of the room. "Hey, congrats, Walt. Ya did it," from a few of the guys later on.

Shame, Walter reflects, looking back, is hard to erase. Another one of those accidents of nature that leaves an ugly bruise, just one more in the dog-eared business of an indefatigable memory bank.

~

"How are we doing today, Walter?" says Irma, "we" meaning how he fares she will too? More likely it's not a question. He should be as she is, upbeat and onward bound. "How about a scrambled egg with lots of butter?" He has been relegated to much softer meals but more frequently served. Gradual constriction of the upper alimentary canal, which he'd rather not visualize: one more neurological inevitability, as in a stack of vertical cards falling until they've all collapsed.

"Great," he says to dismiss her, not in the mood for banter. The thick blond pigtail bisecting her back brings to mind, given his grumpy demeanor this morning, a menacing sea creature with a poisonous rear end. Irma is of Hungarian extract, which is borderline Germanic. He understands people of that persuasion, which included many of his better-heeled yard-care customers in their hometown. Determined to work hard, determined to have fun as in a raucous Munich beer hall. Irma is imposing, to say the least. Although Walter slept through most of the few operas Polly got them to, he associates this emphatic good woman with Brunhilda or some Wagnerian majesty overpowering any men on stage by dint of her voluminous girth in addition to her voice.

Irma is straightening the blanket, fluffing the pillow, lingering to say more, the continuous tending belying a hesitation to expressing her thoughts, not her usual mode. He is starting to wonder if the lines distinguishing her from him, being ever more dependent, are obliterating the little that's left of his personhood.

"There is someone who has asked to see you, Walter," she says at last.

"You're not sure if this is a good thing."

She sighs, chubby hands shoved into the pockets of today's flowery apron. "It's the son of your former business partner Will. I know that relationship did not end happily for you, and it seems inappropriate given…"

"These circumstances. It's okay, Irma. I'm sort of defenseless, on the one hand. I tell myself I've got my wits intact, on the other."

She gives more details of this Adam character, Walter clearly remembering the one of Will's two sons that was a layabout like his latter-day dad. "Go ahead, Irma, you can arrange it. I could use some relief, going steady with myself in here."

It's fine, Walter thinks as Irma leaves to fetch his breakfast. *What can possibly get my goat at this point? Adam and I can have a nice post-mortem and recycle choice tales of his father and me in our prime. Another trip down memory lane except this time, instead of me rehashing so much about Will, it can be by proxy, in person, for real.*

~

"I don't recognize you, Adam," says Walter a week later. He is still able to sit his top half almost upright in bed with his knees hiked to chest and grasped with two arms—a radical departure from his ordinarily being prone.

"I don't recognize you either, Walt. And I'm sorry for that." The man is nondescript in a pasty, middle-aged way. Walter squints for a glimpse of the teenager who was in the picture back then, but confronts a face speckled with starbursts of tiny red capillaries disfiguring overly rosy cheeks. The swollen nose, the puffy lids, tell-tale signs drummed into Walter of the litany of sins resulting from alcohol.

"Have a seat, Adam. Irma will offer you coffee or whatever," says Walter, suddenly the host, the boss again, the guy in charge. Adam extends a hand to Walter, who reciprocates. "Sorry about the tremor. Some good days, some bad."

"I…I thought it would be a good thing, Walt. A chance to—see you once more, old time's sake." He cannot get comfortable despite the oceans of goose down into which he has sunk. He grips the ends of the armrests.

"I've had lots of time to think of your dad, Adam. Boy, we were jazzed up. With ambition, ideas. We fed off each other in that way. Our sum was greater than its parts, so to speak. I remember your hanging around the office after school. Your brother, I believe. Didn't he become an intern with us one summer? Mechanical engineering, yes?"

Adam swallows whatever his first reply, as if fumbling for something more amenable than his super sibling. "Eli was the go-getter. I was more into playing ball. Girls." Here he smiles, his sources of pride.

"I recall Will arranged a job for you after high school, you wanting to wait and see about college? Testing new products, the mowers out back. Gosh, good money we paid, but hard to keep at it, hour after hour."

"I did okay working after that for the brewery, driving a truck at first, you wouldn't know about that. But it led to deliveries, sales, new customers. Paid the rent, paid for the wife and kids."

Walter nods, lets him continue. To what end heavens knows. Adam glances about the room—the elaborate woodwork, the carpets, the art. The bulges around his belly match the billowing cushions of the armchair.

Walter breaks the growing silence. "It must have been hard on you, and your family, your father's decline."

Adam is staring at the floor. His jaw is pressed, making folds of the excess flesh. "I never understood at the time, I was just in my early twenties, that—that Dad's drinking problem was a result of—" He pauses.

"His disappointment over how our partnership fell apart."

"How you fucked him over, Walt." Adam's glaring eyes are ignited red like the rest of his face.

"I'm sorry you see it that way. Will did, too, at first. And then our lawyers intervened and got it all resolved. Will readily admitted his own weakness, letting go of his hold of the reins. He was ultimately grateful, Adam, that I carried on. He got his value for the shares, then you and your brother soon after when he died."

"You bought out his initial shares when he needed cash instead of axing his salary for the time being. He could still have claimed his original half, his rightful stake. In spite of his drinking problem, he was getting help."

"That I paid for." Another silence ensues that is filled nevertheless with this man's vitriol. "Look, Adam, there's no point. It's all settled long ago."

"Not for me it isn't, Walt. I'm not here to redo any legal shit. I'm here asking you man-to-man, out of the goodness of your heart. You're a decent man or were at the beginning. You've got to feel like a bastard for outfoxing my father when he was down-and-out. On his knees. Pleading with you to be generous, for Christ's sake, you held all the cards. I'm giving you a chance to make amends. Before it's too late."

"Get out."

"You see. You're a cutthroat son of a bitch, Walt, bottom line." Adam stands abruptly, quivering.

"You had a roof over your head thanks to my bottom line."

"Did you want some coffee?" thunders Irma from the doorway.

"Adam was just leaving," says Walter firmly as Adam stomps off.

Walter grabs one hand with the other to quell the shaking of both, his tremors not having ceased through the whole of the encounter. He reaches for his pen and notebook; that might help.

You're some weird kind of gold that wants to stay melted in the furnace, so you won't have to be coins.

Chapter 6

Words let water from an ocean, infinite ocean,
come into this place as energy,
for the dying and even the dead.

SOMETIMES HE READS THE Rumi poetry, less often these days does he manage to scribble a few lines down in his bedside notebook. He likes this one. Blurring the line between where he is now and where he is going. No life after, but somewhat dead right now. Looking up from his book Walter asks himself: *How is this moment any different from ones the day before or decades ago?* Just because he was fully alert at his workplace, less so at home, he was completely occupied by the outline of himself, not whatever composed him deep down inside. Is there one, irreducible thing that makes a person different from every other? The salmon swimming upstream against all odds or the goose driving through a gale—it's the force of the fins, the machinery of wings in high gear that powers them to the exclusion of any other options. *Whatever fueled me, minute by minute?* he wonders. *Washing the berries and salad greens after Polly was gone, for instance, because of a pronouncement from Paula that commanded this is what must be done…deciding one market in which to advertise, another not, because I've made a lifetime of such decisions, the next one fitting atop the others like so many perfectly stacked stones. The minutes aggregate into a day as the one before and the one to follow. Just because humans can think does not ordain that we do.* Dolphins, he watched on the nature channel, surround a birthing whale to fend off sharks attracted to the gushing blood. Where does one draw a line between a man and his hallowed mind—meaning brain plus or minus whatever conscience is engaged—and those magnanimous dolphins or a brace of fowl mated for life? As if we're the only living thing that matters. Sure, he had mattered to himself and a few more souls. But really, he should put this in perspective. Interesting he never did so before, an unheralded benefit of the deathbed. All of this is helping. He has got to let go of what he has been. He's beginning to see the stuff inside himself as indistinguishable from that within all others. And that substance is essential, the origin of life. The shell, the persona, the pigment, those are after the fact. How many multiple thousands of insects? Just the mosquito…you see, we're blood brothers! We all wine and dine on each other, part of the master plan. What plan, whose plan? There is no plan. It all just is. Another item washes over, he recalls it verbatim, what else does he have to do? A newly reported galaxy by NASA is over thirteen billion light-years away… the Hubble telescope now stretches its range to thirty-two billion light-years because of the expansion of the universe just in the time it takes the new galaxy's light to reach the telescope. Mind-boggling, he thinks, and that's the point. There is no end in sight. The present state simply exists as proof, living proof, that whatever he can see and feel and imagine, in all its humanoid glory, is a mere speck in a scheme so vast that, of course, it is beyond his limited comprehension. How magnificent! But no one individual is insignificant. Every organism is in service to the cosmos, one's planned obsolescence accounted for by its newly minted replacement. How clever the chemical stew on perpetual simmer. How reassuring his present role in the orderly, ageless confluence of things so far beyond any emperor's (let alone his, a widget maker's) capacity to control. How precious this opportunity, in limbo on death row, allowing him to discover the beautifully precise end point, this placement of the last piece of the sprawling, intricate puzzle he's made of his life. How numb have become his limbs permitting his mind to more than compensate in overdrive. How expansive this slim book of Rumi poems.

When I die, lay out the corpse.
You may want to kiss my lips,
just beginning to decay. Don't be frightened
if I open my eyes.

I am ready, Walter thinks, even if the body carries on, yet another organism with a mind of its own. Irma comes and goes. More caffeine. More fluids. More salt. His carcass pays her attention but he is elsewhere. The visiting nurse, no longer Valerie, he loses track, and the nail salon lady, a few others here and there, "checking in," offering a word or two of reassurance, condolence in truth, at his obvious deterioration. He no longer chuckles inwardly at this ritual for their benefit. Everyone is kind. The world could use more of that.

There stands the walker-cum-chamber pot, idle. The abdicated throne. *By this gate kings are waiting with me,* he recalls. Does Irma help him to the loo? Is it all in these pads? Not his concern.

The window, the "picture window," his eye on the great outdoors, has lost its luster. For hours, apparently, he can follow the tiniest spider hustle and bustle about its business along the windowsill, the flimsiest of webs lucky to ensnare a flea. And this will trip him into another maze of reflections, dead ends aplenty, no arrival at its center nor does he want traipsing the circuitry of paths to conclude.

The dining room is no longer. There is the living room, out of sight. Ha, he thinks. Whatever living happened there? More happening, for me at least, right here. The dying room.

An inner voice cracks, *Nice going, Walter. When in your life did a concept like irony cross your path? Never too late to learn…*

But for endless hours he is on hold. He is slipping ever deeper into decline. This is good. On track. No pain, above all. Feet forgotten. Most of the time, best he can tell, even his thoughts have slid off the radar. His self-contrived entertainment is losing its charm. So much chatter.

He sleeps. Occasionally he dreams. He hoists open eyes. Paula come again? Gavin? The disagreeable one, Will's son, did his assault demanding money actually happen? Was it another fantasy from shadowland masquerading as real? All a blur. And of no consequence. He has made his peace. There is nothing left. The odd poem.

This talk is like stamping new coins. They pile up,
while the real work is done outside
by someone digging in the ground.

~

"You sound awfully hoarse, Walter," murmurs Irma, overcoming her tendency to let him doze when she sees fit.

He swallows with difficulty. "Think I'm coming down with a cold. Immune system bombarded. What do you expect?" He reaches atop his bed stand.

"No, forget those pills. You take enough. I'll fix a few shots of cider vinegar laced with honey. Good enough for the Old World, good enough for you."

"Vinegar?" he cringes. "I like the honey."

"Both."

"You know best, Irma. No quibbles there."

Enough with the pills? Is she giving me permission for the ones I'm stashing away, the bottle hidden in a sock at the rear of the drawer she never checks? A sliver of satisfaction seeps into his system. Taking orders from Irma is on the surface. Ultimately, I'm on my own in this business, the way it should be.

~

He is washing pots, no, scrubbing them, until his reddened fingers are on the verge of becoming bloody pulp. No sooner does he finish this stack when the cooks haul over more. They're dropped onto the metal sink platform with ear-splitting clatter. The crud is now deeper, darker, more stubborn. He needs the wire brush, the one with misshapen prongs that stab him if he's not careful, if he stares too intently at the diners he can glimpse for a few seconds by harried waiters sailing through the doors. The chandeliers sparkle like white caps on a moonlit sea, the men erect in their jet-black tuxedos and trim beards, the women draped in gowns exposing their snowy shoulders, perfect to display brilliant sapphire blues, dense emerald greens, fiery ruby reds. His gaze lingers on the gems set ablaze against the elegant necks and pale upper breasts, succulent as the tender morsels mostly to be left on their plates. He readdresses his work. He is never able to un-cake the pitch-black grease under his nails. This is what he must do to make a buck. He will be lucky to squat all day in an office, no steam, no sweat, no shouting, no hands rubbed raw, someday, just enough money to get by, no suits, no jewels, a cubicle all his own, alone…is this asking much? The frying pans defy him, the most miserable of the lot. The faster he works, the sooner they pile up, as if he's being punished for busting his butt, no end in sight.

His pulse pounding, he suddenly sits up. Was this a dream? He once did work in a hellish kitchen, but never remembers anything so dreadful. Is he making this up or was it shoved into a dustbin to be forever kept out of reach?

Walter is feeling helpless, vulnerable, and utterly alone. *How vaporous is the veil,* he assails himself, *as if I could spin my own fine cocoon and lie fallow until the end. I'm absolutely alive, forget the flesh!* As if for the first time in his illness this thought seizes him in a chokehold. He can breathe, but barely. *You thought it could be so easy, just wafting off with the help of some Eastern teachings on a magic carpet,* the attack continues. *Such tidy packaging of life and death goes against every grain our culture inculcates from Day One. What makes you, lord of the heap here, any different?*

~

"Walter, there's a young man, well, boy, early teens, who would like to see you. He said you sponsored him a few years ago for a town art project. He's raising money for…some kind of youth art exhibit. Seems so sweet, but…how are we this afternoon?" Irma looms massive like the Statue of Liberty over a tiny tourist at its base.

He swivels his neck. That still works. "Oh, that's fine, Irma. Art is good. Whatever do I know about art? Something new."

She withdraws and is shortly replaced by a tall, thin boy. Dark expressive eyes, what can show under the curtain of light brown hair wrapping the whole of his narrow head like a boxer's helmet to withstand a barrage of blows.

"Sit down, son. I know you, Irma says. From a school program?"

He looks both terrified at confronting the terminally ill, likely his first, as well as fevered with the mission that got him here. "You let me have lots of metal parts in your factory repair shop so I could build my sculpture."

"Really? Don't remember. What was the sculpture?"

"A horse. Mostly head. I didn't know welding or anything. I was eleven. But I wired things together."

"Marvelous."

"I brought a photo to show you. Here." He holds it to Walter's face. "It won first prize. Even beat lots of adults." Quickly he reclaims his seat although balances only on its edge.

"Good grief. At eleven. Whatever inspired you?"

"A trip to the Museum of Natural History. A year before. The way they reassembled dinosaurs. It was magic! But it was all bones. I got curious about what's underneath a humungous animal like a hippo or even a horse."

Walter shifts his shoulders to get a better view of the lad. "And now you're what, fifteen, sixteen?"

"Fourteen. I'm tall for my age." Finally, he brushes his bangs to the side, allows the slightest of smiles.

"Your name, son?"

"Alexander. Everybody calls me Alex, but I like Alexander."

"Good. Good for you, Alexander. You're a serious young man. So what is your art like now?"

"I'm obsessed with drawing, painting, any materials I can get. Not much in school. Mostly I do stuff at my friend Becca's house. Her mom has a proper studio. My mom, well, we don't have much space."

"I can imagine if it's in your blood to make art, it happens somehow or other."

"You can see I'm not really built for sports. I hang out someplace, the bus station, wherever, sketching faces, people in motion. Instead of playing ball." He turns shy but only to a point, and continues. "I used to get kidded a lot. Mostly they ignore me. Fine with me. I'm really happiest when I'm at work with my art. Nothing else is going on. I get totally lost." His fingers are in constant motion.

"I'd enjoy seeing some of your things." Alexander is poised bedside like an alien creature, as if he'd been miraculously deposited from outer space. He is so unlike anything Walter can relate to from his own youth, certainly thereafter. *But hold on. Didn't I too have blinders to so much?* he thinks as the boy's gaze takes in more of this old man's clinical, creepy surroundings. Beyond sex and money, what else? As for art, Walter had left that entirely up to Polly. To every chair or drape or dish he was oblivious. Despite Alexander being rail-thin and prepubescent, he is exuding the tensile strength of a vibrating power line.

"Thank you, sir. That's very nice of you. Maybe I could bring…I could show you a few of the smaller paintings I hope to exhibit. In the new space we hope to have. That's why I'm here, to ask for a donation."

"A building?" Walter reacts, shrinking like a slug that's poked, a building the likes of Paula's enterprise.

"Oh, no. A group of us, well, mostly older high-schoolers but we hang out together, want to rent a room for a month, a meeting room at the Ladies League. They'd give us a bargain because we're kids. They have ballet recitals there, stuff like that."

Walter nods. He notices Alexander has a large bound notebook of sorts, which is now pulled atop his lap.

"I keep drawing faces," says Alexander, excited, prying open the book. "For ages I tried to get it exactly right, like the angle of the nose and the chin. Did you realize each eye is totally different? One eye can look calm and the other weird. Two different sides to a person! Here, let me show you." And he does, displaying a page with a woman's face filling the whole. "Here, see when I cover the left eye and that side of her mouth? She's kind of pretty. Relaxed. Now look." And he covers the right half of the portrait. "Angry! Depressed. Isn't that cool?"

"Amazing," Walter summons the strength to utter, as if the boy is sucking up all available ions of charge in the room. "You'll be like Picasso if you keep this up, Alex. Alexander. Just rendering what…"

"What the artist can figure out under the surface! I love Picasso. And Braque. Modigliani. It's not what everybody can see and agree on. I don't want to do that. I want to…cut loose!"

"Orange hair and purple eyes," says Walter.

"Yes! Actually, I did that in Kindergarten. But later on, you know, I tried to copy the masters in junior high art class. The ones in museums."

Alexander flips through various pages for Walter's viewing but Walter reaches the point of overload. "I am really impressed, Alexander. You're extremely talented, and articulate. And so motivated. Your parents must be very proud."

Alexander shuts the portfolio. He starts to sit back but hesitates, as if he's sensitive enough to suspect he's overstayed his welcome. "I live with my mom. I think she's relieved I pretty much take care of myself and don't bug her. Dad, he's out of the picture. Except for…" The boy pauses.

Walter interrupts. "Let's get back to your seeking donations for the exhibit, son. Did you mention the cost of the rental?"

"I—I didn't, sir. It's five hundred dollars, but any contribution would be great. Twenty-five, fifty—"

"One second, son. Let me twist over here." Walter fumbles for a checkbook, the nearest, and then a pen. Thank goodness for the occasional journal notations, keeping the hands from gridlock. "To whom do I make this out?" Alexander answers and Walter quite legibly follows suit, and with the number, letting his signature flow as an afterthought, a squiggly line, all that's left of him anyway. He hands the boy the check.

The dark eyes widen in astonishment. "Holy cow! Really? All five hundred dollars? This is so terrific! You are way too kind."

"Not really," says Walter, sinking back into the pillows. "We have a history, do we not? Apparently, I was a patron of the arts, your horse sculpture years ago. It's only fitting, Alexander. I do hope you'll take photos of the exhibit for me to see."

"Of course!" He is poised to flee but he's held in place as if by the stunning miracle of this turn of events. "I should tell you, sir, although my father, he is out of the picture, but recently he came to see you. It was him who suggested I ask for a possible donation. But not in my wildest dreams could—"

"Your father? I know him?"

"He's Adam. Will's son. Will, your early business partner. Dad visited with you a few months ago, maybe you've forgotten, you must have so many folks…"

"No," Walter whispers. "I haven't forgotten." His vision returns to its usual disposition of dull fog. "Please thank him for suggesting you come see me," Walter adds without thinking. "Please do give him my best."

The boy departs. Walter assails himself. *Give him my best.* What a feeble excuse to assuage my guilt. Third generation. Weaseling a handout.

Chapter 7

Poles apart, I'm the color of dying, you're the color of being born.
Unless we breathe in each other, there can be no garden.

POLLY, OF COURSE, ORCHESTRATED their vacations, insisted it was good for Walter to have a break. In foreign countries he could be "passive-absorptive," according to Polly, which not only would recharge his batteries for the workplace battles but enlighten him to the wide world of other ways. Especially solo at the helm of his business after Will's departure, he should foster "lateral thinking," Polly quoting the approach promulgated by a famed British psychologist, Edward de Bono, who encouraged the creativity and innovation that occurs naturally to children but is stifled in adults. For Polly herself, any adventure was really a continuation of her passion to help the neediest, "the little people" Walter's partner Will would dismiss as being unworthy of their marketing forays. Polly, Walter is recalling, was euphoric in Nepal.

Here we are in truly a fourth-world country, Walt, and just look at their determination to better themselves!

He admitted the women somehow hauling on top of their heads gargantuan crop bundles through the fields and along the dirt roads were workhorses. He didn't know about the menfolk slouched under shade of the eucalyptus trees, smoking whatever relaxant herb or root.

We must buy one of these rugs, Walt, exclaimed Polly at the carpet-weaving center. *Talk about resilience,* she went on, fingering the samples, smiling at the women, unlike them, with her perfectly white American teeth. *Refugees from Tibet, they are here in this dirt-poor place,* she said, *but it's salvation for them. With their native wool, lush Tibetan wool, the colors, earth-tones, aren't they gorgeous, Walt? Such intricate patterns but they don't shout. Pearly pink, grayish seafoam green. Oh, my God, this! Such a sublime rose. We must special-order it as a runner for upstairs leading to the guest wing.*

Polly was like a politician plunging into the crowd, seizing the head woman's forearm to underscore her admiration, inquiring of another about shipment. And then she hissed at him: *Do you realize the Chinese burned their Buddhist priests along with their ancient manuscripts? The utter horror. And here they are, welcomed next door in a land with next to nothing themselves. She fished out the wallet from her purse, attracting a few more helpers from the staff.*

For his part, Walter remembers being transfixed by the darting fingers of the children, no more than ten he supposed, fingers flying over the complex loom, threading the yarn with such precision. Of course, the smaller the fingers, the faster. But still. And as he stared, now recreating the scene, for all of Polly's exuberance he was totally inert. He watched but felt nothing. Not a shred of Polly's gushing sympathy. He was in his world and these people in theirs. He could not bridge the gap between their life-saving gray porridge and his sirloin steak. *Yes, Polly,* he likely thought at the time. *It is good there are people like you, one moment at home in these mud shanties and in the next breath a plan for feathering your already opulent nest. Me, I do not feel the lesser for acknowledging my vaulted place on this earth. I pay my employees much more than minimum wage. You're the better person, no question. But I thank my lucky stars for being emotionally retarded, along with most males, according to yet another women's magazine at the dentist's. You're the queen bee, sweetheart, and I'm the worker. It takes us both.*

~

WALTER'S GAZE IS HELD by a tassel of the dining room's carpet. *Is this why I'm obsessing about Polly? She is so long gone.* Yes, she was his first love, his true love, his only love. Fair enough she would continue to dominate his dreams, even his nebulous daydreams that flicker on and off like an original home projector when a sprocket would get stuck and then resume.

I'm not saying you're central to Gavin's problems, Walt, but at his age, just eleven, the house fire is as much an alarm for you, for me, all of us. Paula, too. You cannot simply shrug and say it will pass—his plea for attention. This is far graver. We could have been killed! I likely stood there but avoided her dark brown eyes attempting to lock onto mine.

A boy but already part man is our son. You are a man, Walt, and expected to possess a backbone solid enough to withstand adult onslaughts. I'm just one half of his parents, and I know I talk too much. I'd like to think action speaks louder than words, as they say. Yes, Walt, you're a man of action but I think in your case a man with far too few words. Gavin needs to hear you, too, say things about right and wrong, not just from me. In your tone of voice, fine, which is calm and poised. I know you do think before you speak. But you do need to emphatically say it is right to read good books and play baseball, it is wrong to give in to impatience, boredom, destructive distractions, blaming his sister for all her good grades and how could he ever match up. Maybe, Walt, now and then you need to raise your voice. Call sulking up from the table and slamming shut his door bullshit. I don't swear, ever, nor do you, at least in front of our kids. Maybe you should!

The dining room Tibetan carpet upon which his bed is now centered is a harmonic blend of an ethereal orange—he's never noticed it in isolation—and a delicious soft apple green. Maybe actual fruit was used in the dyes? He's presently studying one square foot. The weaving together of both straight geometric lines and carefree swirls in the overall pattern has held him captive for...hours? But the longer he looks, the more the carpet the length and breadth of the room becomes a cloudy mist, pleasing but preventing sharp focus on the foreground. Such detail, right under his nose all these years. What else? The old mahogany table is collapsed against the far wall. Prior to its displacement by his hospital bed, with all the extensions the table seated over a dozen. He recalls those gatherings, Polly in her prime and him glancing off from the head of the table half-listening, if that, to the vacuous if voluble conversation. *Me, I was likely dwelling on the postponed shipment of zerks from the Cleveland supplier, the pending rate increase for UPS...*

But now Polly comes a-calling once more, God love her, never idle for a moment, never a void she wasn't eager to fill, like the most eager kid in class frantically waving a hand before the teacher could even complete the question.

Oh, we did have fun, Walt. At first, she adds. Isn't that what bodies do?

Well, our bodies sure knew what to do without asking permission.

In our youth, she restates.

We were factory-fresh, he replies. Gleaming and lubricated and designed to reproduce. I had my job, you had your clubs and causes and book groups and God-knows-what on your to-do lists. But right off we made our kids.

You make it sound so—unthinking, like animals, Walt.

We were! he exclaims.

I loved our babies. I loved breastfeeding, she sighs.

And that was your next mission, Polly. Flaunting it in public to take a stand! Even the women at church were up in arms against you.

Yes, hiding like Muslim women under burkas, never to reveal the lowly sex, Polly sneers. Remember when I got single mothers at home with infants to sew nursing shawls? They earned their living and we could donate funds to the new chapter of Planned Parenthood.

Oh, Polly, you were incredible, getting that off the ground with your women friends.

And Walt, my dear, you were so generous as our chief donor. Overriding Will for a change, I might add.

Thank you, Polly. All this is ancient history, but I'm pleased you haven't forgotten.

He turns his head. Earlier today he was mired in despair. Thick with self-pity. A new pain in his middle spine he hesitates to mention to Irma, let it be. Feel the pain. Then force yourself to ignore it and stay centered in…something else, anything else. Memories, he has learned these many months, can enfold him with warmth and sweetness much as a mother must infuse the infant upon which no possible distress can intrude.

Remember that time in your office, Walt? Talk about our youth. Talk about before the family. As usual you were staying late. Not a soul about. Your light was the only one, I could find it with one eye shut in that vast monstrosity. I knew you'd forgotten our theater date. I hardly felt stood up.

You crashed into the office, he says, and literally pounced on me. You yanked me by my necktie and forced me onto the floor.

Fortunately, it was well-padded. I'm sure I was responsible for the shag rug in that otherwise regrettably bleak building, says Polly. But I didn't even bother with your tie and shirt.

You went right for my belt buckle. You practically ripped off your panties and my boxers and trousers maybe down to my knees if that. You didn't care about finesse on my part, not that night.

We missed the gourmet dinner, too, Polly reflects smiling, her lips forever painted bright red.

We went to the diner for a burger and beer, says Walter.

More than a few, she adds. Later in bed, cuddling at our best, could have been the night I conceived Paula. Walter, I did know what I was getting into. I knew perfectly well you were a free one-way ticket to my own career, no-holds-barred. I loved you for that. I needed and wanted a mate who valued me for my mind, my independence, my energy.

Don't forget you were gorgeous, Polly.

Oh, my God, who isn't at that age? she retorts.

Me, he responds. Okay, so no more slide-rules but worse. Bulging briefcase. Ever-thicker lenses for my eyeglasses. Nerd reincarnate.

Polly shakes her head no. Her lively mop of curls, those untamable curls from girlhood to prematurely gray never stopped springing into action, as if the hellion in her could not be contained and oscillated in every last strand of her hair like a leaf in a gale-force wind. I have to remind you, Walt, I did not enter a convent. To me you were adorable. I didn't care about your body like some girls with their fullbacks and what-not. I, too, was interested in your mind. Yes, you didn't say much but you could be pithy. Witty. A bit snarky, early on.

Really? I know. So long ago. Before the work was all-consuming. Before…before…oh, Polly. With us I've tried to focus on all that was good, in the early days.

Walt, do you realize you were good in bed?

I know. Before.

No, for me you were great. You did everything possible to please me.

About which you explicitly instructed me, he interjects.

Well, yes. Women are more complicated that way.

You're telling me? And not just the plumbing. That's only for starts, at least in your case, Polly. I remember your tale of you building a puppet stage for Hansel and Gretel when you were seven or eight. Sewed the curtains, the costumes, painted the scenery. Used your dad's black boot polish for the witch's kettle. And you made everyone in your family attend plus the families of your best friends in the neighborhood. And you held up boxes of soapsuds between the scenes and delivered commercials! And you charged admission and printed tickets.

Polly giggles.

You see, my dear wife, you married that part of yourself—the mad entrepreneur—there simply was no room left for.

Polly goes Hmm, for her, at a loss for words.

Polly, you became the salesperson extraordinaire that I partnered with Will for—not in my bones. You would dish out two or three proposals at a time. Art supplies for the school, escort volunteers for the women's health center when the abortion wars began, testing for asbestos in the old, ramshackle squalid homes, raising money to fight the slaughter of baby seals. Plus, eagle-eyed over our kids.

How can I shut her up? he questions. *Whoops, I mean myself. Did Irma say something about Polly the other day, this morning, whenever? No way to tell. Here when I'm down-and-out she has a way of creeping in, a draft from an ill-fitting window lashing at me in an icy stream.*

Polly's back is now turned. In the kitchen. Bustling on the phone. Even in bed.

Don't go there, Walter, he cautions himself. Instead of splitting apart the calm, uneventful day-tripping of your mind, reinforced by Rumi, with the saga of Polly like a migraine, try with all your might to zero in on the present and future in which she doesn't have a part.

"Did you remember, Walter," says Irma, serving him watered-down carrot soup with a straw, "that Polly is scheduled for her visit this afternoon?"

"Oh," he mumbles and sucks on the straw.

His mind becomes a blank. Of course, that was always his habit with her. Let her rave, let her stomp an angry flamenco, especially near their end. Standing perfectly still, he managed to survive.

~

"Walt, hello," says Polly, uncharacteristically demure in lower decibels. She heads to the cushy armchair, rearranges the cushions, and before sitting strokes one of his shins and then more lingeringly the crewelwork upholstery of a wingback chair's armrest in need of repair. All of this, it strikes Walter, is like a dog circling several times to get it right before finally plopping down. "You look less peaked than the last time."

"There was a last time?"

"You were very groggy. Probably a new med."

"I'm sorry."

"Walt, you need apologize for nothing." She is snow white but the curls have not diminished one whit in frolicsome bounce. Maybe a trifle more compact.

"You look vibrant as always, Polly. Obviously, you've got a full plate. As ever."

She smiles, barely lifting one side of her lips. "Oh, you know all that. I want to know is how you're faring. If you're willing to tell me."

"Thanks. After so many months it's the doldrums, imagine, that keep me going. Time to think."

"Oh, dear. I hope that's not too down in the dumps. I can see perfectly well, Walt, plus the visits before, that you've made peace. Paula fills me in."

He holds up a few of the slim books. "Poetry helps. Can you believe it? They're from Paula."

At this she stands, arranges her dressy pink sweat suit that has bunged up her crotch. She's portly now, of course, but was never much concerned with her weight.

"Oriental. Buddhist, Hindu?" she says, reviewing the titles, then retreats. "Good for you! On to another realm. Sorry, you know what I mean."

"No, that's exactly what they're about. Paula hasn't talked to me specifically about confronting the end, but in their way, the books she's brought me do. For she herself to broach the subject...she's too blunt."

"That's our Paula."

"Your Paula. She got all that vim and vigor from her mom."

"And now she's the business maven?"

"All right. I'll admit, for a change. We, underscored, did good. As for Gavin..."

Polly's forehead, no longer encased in rambunctious curls, exposes a network of frown lines. "Now you brought him up, I did not."

"He was here. I'm sure you know. Seemed, well, almost normal. His yachting thing. Poor as a church mouse, he didn't need to tell me. He didn't ask for a cent, Polly."

"But you doled a nice chunk out to him. I know that, too."

"Well, shoot. Paula can't object. She has it all."

"We just hope he can stay on this course, Walt—semi-independence, all right, the woman's money, but for him, and without leaning on you, maybe he could go straight."

"Have you seen him?"

"No. But that's his choice." Her shoulders, already rounded, sink lower into resignation, not relaxation.

Walter is now on high alert. This is taking every ounce of his attention and his wherewithal. In response to Polly about Gavin he simply nods. If he is to make amends with Polly, their son is not central to that. Years ago, yes, but now is a different story.

"How is Jack?" he says, he hopes without a trace of opinion one way or another, as if he's not himself but a casual old acquaintance of Jack's passing on the street.

Polly smiles, this time in earnest. "Thanks for asking, Walt. He lives on the golf course. We connect at happy hour."

"Sounds like us in our day. You having been in a whirlwind beyond the house and me as well."

Polly is immobile in the armchair, seeming to review what she will say. Any pause, certainly with Polly, eyes unflinching, only heightens the impact of what is said next. "I worry about you, Walt. I mean, I worried about you all these years. You're the father of my children."

"Till death do us part?" he attempts as a little joke but he knows and she knows he means it.

"I did not suffer guilt at leaving you. It was a two-way street. We each knew it was time. And thank goodness we separated amicably. Paula and Gavin hardly seemed to notice. They were happy for me."

"They adored Jack right off, how can one not?" states Walter.

"But they did not preoccupy themselves with your heartache. Nor did I, even though it was plain as day. You admitted—"

"That I'd long since paid you serious attention. The sex was standard issue."

"Sex is not the key element for couples, we all know that. You never, not once, had anything but the hard-on from hell." And here she makes a rosebud of her bright red lips, too bright for her matronly self, but Polly's indifference to those details was always part of her charm, and her power. "But you did worship that darn thing. I suppose every man does. The Holy Grail." She halts, abruptly, straightening the fabric of her rumpled pink slacks.

Walter takes his deepest possible breath. "I know why you left me for Jack. It's very simple. He was more fun. I know that, Polly, because for me, from the beginning, you yourself were so much more fun. Me the cog in the wheel and you gloriously whipping everything left, right, and center into shape. Good grief, the tango lessons. Remember those? And dressing me up in drag that time, all the guys, and the women in pants and ties at some protest at the shoe factory for equal pay?" He seizes up with a coughing spell.

Polly stands, yanking down the shocking fuchsia sweatpants more in keeping for a Pilates instructor. Her sneakers fit for a marathoner are also, he realizes, the sensible, overbuilt shoe for the aged. He has plenty of his own, now idle. Polly's being consumed in their early married years overseeing this neocolonial as Williamsburg-perfect was simply a phase. She is one woman for whom surfaces have their place but issues are essential.

"I can see," Polly says, "this has been plenty enough activity for you, Walt. I'll come again I hope—" She swallows the thought.

"Before the end," he finishes. "But really, Polly, all the way from Philly."

"It's a nonstop flight. I'm catching up with friends. And it's lovely to see the old place shipshape." She picks up one of his limp hands, nary a trace of a mirth or frown of sympathy.

As best Walter can, he gives her hand a squeeze. "I forgive you, Polly."

She squeezes his hand in return but with her forehead locked in a frown.

"Nothing you ever needed forgiveness for," he hastily adds. "And I'm fine. Always been. Even after."

His mouth has run dry, but Polly waits as if sensing he's not finished.

"I love you, Polly. Lucky for me that lasts."

At this Polly nods, finally allowing her lips to form a slight smile, acknowledging his sentiment, he figures, but holding whatever may be hers in reserve.

Chapter 8

Late, by myself, in the boat of myself, no light and no land anywhere,
cloud cover thick. I try to stay just above the surface,
yet I'm already under and living within the ocean.

I FOUND A PASSAGE I thought would interest you," says Irma during one of her increasingly frequent bedside visits apart from pills and food. She's paging through a book he doesn't recognize.

By way of response, Walter simply adjusts his head and neck her way with a tentative smile. He can sense the occasion is for her benefit, not his. And good for that. It's she who could use a lighter moment or two midst her manual labor, plus managing the mail, the crew, the calls, him.

"He's a contemporary author, very well-known and regarded for making Buddhism and meditation relevant. Jon Kabat-Zinn."

"I'm kind of hooked on the Middle Ages. I don't know."

"Now here he's talking about shutting off the flow of mental gibberish like a faucet. Just listen: 'It's as if you died and the world carried on…all your responsibilities and obligations would immediately evaporate…they'd get worked out without you…By—quote—dying—end quote—in this way, you actually become more alive now. This is what stopping can do.'"

Walter lets this sink in.

"'You don't have to wait until the end of your life,'" she continues reading, "'you can get a fresh take on everything right away.' Isn't this what you're appreciating about the poetry? A whole lot less of more of the same hogging your thoughts?"

He signals her to hand him the book. "Thanks, Irma. Head of the class, you are. But we already know that."

"I'm sure Paula has digested a lot of this material, subtler than the simple self-help books. Beyond her yoga, Walter, you must give your daughter credit for more than running her business. She's a complicated lady."

"As are you."

~

"Hello, Chuck. Walt here," he says, long ago having switched from Charles, claiming his investment manager as what amounts to his only close male friend. "No, nothing has changed, I just lie here…oh, I've got some books, the television…gosh, the other day I think it was, 'Auntie Mame,' so funny, Roz Russell, the technicolor like a century ago, I almost thought I was back in the fifties or sixties or whenever…no, Irma's doing all that. She does everything. There must be three remotes, I couldn't decipher just one! But I can handle the laptop…the portfolio? Haven't bothered. Oh, no, that's your job, Chuck. What do I care at this point? All for the kids…What about him? Horace is still the tax stuff, estate plans, but done all that…it doesn't matter, Chuck…besides, you know all those things that Horace has put into fine print, I only need you not him at this point…well, maybe…I've been thinking of a special…donation, gift, whatever…no, it won't affect the trusts, but the way it's set up I couldn't write a check, we'd need to transfer funds…no, Irma can help with all that, just fax the forms for me to sign, she can get a notary here if necessary, no big deal. I know, Chuck, cool is it not? Me with a cell phone! I can place calls but can't answer them, that'd be like doing a pole vault…yes, I thought I've maxed out the lifetime gift exemptions…well even if this would be taxable to me, so what? Oh, Chuck…I do have a clear head, the voice and hands work, you'd be surprised how active my days are. I can't believe it myself...incredible, isn't it? Never exercised. Maybe my body is used to being a slug and it keeps on going as if everything's normal! Oh, yes, you the jogger... if you were like this, you'd waste away in no time...used to being a well-oiled machine, idle you would rust. Somebody told me years ago, probably Paula, that fitness was ninety percent what we put into our mouths. So, of course, I count out the seven raw almonds, never less, never more, never salted or roasted, kills the nutrients, I just do what I'm told...right! You don't argue with Paula...sure, she's paying the bills, handles the accounts, as you know, or one of her assistants I suppose...all this is down pat...no, you don't need to see me, this way is fine. I like my solace, Chuck. The fewer interruptions the better...thanks, Chuck. You've been such a good mate as well as all the investment business. It's been great we don't involve any others... oh, the craziness with Will, everything at the company for so many years. Nice that it's now so simple. For me, anyway. You worry your tush off with the ups and downs, your job. Mine's done...sure, I'll let you know about that transfer if I decide...I'll keep in touch."

~

When Walter interacts with the world—his financial advisor or the visiting nurse checking his vitals—his brain if not his body hums along as would his Mercedes at seventy-five in the car-pool lane. With Paula and Gavin, however, he has to slow down and stay attuned to the extra effort required of shutting up. He must be watchful and wary, supportive of what's bugging them. They trot slightly ahead like pedigreed pets with him holding the leash, but in fact he's completely engaged for the time being with their needs and not his own. This is certainly true now with him the passive invalid and them mobile and in their prime. What's the difference going back decades? it pops up to ask himself. Early on, he adopted his stance as a parent by fleetingly side-stepping the crushing concerns of his business to listen to theirs. He let them roar ahead even when he had doubts. Learn from your mistakes! And this held true with Gavin once he was ostensibly back on his feet, a half-year after the latest rehab. Did this do them a disservice? You bet, Polly surely argued. For now, Walter not only harbors zero regrets but doesn't really care. All in the past, over and done with. But still, here with his adult children bedside, he finds himself recreating his forever mindless role. It's like reciting the Lord's Prayer without paying it the least attention. He listens to Paula and Gavin. And he plays his part of all-powerful parent who doesn't cross-examine, keeping his thoughts to himself. But, try as he might to remain neutral, he becomes very much embroiled of late, perhaps even more so straining to stifle give-and-take for the sake of returning to his realm of repose.

As for Irma, when she doesn't suggest an interlude of reading or exchanging his or her more serious thoughts, she glides in and out without notice. She has become an extension of his most inward being, that unnamable, vital component that operates alert and alone. Like crystal up close, it's something so clear as to lack even an outline, but it's as substantial as stone. This makes Irma so wonderful for him. When he slips into curiosity about her past, which she's reluctant to share, he is compromising her privacy. He knows she came to the States from Hungary, but possibly some of her stock is from Slovenia? Rumania? Croatia? For him it's all the morass of a newfangled map, polar opposite of the one he mastered in third grade. He knows she married an American GI. They split up, no kids she's ever mentioned, but she's mum about all the rest. In addition to their toying with the semi-spiritual, Irma has become the physical self he can no longer control. He is like an autumn leaf fallen from the tree, withering but still partially intact on the ground, while she's the mighty trunk and limbs standing tall and will do so right through winter.

By spring I'll be gone. He is picturing himself as a cat knowing life is to end but with no complaints, and simply, slowly, walking into the forest and curling up out of sight. The aggrieved folks at home wail away…for a bit…before the replacement, but for them life goes on. In truth, is it so different for any of us? Bleeding heart for the spouse of fifty years…or not…certainly a hole for all others easily filled with the flux and flow of their lives. What was there in Paula's book, the eerie one about the Hindu system? The sequence of four ashrams: student, worldly service, retirement, finally true dissolution as a wandering saint in the outback. Walter likes this. Here he languishes, for the most part, swallowed alive by the mists of his mind. No longer a renunciation. He's done that. He's arrived in the thicket, circled around himself like a sleeping cat, still purring but ever so faintly, eyes already closed, with one quiet, shallow breath at a time…

~

"Walter, the young fellow Alexander has stopped by. Is this a good time?"

"Alexander?" he mutters.

"He's the artist you supported," reminds Irma. "He's brought an armload of material."

"Oh, yes. The exhibit hall." He cranks up the bed, less able these days to hoist himself upright with elbows.

Irma is momentarily replaced by the tall, eager teenager. They greet. Walter struggles to reassemble their prior exchange—him dazzled by the kid's confidence then pissed off by the outstretched palm.

"Can I place some papers on the bed?" Alexander asks.

"Pile 'em on. Can't feel much of a thing down there, below the knees anyway." Being pleasant is Walter's fallback habit, slipping between the cracks.

"I thought before the watercolors were mounted and the oils framed, I could show them to you, the ones going up soon." He's had a haircut, no longer with the helmet hiding all but his mouth. The boy holds aloft one drawing after another. Well, if this doesn't hit a pause button from the world Walter knows. "I've been sketching women, girls, a few men, in the women's health center waiting room," the boy explains. "With their permission, of course. They're usually too distracted to mind me."

For some dumb reason Walter thinks of the Hitler Youth. Brazen, blond, saluting and leaping into the fold as if they could comprehend the depth of what they were doing. "Do you know about abortions, son?"

"We have sex ed starting in fifth grade. Actually, I was getting bored sketching at the bus station. The people there, well, they themselves looked really bored. I thought of the women's center because the faces and the body language—relaxed, tense, the whole range—would be a real challenge. And exciting! It was."

"I can see. These are wonderful, Alexander. Perhaps you should have an exhibit of just these drawings someday?"

Meanwhile Alexander is uncurling various rolled-up canvases. Walter is not as fond of these but, of course, doesn't say so.

"This one I did in the park. At first, I wanted it to be sunrise. Or sunset. Just a chance for orange treetops, a rose-colored sky, deep black tree trunks. I kind of went crazy. It's all purple and blue. Not really trees and sky."

"How good you are pushing yourself into new territory." Suddenly Walter is shoved down into a pit of despondence. Here is life, and I am its opposite. So much for a nice change of pace. So much for pretending my life is anything but spent, soon to be discarded. He shudders and squints tighter upon the artwork. He's becoming more capable of cutting himself off, perhaps thanks to that Zinn fellow.

"This one here of the pond. People said, 'Alex, you should put in some birds or ducks or people in a rowboat.' I used to do that." He wrinkles up his nose. "Sugar-sweet like a Hallmark card."

"You're sure focused on colors. Isn't that what you're after? Just the hint, the idea, of a pond? It forces me to complete it myself. To picture a pond or a puddle or, I don't know, a mood I can identify with. For me with this painting, it's all very quiet yellow tones. I could lie here and meditate on that one." In fact, his breathing has slowed as Walter becomes ever more curious about what makes this kid tick.

"Did you ever draw or paint, Walter? May I call you Walter?"

"Of course, you can. But goodness, making art never occurred to me."

Alexander is collecting the materials but then he has more, flat from a portfolio case. "What about music?" the boy asks. "Did you play an instrument? Or sing?"

"Heavens, no. We each do our thing. Splendid you are finding yours." Yes, he did *his thing*. Walter refuses to flagellate himself as the bottom rung of the ladder that places fine artistry at the top. There has to be something good if not lofty about pouring oneself—stamina, brains, every breath—into not just a job, in his case, but the whole of one's being. Look at this lad eye-to-eye, don't crane your neck upward as if in awe.

Alexander has withdrawn several sheets Walter can tell are watercolors. "Actually, I want to be an architect," he states buoyantly. "You need lots of drawing skills and all that. But I like the idea of building something massive out of thin air!"

"What about sculpture?"

"Nah. No way to make a living. Not gonna mope around like my dad. And I can always have art, Walter. You can have a hobby, right?" He's displaying various watercolors around the bed. "Here I'm just playing. I toss colors every which way. I love how they bleed into each other. There's no predicting what will happen when it dries."

Now with these Walter is at home. Muted. Mellow. Undemanding. Lyrical, the louder ones. But all of them soft and subtle. "You know, Alexander, these are so different from your bold oil paintings. And the very realistic portraits of the women. It's another whole dimension that you're experimenting with." He lights up. "The watercolors, they're like the poems I've been reading for ages now. They don't assert themselves with words and images that are logical and understandable. But they get under the skin. With these paintings you're suggesting not stating. Nice!" He moves a hand like a wand over the most enticing, as if he could call up some of the magic.

"You should try watercolors sometime, Walter. I could bring my supplies. It's very simple. Playful, like I said. Others have told me they're not serious like my oils. Or my drawings of people. That bugs me to keep going with them. Every medium has something really cool about it. I just tried pastels for the first time. What a mess! But the wild colors—the brightest blues and reds ever!" He returns the sheets to his flat portfolio case, gingerly, as if each has been a labor of love.

Walter is filled with admiration, even wonder. It really is miraculous, he thinks, somebody delving into such work. And this by no means diminishes Walter's own skills and accomplishments. His flash of self-effacement beforehand, a plague at times in his life, now recedes as a momentary lapse.

"Did you say how you got the idea for the women's center drawings?" he asks. "If so, I've forgotten."

Alexander stands tall—he has not sat at all for this visit, and points the sharp nose of his fair face out the window. He is like a newborn colt ready to take off, not even with a nudge. He says: "My mother told me not too long ago about something I should know. The baby she had after me when she was still with my father she gave up for adoption. By then he was beating her badly. He was jobless and drinking. I guess you know all about my grandfather that way, the drinking at least. But even though my parents got separate places I remember this, her and me on our own. He would come storming in and try to make up, she told me. She says I'm old enough to understand. Far as she's concerned, he raped her, and she had to have an abortion, no way would she have another baby. He wasn't allowed to go near her after that, and he only had visits with me now and then. But they never amounted to much, the visits, and he stopped altogether. But a few years ago, I was twelve and working after school doing yardwork. Out of the blue I called him up, and we went for a walk in the park. He said he'd stopped drinking, went to AA meetings, got back his truck license." Alexander takes a big breath. He has apparently brought his story to a close, or reached the limit of what he is comfortable sharing.

"I'm happy for you both that you're back in touch. The way it should be. Did you happen to thank Adam for sending you my way, for the exhibit donation?" Did I really say that, this question a reflex to cancel the inadvertent courtesy?

"Oh, yes! He was excited that you're sponsoring the whole rental. He's looking forward to it."

"Did you—tell him I sent my best?"

"I did that, too. I know and Mom knows he asked you for help and all that, and you said no. She was glad you did."

Walter's mind collapses into utter chaos, a traffic jam with each contradictory thought a blaring horn.

He has said enough. More than enough. So has the lad. "I still want to see photos of the exhibit, Alexander. Your artwork all nicely mounted and framed." He can't stop himself. "Who's paying for that?"

"My dad!"

Walter swallows hard. The boy is poised to depart. "Alexander, one more thing. Just before you got here, I was staring out my window for hours, letting the gradually shifting clouds compose kind of a watercolor, in their way. It fascinated me, Mother Nature at work. Gray-blue, gray-yellow, gray-black, and on and on. Maybe someday you'd let me take advantage of your good offer. To bring your watercolors here. I could try my hand. The hands still work! Or at the least, you could do some painting yourself so I could watch. Irma could set up a table and so forth. What do you say?"

He answers with the broadest grin the likes of which Walter hasn't beheld for many a moon, not counting the several beamed by

Mary Martin in the rerun of *South Pacific* that boosted his spirits for two days straight.

Does he say what he means…does he mean what he says…

Walter returns to the beatific silence of his tomb, living tomb, call it what it is. A burst of life is fine now and then, even if it does shake him violently by the total contrast to how he now resides. Maybe he can lie in the eye of a hurricane, but if the barricades are secure, storms can come and go.

Chapter 9

Thinking of the phoenix coming up out of ashes,
but not flying off.
For a moment we have form.

He's like an African child Polly once read about, a child of six or seven squatting on a rock and sitting still for two, three hours or more, motionless. This child was absorbed by the comings and goings of a little lizard, the reptile itself often frozen in place, perhaps waiting for a fly to pass by. The scene was observed and reported by an English woman whose leg was in a cast and was forced herself to be stationed for hours on end upon the porch of a landowner's house in the veld. As she stared at the child, she became incredulous at this native boy's capacity for…amusement, entertainment, maybe nothing so enlightened and downright unusual as it was for she herself. For her, the experience was remarkable in its contrast to not only her ordinary habit of being, but especially for children, young ones at that. What six-year-old from her culture could sit still? What parent could only restrain their child approaching bedtime, in bed with a book at the ready, and it better be captivating, illustrations and all. She could not imagine such utter lack of distractions in her world. Is that better or worse? Walter is presently contemplating. So, the props are different but perhaps the play is the same. Children as best he understands soak up everything in their rush to learn, to satisfy the brain cells thrumming to be filled. Early on, the adult hunkers down onto the singular racetrack of his own making. I sure did, he thinks, recalling more of Polly's typical dinner table talk. But what if the stillness of that little African boy did indeed indicate a higher capacity than what is imbued in folks from the West? To burrow so much deeper into the lower stratosphere where the gemstones and nuggets of gold are stashed away. *Now, Walter, that's right out of Rumi,* he tells himself. Heretofore, he never gave such thoughts as these but a passing glance. Usually it was Polly's lecturing her husband and children at that pause before the dishes are cleared, seizing those precious few moments of a family assembled to share a lesson worth repeating. *But here it is I who lies still, complete reversal like it is for me, if not of my choosing. It seems like we've short-changed ourselves with nonstop busyness, like addicts hooked on maintaining the high. I've come to relish the peace and quiet,* he continues. *I want to empty the mind. Isn't that what these Buddhists advise? Stop hunting. Step on this net.* He gets the drift. The absence of negative emotions. Forget desire. Forget any sort of wanting, which includes reaching for the nirvana of a blank slate, he adds. All of it must go. And then what? What kind of life is that? Death is easy but what about life in the meantime? True, he's been busy enjoying selected scenes from his past, which he acknowledges is rewriting history. Some of the bad, a lot of the good. Consider the should-have-dones but strictly from a clinician's view, peering through a thick one-way mirror in the lab at the unsuspecting person, slumped on a stool, up for review. He's simultaneously the one slumped and the one peering. There have been enough visitors, family and more, tiptoeing through the Dying Room who prod him ever farther from the fray. He can see himself a spark tossed from the bonfire well apart from the blaze, very quickly a red-hot ember cooling off into ash. But he shouldn't even be using separation from others as a means of clarification. It shouldn't matter whether he has company or not. He's to reach beyond, dig deeper, where solace is so profound that he, as he's known himself, ceases to exist. He would not be alone, he would be nothing, aloneness necessitating a person to like that condition or not. Walter pauses. This line of thought makes no sense. He thinks of Irma tending him night and day as selfless. But she has him! Blessed Irma has probably survived a minefield of miseries but here she is, devoted to him beyond any reasonable measure to provide for her own circumstance and basic needs. He believes her to be extremely content if not bubbly happy, as close to an uncompromised soul as he has ever met. That she says so little, in her case, suggests she doesn't need to. This exudes a power of which, of course, she's completely unaware. *Forget yourself, Walter. I must look deeper at others, clues right before my eyes. I mustn't go to sleep. I mustn't let the ember collapse yet into ash.*

He reaches for his pen and notebook, finds that one from a day or so ago.

Let's go to those strangers in the field
and dance around them like bees from flower to flower,
building in the beehive air
our true hexagonal homes.

~

"Do you need a stool, Alexander?" says ever-cordial Irma.

"No, thank you, ma'am. This card table's fine—I like to paint standing so my arms whirl away."

"Walter, are you comfortable with the bed that raised up?" Irma is hovering over the scene as Alexander assembles the watercolor blocks and brushes. Irma has delivered several tubs of water to the table at Alexander's request.

"I can have my meal tray over my lap. Will this work, Alexander? Upper body still with good range of motion," Walter says.

The tray in place, Alexander positions the smallest of the blocks, eight by ten inches, easily within Walter's reach, plus two cereal bowls of water and his palette, which to Walter is a rainbow of every conceivable hue.

Alexander perches on the ample side of the hospital bed after declining Irma's repeated offers of tea, water, soda, snacks. "Let's do the first one wet-in-wet. Water down the whole thing. No, not the tiny brush, Walter, the biggest! Yes."

Walter begins, gently dipping the tip of the inch-and-a-half wide brush barely breaking the water's surface.

"No, soak it! Slosh it right in."

Finally, Alexander cups his hand over Walter's and leads him to the task. "Okay, you're ready for whatever color comes to mind. Now you can take the tiny brush. No, not tap it on the cake. Wet it and really slide down into it, grab all the color you can. Good! Prussian blue. Brilliant at first but wait to you see how it's going to wimp right out."

Walter watches his dash of dramatic inky blue disappear as down a drain. "Oh, dear. You're right."

"No, this is good. It's all pale at first. As the paper dries, you can add deeper and darker shades."

And so they carry on. Alexander mops up a big puddle with a tissue to speed things along. Eventually a purplish section dries enough for Alexander to suggest some jagged lines.

"Take the end of a brush, Walter, and drag it through the dark purple…see? A mostly white line, the color pushed aside and the paper showing again. Here, like this." And he scratches a crosshatch of intersecting squiggles.

"No," states Walter. "I want to keep it quiet. Like the clouds but no storm in sight." He takes a medium sable, suffusing it with a reddish-brown that he swirls on the palette's clean center, and blots out Alexander's sharp marks.

"Rinse in the dirty bowl then dip into the clean, for another fresh color…attaboy, Walter!"

Walter, inexplicably pleased, does feel like a boy.

Irma peers on and retreats, never intrudes. An hour easily passes. "Goodness," Walter declares. "Look at this mess."

"So, it's threatening clouds. It's just a start."

"It's a reddish-blue bruise. A self-portrait."

"Huh?" questions Alexander, setting up another block.

"No, let me watch you paint, son. That was quite a burst of my limited energy."

Alexander arranges a larger block on the table, "hot press," he explains, compared to the more absorptive cold press he chose for his pupil. The hour stretches to another, Walter half-listening to the boy's earnest accompaniment to his painting as he discusses technical details—round brush versus flat, defining shape through negative space, painting only the darker background. "This keeps an interesting balance so it's not all positive outlines that can get boring." The furrows of his otherwise unmarred face lock in concentration.

It fascinates Walter that this boy is only fourteen, yet he's been serious about art forever. *I, too, was serious at fourteen,* he reflects. *There was purpose, but any pleasure?*

"Your father Adam was always in the trucking field?" Walter remarks without knowing why as Alexander is winding down. There is the vaguest family resemblance between the boy, his father, and old Will, Walter's nemesis of so long ago. Same kettle, each stew a different dish. Walter has dismissed his peevishness at the boy's asking for a donation being a mirror of his father's brash request.

"Oh, yeah. It's a rough trade, suits Dad. He's always bitching but I think he's doing pretty well these days. I know he's bummed about a pay dispute, they owe him extra, but refuse to pay overtime he says he's due. Hard to know with Dad," Alexander continues as he tidies up the table and Walter's tray. "There's probably another side to the story. I do know he's talked to Mom about wanting to run his own business with his own trucks. He has lots of customers who've only dealt with him, not his boss."

"Good your parents are talking again," says Walter. "I guess, good for you?"

"I'm not at home very much, can't wait to get my license. Neither of them has a chance to chew my head off as much as they used to." He grins, a sign of elation about what is to come.

Walter manages to slap his hands together. "Golly, that was fun! Mostly watching you, Alexander."

"Fun for me. First time I'm the teacher!"

"You know I'd be tickled for a next time. No rush, now."

He smiles broadly, clutching the armload of supplies. "It's so nice and quiet here, Walter. Nice for me for a change."

How pure and unblemished is this youngster! Walter's heart misses a beat. A hunk of gold, Rumi would say, before hammered into coins.

"Listen, son, I know those blocks of French watercolor paper that you said were the best—they can't be cheap. Please let me return the favor of your kindness to pay for a few." Without waiting for an answer, Walter grabs a checkbook and makes one out for—fifty, no, a hundred.

"Thank you, Walter! I'll bring a bigger block for you next time. More room to play."

Alexander leaves. Walter lies flat again on the bed. Yes, it was play. A spirited youth, intoxicated with potential, a completely new breed of person than the people in his orbit who are so much like himself. And so totally opposite his grandfather Will. No, don't go there.

Aloneness descends as the darkest of clouds. Walter blinks around the room. Nothing comes into focus.

~

Days later, more sinking into than floating above the murk, Walter has the sense that, true to the Buddhist teachings, he may have exhausted his reservoir of "monkey mind" interferences, if for the wrong reason. There are so few ideas left for him to toss in the air and grapple with. Instead, they flutter, ungraspable as dancing milkweed seeds, and disappear or fly beyond reach.

~

"Where is Elena?" he asks, he hopes politely, of the new and strange young woman to tend his nails, although she too is brown. To a man of Walter's background, deviations from white skin are captivating and exotic, of course at a distance.

"Elena's retired. They didn't tell you? But not to worry!" she chirps in a lovely musical voice. "I'm just a sub for today. You can tell your housekeeper if you'd prefer another gal next time."

She is prancing around as if this was her own bed, unfolding the napkin of utensils practically on his crotch, humming to herself, and to him, of course. A Latin melody. Salsa? How would he know? Although her face is a very light tan, he judges her hair to be African, with beautiful Mulatto skin a pale milk chocolate. She is petite and girlish at first in her coral dress uniform circled with a ropey belt braided with scorching-bright colors, which seems a teen-girl exaggeration. Enormous thin gold hoops pierce her ears. But there are worry lines about the otherwise fluttering and welcoming dark brown eyes. She's been around the block.

"Let's start with the hands, Mr. Walt," she sings. "Shall we?" But that is hardly a question.

"You're in charge. Your name, please?"

"I'm Tressie. It's short for Theresa. One of the few things, my nickname, they allowed in the convent."

"Convent?"

"Well, Catholic school, but some of us lived there. We girls kidded amongst ourselves, all of us given names of saints. That was a joke! Boy, it was strict but, frankly, Mr. Walt, I loved it after being stuck in the projects with an aunt, well, a wonderful woman, but six boys and me sharing the same stinking john. Not even my brothers." This, too, she made lyrical with a lilting voice that varnished the content of her words.

"You can call me Walt, Tressie. If I'm paying you, that is my wish." He fights a foolish flash of repulsion at her skin color: dark is dangerous.

"Okay, Walt," she croons, precisely clipping one nail after another. She is in no rush, nor is he. She squints at her work, emphasizing her frown and laugh lines. Her own fingers, to him, suggest the agility of a pianist. Maybe she plays a piano like Ana the cleaning lady's granddaughter. What do I know of the way the world now works? Perhaps the guitar, to accompany herself. Walter is sliding into an unfamiliar limbic zone, a boat adrift without direction. How often is anyone touching his body these days other than with medical prods?

"Such soft white hands. No calluses," she whispers.

"Been ages since they did anything more than place a phone call."

"But you're a white man compared to coarse dark skin. And I don't mean because you are privileged—"

"Although my race and I certainly are."

Tressie shrugs, moving on to filing. "The pigment, a reason for black folks who come from the Equator. Something like that doesn't change overnight."

He hesitates to speak his next thought but wonders why he's reluctant. "You obviously have white blood. Your own skin looks smooth as a baby's."

She puts down the file and takes his free hand. "Feel it," she says, placing his fingers atop her hand. She scrunches up her nose, now cute as a schoolkid. "Plenty rough enough. But yes, I have my mother's silky face. So I was once told. Never met her. Or him." Nary a trace of complication for her, at least anything that shows above the gently rocking rhythm of her comments, the continuing ballet of her fingers pirouetting from sanding one fingernail on to the next.

"There! Nice 'n smooth. On to your other hand," and Tressie does a little jig around the base of the bed and angles her curvy bum onto the opposite bedside. She may be somewhat Caucasian on the surface but with enough of a coffee cast to make a contrast with her snow-white teeth on constant display. This woman likely wears a smile even when she sleeps. Walter knows enough about basic human wiring after a year-plus of mental gymnastics—his own private boxing match it's been, that Tressie has constructed her presentation to the world from the inside-out.

His other hand also becomes her partner to a song-and-dance routine, much to Walter's delight. She cannot help but make music. They prattle on, about his kids and hers—a boy she's raising solo. This is no surprise to Walter, who has lived his life imprisoned by stereotypes for convenience sake. But still his admiration of her swells. He fights not to show it. He understands he is needy and vulnerable to the slightest physical touch, let alone this effusive and genuine capacity for affection that appears to be welded to her spine. And given just the initial information about her, Tressie certainly has a solid one of those at her core.

"Oh, dear, Walt. I'm finished with your nails but no time for the toes! I can come back next week. That is, if you are up for a repeat. There are plenty of us girls in the salon. Mostly Chinese, and they don't talk a blue streak! Sorry." She pats his hands, no, strokes them. "I didn't even finish off with the hand lotion! Cripes." And quickly she thrusts into her bag for the bottle.

"Oh, my," Walter sighs as Tressie commences with the final business of his hand job. Listen to me! But he shuts himself off, shuts his eyes, aware of his own slight groan reaching his ears but well below Tressie's humming of a lullaby…spiritual? Whatever, her voice with its angelic timbre matches the velvety presses and slides of her massage.

She becomes demure, smiling now without flashing the sparkling teeth, readying her things.

"Thank you, Tressie. This has been—divine. Of course, I'll tell Irma to make sure you come back."

She has left his hands folded across his chest. Not quite ready for the coffin, Walter tells himself, returning her parting wink with a wide smile of his own.

~

"Chuck, Walt here. I'm toying with a gift of two-hundred-thou. I know there's plenty in the cash account, but thought I should give you a heads-up."

~

It's roaring again right at him, the wheels so huge he can barely behold the truck or tank itself. But he does lift his gaze and meets the impassive glare of the drivers, oblivious of the boy in the middle of the road. The tricycle. The boy oblivious. Am I the little boy? Am I watching from the curb, could I have saved him? Am I the driver? Is this a dream or did it happen and crashes like the massive rushing truck through my deadened brain to rattle and remind me?

Walter, sweating, wakes with eyes in the dark wide open. The same old horror movie is meant to be forever shoved aside, but plays again and again.

Trixie. Dry mouth, desperate for the name. Tessa. Teresa. *Tressie.*

He slips back into damp sheets. Eyes now closed, lids still quivering.

Chapter 10

There is no need to go outside.
Be melting snow.
Wash yourself of yourself.

"There!" exclaims Irma with satisfaction. "Back in the wheelchair where you belong on a beautiful sunny day like this." She has lifted him in place with the ease of arranging a baby. She tucks in blankets over his lap and feet.

"Ha," chuckles Walter. "Imagine consigned to a wheelchair an advance in quality of life. I must say, Irma, I distrust that overused phrase. Quality of life. They hang it over people like an ultimatum. You'd better live up to some standard or other, or cash it in."

Irma carefully maneuvers him onto the terrace flooded with light, but the baseball cap is sufficient shield against the glare.

"Golly, rolling outdoors here, Irma. I feel like a kid on Christmas morning, dazzled by all the goodies. Look, the trumpet vine over the gate is still going strong. Last year there was some kind of bug."

"Is this too much breeze, Walter?"

"Gosh, it feels great."

"I'll check on you in a bit. The temperature okay in your heated gloves? You can turn them up or down or off."

"I should wear these in bed. The circulation in my fingers—now perfectly normal!"

She bustles off to her apartment above the three-car garage, probably to sort through his mail. Also, prereading the latest books Paula has brought. He knows she appreciates being so much more than a cook. Just the other day she dealt with Bruce the head yardsman on his algae problem with the pond. "Don't bother doing an overhaul," she reported to Walter her directive to Bruce. "No one's swimming there anymore, I told him. Not the boss, that's for sure." Perhaps Irma is common sense personified, considers Walter, since she seems devoid of conflicts and distractions of her own. However does she do it…

Why does he harbor a lingering bug that questions her near-divinity? Months ago, he'd had the willpower to poke into it. No more.

Walter draws in a deep breath. The cool air stings his lungs in a good way. Does he wish the doctors would make up their minds as to his prognosis? Not really. He's become accustomed to this state of indefinite limbo. And now, a green light to get him somewhat mobile again, what need to spell it all out? Back to that motorized walker that swiveled his hips? Or one of the many wheelies Paula had inundated them with at the first of his faltering? Dream on. For now, after months of the dining room window, this view of just a slice of his estate—a few of the ornamental cherries, the wisteria smothering the trellis—has exploded his take on the globe like men looking back from the moon. He adjusts the peak of his baseball cap to better squint at the kitchen-side herb garden, kept picture-perfect as ever by the yard squad as if the bedridden master is still of concern. Irma has the crew help themselves to the harvest. The sprawling lawns, the majestic trees, the ever-blooming shrubs, they all have lives of their own. Or, another way to view this, he personally was never part of it in the first place.

So, what happens to it once I'm gone? Unfinished business? Can't for the life of me remember how it's set up, apart from the portfolios.

~

"Dad, this is Trudy. My partner." Gavin has stirred him from sleep or a drug doze, what's the difference? She has short, platinum, obviously altered hair capping a sharp, sculpted face with the lines of a hawk. Twice Gavin's age, whatever that is, Walter is thinking during the introductory babble. Of course, Gavin is in his forties and looks twenty-five, astounding given the onslaught of abuse he inflicted on himself. Or maybe while the drugs were frying his brain the body was in stasis awaiting the real ravages of age. He did keep up the sports, like a kid. And now, obviously in service to this formidable woman, herself with the body of Barbie, he boasts muscles and stature as never before. These are hopeful signs.

"We've tooled over from Boston," drawls Gavin, flexing chiseled cheekbones from whatever source, Walter has no idea. "Just delivered a boat to Marblehead, and we're between gigs." Trudy has tucked legs under herself, squirreled into the cushy chair, with Gavin perched on an armrest. She sits there expressionless like a queen, Gavin her grinning consort. Good for him, and her, Walter thinks as his son outlines the intricacies of one yacht or windstorm after another. Trudy, the old pro, has a deeply tanned and weathered face. Gavin brags about her nautical accomplishments—"She grew up in Newport with the fanciest-possible rigs"—as his father assesses her history much like his own: one track from the start.

"Gavin has the strength to wrestle the masthead."

Steely, she is all business. A she-fox has claws in her manservant for that other essential physical prowess, as well. How wonderful for Gavin to be gainfully employed, sex cementing the deal. While it lasts, Walter thinks, but then whatever does? What is any single life but a path of stepping-stones, each somewhat separated from the ones prior and ahead but connected all the same?

"You're looking better, Dad. Imagine that!"

"I get back outside. Irma props me up in the wheelchair like a toddler in a stroller."

"I'm sorry we can't get you on a boat," says Trudy sincerely. "Maybe a ride in your Bentley coupe. Gavin let me peek in the garage."

"Afraid that's a tad too snug," responds Walter. "Haven't seen it for ages but hate to let it go."

"That was your sweetheart," says Gavin. "You fancied your elegant autos."

"I try not to think about that these days. Can make me gloomy."

"We're gonna visit more often, Dad. Irma is fixing the most incredible lunch! Joking."

"No, you're not, Gavin. The two of you, come and crank the place up. I'm serious. The pool, the jogging trails, the tennis courts. We'll drain the pond and get it back into shape! The upstairs must look like a long-lost museum even though I know Ana wouldn't leave a cobweb in sight."

"Thank you, Walter, but that's not likely," says Trudy. "My son Jake is my top priority at this time. He's worked his way through high school, got top grades, but hit a wall in terms of financial aid going forward. No résumé, no sports and extra stuff. He's applied to junior colleges and would hope to move on. I help him out all I can but... I'm doing what I love instead of working nine-to-five. Your son is my life-support system." All this is spoken matter-of-factly, a way of applauding Gavin, certainly not making a plea for Walter's sympathy in terms of her being pinched.

Walter is not about to reach for a checkbook like he did at the end of Gavin's last visit. Topmost for Walter is his son's new lease on life. A job, any job—building blocks of the work ethic! How great this gal is mentoring my son. Walter is sharp enough to smell any whiff of somebody out to fleece him. Been in that mode for most of his life. In fact, Gavin's dependence on this woman's savvy and fearsome physicality if anything has displaced Gavin looking to his father to bail him out, is the way Walter sees it. Sure, Gavin knows of inheriting a bundle when Walter passes on, but he truly appears in no hurry for that. After what's been his cockamamie crash course from boyhood, right now, day by day, he appears to be holding it together just fine. They chat on.

For so many years, Polly studied addiction and the counsel of its experts, convinced it was a disease, at least as manifested in their son, and far beyond his ability to control, let alone be subject to blame. Yet some seed of insistence stayed lodged in Walter that his boy was part *him*, made of enough sturdy stuff that should suffice to build recovery upon. Look at Polly. Look at Paula. Look at himself. People achieving in the world with enviable, privileged sets of skills. Practically no excuse not to succeed and none to fail. If anyone was to blame, it was Walter himself for not seizing the situation as yet another catastrophe to resolve, instead of abdicating to Polly and endless shrinks, happy for the recompense.

They share a magnificent lunch outside under the pergola. More specifically, Trudy and Gavin devour Irma's seafood salad while Walter sips the fresh pea minted soup from a very large tablespoon, graduated from months with a straw.

There's a pleasant pause, mouths tapped with linen, as they admire the manicured spread. Even to Walter it seems more a theme park than a home. And don't accuse Polly. It was primarily his own doing, as if simply affording it was reason enough, not a passion for splendid Colonial architecture situated on grounds suitable for a fox hunt.

"Take it, Gavin. Take the Bentley."

"What?" His boyish self is suddenly stern.

"Take the car with you. What's the point otherwise? Irma will get you the keys, whatever paperwork. I'm sure it's all up-to-date."

Trudy rests her sterling silver fork on the English bone china plate, other extravagances from yesteryear sitting idle. For the first time, she loses her composure and smiles wide-eyed as an adolescent.

"Trudy can drive your car back to Boston, you take the Bentley, Gavin. Keep it in a good garage while you're traveling. I'll give you a check to make sure you can cover that. It's in impeccable condition. One of the gardeners tinkers with it and takes it for a spin every week. I don't know if you should race it on the interstate, but you can have some fun in the country. Whatever, folks. Just understand I'm downsizing. About time."

"Jesus, Dad—" And he's speechless.

"Can't sell it, though. Still in my name."

They take off, elated. Walter is plunged into depression. *Why did I do that…desperate to make things all right and rosy for my son… but that was all about me,* he continues, *not him, let alone abruptly shifting gears into sugar daddy will do any of us a damn bit of good.*

~

THERE'S THE FAMILY DOCTOR and the blood doctor and the heart doctor and two neurologists plus the consulting one from the Mayo Clinic whose latest report conflicted with the teams at Cornell-Weill and Sloan Kettering. The more complicated it becomes, the less Walter is able to comprehend. Or to give a hoot. Long as Irma can sort it out, along with the daily flow of visiting nurses, which vein to draw from next, which pill to pop and when. Sensible, rock-solid Irma runs the show, him the dish du jour on display. As long as he gets rolled outdoors on nice days and stretches his lungs. It can seem almost normal, forgetting he's strapped in place like in an electric chair, instead casually counting the varieties of birds in his yard. Cedar waxwing one moment, a rose-breasted grosbeak the next. And, on special occasions when he's least expecting it, a brilliant cardinal followed by his muted female will sail through the scene. In that instant, Walter has won the lottery and forgotten all else.

~

NOW WHEN IS THAT Tressie woman from the nail salon returning? He hasn't forgotten the name, no sirree.

Who is the luckiest in this orchestra?

The reed.

Its mouth touches your lips to learn music.

~

"PAULA, HOWEVER DID YOU find this rig?" Irma is helping Paula buckle him into the latest contraption of her doing, well beyond the simplicity of his wheelchair, more to Walter a Rube Goldberg machine.

"Dad, you are not the first invalid—"

"—or the terminally ill?"

"—to have some time for fresh air. And fun!"

Irma looks skeptical but would never contradict Walter's daughter, Paula having made elaborate arrangements for the delivery of the buggy from a horse farm near Philadelphia that raises trotters and pacers. One of Walter's handymen fashioned the connection to a mountain bike, which Paula also specialty ordered. This is its trial run, just around the driveways. Irma single-handedly as always lifts Walter into place. She has approved of the extra belts and harness to surpass such restraints on surely the wildest of rollercoasters.

Paula is sporting racing gear, those black skin-tight shorty leggings, sleek helmet, plus ferocious-looking black sneakers streaked with phosphorescent orange lines, like the gums of a snarling leopard. Who is he to have doubts of his safety, manhandled by the likes of his Amazonian watchdogs?

Off they go, probably at a snail's pace but to Walter's frail face he is being whiplashed as if this chariot was indeed on a racetrack. He can feel tears streaming down his cheeks, not from joy but from his stinging eyes. Irma forgot sunglasses. So she's not perfect. Nor would be this outing to his team of doctors. The battery-operated warming vest he now wears indoors pushes him to the edge of overheating. Who knows what's being jostled and yanked deep inside that's been quarantined to bed rest? Who cares? He shuts his weeping eyes. He prays she takes another spin, opposite direction, please let this last. She does so. She knows her dad. Afterward, ensconced back in the hospital bed that's built like his old Rolls, Walter exclaims, "The bumps were best of all!"

"Dad, I cannot thank you enough for building the new unit outright. We agreed. I only asked if you would float the loan." Paula undoes the rubber band of her ponytail, shakes her head sideways, stands instead of sits. She is grasping the rail at the base of his bed, leaning into it as would a stretching athlete, although to him she looms like the coach after the loss, assuming the posture for the tongue-lashing about to commence. He crosses arms across his chest, best he can do by way of defense.

"From the bottom of my heart I appreciate your willingness to extend so far beyond the lifetime taxable exemption it looks like you've already met. That's still up in the air. If it helps, I've talked with Charles and Horace about a property transfer from one of your trusts to another, to raise the valuation to an amount more likely when you pass on, so there's hardly any capital gains. This'll compensate for the taxable gift to me now."

He gets the idea perfectly well but is more attentive to the tightening grip of her hands on the rail. She continues with legal particulars and finally lets go of the bed, standing erect as if she's presiding at her board meeting, now with her arms folded crossways as are his.

"Who is Adam Crosby?" she asserts, not asks.

So that's it. "You would have known him as Adam Michelson. Will's son. Before Will lost custody of his boys and they changed their names to their mother's. Eli, his older brother, was probably eager to disassociate himself from his father. Adam was likely dumb to it all."

"Yes, dumb Adam! The derelict. How could you do this and without letting me know? My accountant threw up a red flag in an instant."

"It's only two hundred thousand, Paula. Pocket change for us."

"What the hell for?"

Walter attempts to slide backward into the cubbyhole of composure he's been nestled within for ages. At this he fails. "Adam, like you, is probably close to fifty. He goes to AA."

"So what? How would you even know?"

"I've—I've made sort of friends with his boy. Alexander. He's an outstanding young artist."

"Christ, Dad." She throws herself into the armchair but does not lean back. "Sort of friends."

"Paula, we are sitting here largely because I got to keep it all."

"Oh, my God. They're trying to blackmail you, take advantage—" She runs out of steam, presses her temples.

"Adam is back on his feet, even more so than your brother, I should add. He's returned to his trucking business. And the guys he works for are holding all the strings and limiting him. He wants to go off on his own."

"Dad. We never got to sit here with your ever being a sucker. Every cent you know damn well you were entitled to."

"And you, my wonder woman? You didn't get a head start? It's still going to be all yours. And some for Gavin, of course. You're the one who needs it. You're swelling the wealth. Employing hundreds. Creating capital. So, Adam, he just needs this helping hand."

He has shut her up but can tell the wheels are spinning fiercely. She holds all the cards regarding her father at her disposal, including power of attorney. He knows she knows this gift to Adam is just a blip. He also knows for her there is a crack in the foundation, and she will stop at nothing to patch it.

"Speaking of Gavin," says Walter, "he's looking lean and trim like he would between his—incarcerations, rehab camps, I forget what they were called."

"There were too many to keep track of," she says, tired and slumped now but still teetering on the edge of vexation. Suddenly Paula looks up, startled as a thief caught in a flashlight. "Don't tell me you're going to set him up with another hair-brained scheme, like your underwriting him as a beer distributor. The women's essential oil franchise, worse. Just another way to get laid."

"Paula."

"I'm not paid to be polite. And it's got me way beyond my need for your approval. All of which you do in fact approve of." With her hair down and softening a beautiful face, she is so much like her mother—natural beauty dismissing the need for makeup but masking the dead serious woman on board.

He heaves a sigh. "How are your kids?"

"You want the problems or the platitudes? We're normal. Just like you and Mom and Gavin and me."

"Skip the kids. Are you okay?"

She smiles, finally. "How the hell would I know? Barely have the time to brush my teeth. Sound familiar, Dad?"

He watches her collecting herself, shaking out her leonine limbs, checking her watch, readying her withdrawal.

"Well, I do have the time now, Paula. Not worrying, just thinking. And that includes not just about yourself but your brother. And, believe it or not, your mother, too."

She kisses him as if she means it, as if she approves of the spunk with which he had put her down. And then he thinks: that can only fire her to be ever more vigilant about, to her, his reckless spending.

Today, a mere skirmish. The battle lines have been drawn.

~

"Quite a week, Walter," says Irma, idling bedside with an empty soup bowl. "Both your children in and out. The visits appear to have invigorated you."

"Invigorate? They stir the beans, that's for sure. Odd that Paula was more the handful this time."

Irma cocks a hip, in no rush to leave. "I know you're listening to them, taking them in, shifting yourself aside."

"Do I have a choice at this point?"

"Of course, you do. Acknowledging where they're at, with you of no concern. There was a line in one of the new books quoting the Dalai Lama. 'My religion is kindness.' Both Paula and Gavin after their visits said as much to me—Dad is being so nice."

Little do they know. What even do I know of what I'm about?

Chapter 11

When I hold out silver coins,
take them,
and give me a cup of liquid full of gold light.

NO, WALTER. THESE DAYS I just give talks around the country, Polly said ages ago best he can recall.

You're a motivational speaker! Nothing's changed.

I sit on panels where women from around the region gather to discuss ways to bolster their fledgling or underfunded chapters of Planned Parenthood.

You've never let that one go, Polly, and good for you.

Well, it's more than how to raise money, it's PR. Imagine it has to keep being resold, this most basic of rights. Getting stories out about an abused mother right in their midst, on her own with five kids and trying to make ends meet, desperate to avoid another pregnancy. That kind of thing.

He shakes his head, still in awe of this woman who used to be his wife. And Jack's okay with you hiking all over?

After thirty years he says he loves the chance for frozen dinners. A break from my kale salads and the like! He has his cigars, and can indulge at the club with his golf cronies. He's so easy. Watches Gomer Pyle reruns, can you stand it?

I do, too! He lets that sink in. This woman with two men cut from the same cloth. He says: I admit I was not easy, Polly. Nor were you. We'd both be squirming at the symphony.

Oh, Walt, you always got headaches or an upset tummy the minute we began a vacation. Simply could not relax, those years.

You should see me now, he thinks presently, flat on his back. *I guess you've been here a few times to visit, I've lost touch.*

Paula will send him an email with a video attachment featuring a clip of Polly on some local TV interview, commenting upon the fight to block a state initiative banning abortion outright. Polly always appears so rational, articulate, never angry. Schoolmarmish in her matronly years, a worldly senior whose wisdom you don't question. *But isn't that the role I happily helped her assume at a third our age now? You go your way, Polly, and I'll go mine. What about the personhood of a zygote thing down south?* it strikes Walter. *Was that Polly or more recent? It's all a mash-up the more he attempts to recollect. If I'm going to reminisce about the old girl, why not the few but marvelous times smooching when we each got carried away? Ray Charles in his raspy voice tripping out "Georgia On My Mind," or was that farther back in high school with another girl, him too nervous to notice her name or the particulars? Whatever he remembers specifically with Polly, it was something slithery—Peggy Lee, Nat King Cole?—as he and she stroked and groped but ever so slowly, in sync to the mellow, sexy music. Johnny Mathis. Swoon. The two of them definitely on the same page for that business.*

Suddenly Polly is saying: *We were both absent parents for Gavin. It wasn't just you, Walt, glued to your desk downtown. I wasn't traveling, but soon after Gavin in grammar school, for me it was one project after another. I sure as heck didn't correctly read the early signals for his unwinding.*

Mostly luck of the draw, Walter offers. *A faulty gene.*

But at the time, somehow between the lines, and all the talk otherwise, Polly left open the possible interpretation that pinned much of the blame on the man of the house.

All of this is in the dustbin. Leave it be. Backward glances can become a pain in the neck.

Except what else is there, with no future?

~

THE LATEST MONTHLY BLOODWORK indicates no change. His condition is stable. Perhaps the periodic stints outdoors stimulate his appetite. The doctor seems pleased. Irma his overseer stands proud. Walter is neither disappointed by the news nor hopeful. He remains wafting in otherworldly realms, landing on no one planet in particular. His medical situation is what it is, and beyond anything he can do. As such, he is determined not to dwell on it. On some days, he can even lapse into a state of utter freedom. Dare he call it bliss? It's like being blinded momentarily by a fiery scarlet sunset, seizing one's attention to the point of forgetting to breathe. Whoever he is, for those few seconds, ceases to exist.

~

"NOW WE DO THE feet!" chirps Tressie from the nail salon for Round Two. She prances about the bed as if she's arrived at a disco, ready to cut loose.

"Afraid not a lot of feeling down there," says Walter.

She presses a foot firmly between her two hands. "You feel that?"

"Sure. I've been thinking of the massage you did that first session on my hands. That was heavenly."

"Don't rush me! Massage later. First let's look at these nails." She's not in a uniform, her scant bid for looking professional a simple white shirt compromised by the white skirt barely below her bottom, more like the outfit of a tennis pro. The plain blouse makes all the more vibrant a big red hibiscus, artificial he assumes, pinned behind one ear. But Walter, who admittedly has not seen it all, is blown away by the jungle flower pattern of her tights, an outlandish, irreverent Easter parade of their own.

Tressie works like a surgeon on each of his toes, snipping with precision while her delicate fingers not employed are aiming every which way so as not to interfere. One of his big toes is cocked askew at an alarming angle about which Walter is squeamish. She looks up. "I've seen bunions much worse. Be glad there's no fungus, your feet are fine."

He closes his eyes, the better not to be distracted by her dazzle, by her twitching volumes of frizzy hair, like the whole of her, as if she's inescapably programmed with dance steps, a wind-up doll that never runs down.

He slips into a semi-dream. Polly is hovering over him during their sex early on, taking the lead, giving him permission to let go. That fades and is replaced by remembering that Tressie is a single mother with a son. Or is that Gavin's woman Jody, Tonya, something with a T? Doesn't she too have a son, or am I mixing them up?

"Before I file, I'm going to soak your feet."

"Really?"

"Irma said you can sit up. I'll just swivel you around so you can be on the edge of the bed." And she proceeds to set up a small stepladder and the tub of warm water into which she adds salts.

He is anxious sitting upright unaided. Where's Irma? But he does not want her to meddle! This is Tressie's show. Soon he's engulfed with a pleasure never known. He sighs, slumped, ignoring his precarious pose.

"You like that, Mr. Walt?"

"Oh, yes," he murmurs. "Like once in the Caribbean. But no kids, no wife, no sharks."

"Shush," she croons and softly hums another Latin song.

Eventually, reclined once again, Tressie gently pushes back the tabs of flesh that have encroached over the nails. It hurts but how he is savoring all these sensations! Wiping him dry with a warm towel—where did that come from?—she begins with the filing, clipping now and then a nail that doesn't meet her standard for perfection. She is all business, but every time he catches a glimpse of those technicolor tights, he thinks of the cartoons before the main film at the kids' matinee: perfectly silly, purely for fun.

"Now for the foot massage. Lie back down. Close your eyes. Stop staring!" By way of halting conversation, she hums a tune he is straining to identify. "The Girl from Ipanema." Surely not. Way before her time.

He does as he is told. He sinks into the firm but tender pressure, then release, followed by smooth strokes lapping at him like the undulating water mattress he and Polly once tried to revive their aching backs if not their marriage. Soon he is lulled into submission. The whole of the cosmos is condensed into a single, lowly toe. Thank goodness there are ten of them.

Wetness again. "Are you awake, Mr. Walt? You don't want to miss the finale." She rubs her hands with a lavish helping of the lotion and takes up his left foot. She is massaging a much greater expanse, up to and over the ankle, as she has done on each toe. Again, his gaze is riveted upon her. He is unable to remove this mesmerizing creature from the picture, to focus solely on his feet. She's like ogling he once did as a kid at an exquisitely colored bird in a zoo cage, transported from some slice of jungle a world away, no bearing on his reality. After the right foot, she gracefully lowers it to the bed and then runs hands down the tops of both feet, her touch ever more feather-like until he cannot tell the difference between the final stroke and when she is actually finished.

Her playful clothes, red-painted lips, her dark eyes dead serious upon her work, all of her is gathered now into a calm, quiet stance, much as individually vivid hues blend into the pleasingly arranged bouquet someone has brought.

"Thank you, Tressie."

"No, thank you, Mr. Walt. You're paying me."

"I'm sure not enough."

This she dismisses. "Are you getting physical therapy on your legs?"

"A few years ago. All that stopped."

"No way! You have feeling there?" And she lifts the lower sheet, rolls up his pajama bottoms to his knees, and touches him like a technician, no finesse. "You feel that?"

"Of course."

"I thought you said your legs no longer worked."

For this he has no response.

She raises and bends a shin. "Does that hurt?"

He shakes his head in the negative. Tressie asks if she could chat with Irma and, through her, his doctor. "I'm a licensed PT. Mostly what I do. The nails are for extra income. I work six days a week, but it doesn't wear me out. Grooming nails is so much fun." She cocks her head, the fake hibiscus flashes.

"For my part I'm not sure 'fun' quite captures it. Obviously, you love what you do."

"What else is the point?" She starts collecting her things. "You can get a job and make money doing anything. But both kinds of my work, it helps folks so much. And I get to meet such interesting people!" She pinches a big toe and reassembles the sheet.

"I'm interesting? Is flatterer part of your job description?" He says this smiling. "Me, one more carcass on a slab before the last one at the morgue?"

Her arms drop to her sides although she is still clutching her bags. She sets them on the floor, her bright red lips pressed together along with narrowed eyes. "Listen here, Walt. You are precious to me because you are a person. What is more amazing? How are you different from me or your Irma or anybody running around on two legs? There's still life in those legs of yours and I mean to prove it!" Finally, she touches his cheek, picks up her parcels, and sashays out of his room.

"Don't forget to talk to Irma about the PT business," Walter raises his voice best he is able. Although the door clicks shut, he doubts that Tressie is capable of dropping her mission. He could not care less about PT. Time with her, another matter.

~

"Are you sure, Walter?" Irma is marching around him the next day, her long, thick single braid tapping her back like the strictest of teachers wielding a ruler.

"If I can sit why not stand? This walker is constructed like a Sherman tank. My grip is regaining strength, squeezing that hard rubber ball Tressie gave me."

"All right, but just stand. Please. No inching forward."

"Not yet," he says.

"Not now," she corrects.

And so he presses his feet to the floor and hoists up his torso by thrusting his shoulders back. He does it! True, to aid him upright, his calves are firm against the solid bed. He settles into it. Takes a deep breath. "Even before I do PT with Tressie. How long has it been since I managed to the potty setup over there?"

"One thing at a time, Walter. I appreciate that woman has been a tonic. But let's not overdo and go backward."

"What's to lose, Irma? So I fall and smash apart and have to lie prone again. Forever. I was already prepared for that. Now, please, my good woman, would you kindly back off, circle the room, whatever. Let me just stand for a few more minutes as if you're not even here, as if my body is in perfect working order, as if…as if…"

~

"This is great, Walter. You can sit at the table now," says Alexander, placing in front of him the eighteen-by-twenty-four block of fine French watercolor paper. At Walter's request he has set up a still life of dried flowers, an apple, and a pear. "You can pretend you're Cézanne."

"This is no pretense, son. Nothing to do with the jug and the fruit. This is all about your budding teaching career as an artist. I'm just a go-between. Maybe I'll make that apple orange and the pear black. You said to play, so here we go."

To Walter, Alexander seems much older than a teen. He is tall for a youth, and he embodies that as yet unchallenged assumption of one's inviolable, soaring selfhood. Perhaps it is simply Walter's own vastly shrunken concept of himself at this point, by comparison.

An hour later, the painting is a sopping, muddy mess. They peel off Walter's debacle so that Alexander can take a turn. He doesn't so much as render the still life as use the elements as a launching pad. Everything the boy does is stylized to Walter. More like calligraphy. If the objects weren't there, Walter would have no inkling of what this is about. Maybe happiness. Maybe wild abandon. Maybe no more than the intersecting of opposites, according to Alexander: orange with green, yellow with blue, and so on. Walter loses track of his thoughts and just delights in the display of Alexander's agility.

"Adam, I mean Dad, just cannot believe your generosity, Walter," the young man punctuates their conversation when wrapping up the session. "He's taking his time about how to proceed with your money. Leasing space, maybe. Buying equipment. He's also looking at how he could expand his trucking services to a few towns beyond."

Walter nods. "I'm curious about what's next for you, Alexander. Turned fifteen. On to sophomore year in high school. I'm not surprised your big painting of those psychedelic lines won best of show at the exhibit. Will you keep on with your art at the larger school?"

Alexander has the habit of rapid blinking when he has to think. "Good grades are what I need. If I can get into a college with an architectural program…there's tons of competition."

Walter holds his thoughts, one of the few habits of his own that he regards as commendable.

"Time's going to be really tight. Dad said I could work after school and weekends. You know, desk work, paying bills. Mom really needs the extra cash. And hey—" He brightens. "Maybe I could make a job sound impressive for college applications!"

Walter is suddenly beleaguered by all the tedious work people do. Didn't Trudy—that's her name, Gavin's woman—tell of the limitation of the yachting service, which she loves, in order to avoid drudgery otherwise? Something, too, about her son facing obstacles to financial aid. Single mothers. Tressie another one working like a demon, in her case, joyfully, but really. No wonder I became a multi-millionaire, who's counting, just to make sure I could avoid the crushing, dispiriting, meaningless jobs most of humanity is gripped and squeezed by in that unavoidable vise…

Alexander is tidying up. This youngster is yet his latest visitor swathing him with pleasantries like so many beguilers of the sultan's harem. Where is the boy headed? To more of the same. Drafting another high-rise instead of creating an exultant watercolor like his of this afternoon. Who can possibly afford to be an artist? Walter has paid for Ana's granddaughter's piano lessons. Ana's as well. Bought them a piano. That pittance slid under Paula's radar. What about his own grandchildren? Paula's loaded and doesn't need help with college for her kids. But did he ever offer way back to send them to private schools if their interests or skills led in some direction or other? Does he even know what they are up to? Situated outside of Philadelphia is no excuse. He's nothing more than an enabler to their mom, another soon to be a single mother who hit the jackpot, yes, but with huge help from him. What more does Paula need now? What nerve to bust a gut, he knows she did, over the gift to Adam, Alexander's reclaimed father, so he could kick-start his own trucking outfit. What about Gavin? As Alexander is tactfully critiquing Walter's second attempt at a watercolor for the day—the second one so opposite to his initial mud pie as to be inscrutable and near invisibly pale—Walter continues to goad himself over his minimal support of his son. Gavin is living his life apparently without a spare nickel to the point of tossing aside ever the possibility of earning resources for real. Money does matter and isn't everything but Gavin has lowered himself to settle in the cellar, sober but sealed off from any expectations of his potential. His parents left him with the message he was damaged goods, no fault of his own, redemption defined as no more elevated than sobriety and the discipline to avoid addiction. In his thirties Gavin apparently earned his father's neutrality if not praise, and Walter left it at that. It seems to Walter here and now that Polly wrote her son off ages before the centrifugal force of her own enterprises precluded her paying him any attention whatsoever. Which she did once acknowledge. Too late. And Paula, in lockstep with her mother, still classifies her brother as a retard escaping further folly by a knife's edge. With Paula's own ongoing and hostile divorce from that nice fellow Chad, her younger brother Gavin is but a bad nightmare. Who needs a lifeboat more than my own boy? Walter confronts himself. However to pull it off? Paula of the purse strings would have to agree.

Alexander is bidding Walter farewell. As usual, Walter has run off on his own, ignoring the drift of idle talk when it doesn't suit him. Shame!

"Thank you so much, Alexander! I loved it. Thanks for helping me back to bed. Thank you for all of it. Oh, dear, I feel I should be paying you. For lessons, for the—next time—"

"It may be a while, Walter, I'm afraid. I promised Dad to answer the phone in his new office and set up his files. Just three afternoons a week, but still—"

"No, that's great. My helping him out is helping you out, too."

"Bottom line, it's helping out my mother. We'll see if I can save beyond that. A car! A used one, for sure, but my own wheels! Someday." He waves a hand from the doorway as he exits.

"Someday," says Walter quietly to himself, confused, almost angry at so many people struggling and somehow circling his bedside with such boring, basic needs. He who has everything has created this vacuum eagerly filled by visitors who loom ever more in dire straits. Alexander should be going to art school. His mother should be doing something more than for the minimum wage the boy has to supplement. Adam deserves more than a measly two-hundred K. That'll hardly cover two trucks. Irma deserves a full-time assistant and paid vacations. Who knows, she has family stuck in newfangled Central Europe she won't talk about? Tressie should own the nail salon. He should hire the blasted girl full-time for himself. Gavin needs…Gavin needs…to eventually stop leaning on Trudy who has a big obligation of her own…but if they last as a couple and he loves her—however would Walter know—she too is a life force requiring fuel…

What it is with all these single mothers going solo? They should band together, form a whole so much better than their parts. Polly would like that one. If he's bought their daughter a darn warehouse, the least he can do for Polly with her Planned Parenthood network, Polly a five-star general in the war to help women…

He shuts his eyes if not his mind. *So much simpler when I kept it to myself.*

Chapter 12

When you succeed in controlling the words that you speak aloud,
the words that you speak to yourself
may then astonish you.

WALTER THOUGHT WHEN HE was told, inevitably, several months prior, that he could no longer drive, it would be the worst day of his life. Irma waited until Paula came to visit for Paula to so inform him. Irma leans on Paula for any steely communication with her father, of which Walter is well aware. He is just as content that Irma, his caretaker running the household, be reserved for the ongoing and usually silent calls for assistance. And, of course, their occasional chats about the pearls of ancient wisdom from his books. But the day came to deal with his not driving.

Dad, Paula had said quietly but with unflinching conviction after Irma tentatively broached the subject. *You can barely turn your head to the left to check oncoming traffic. Your right side is nonfunctional. I'm sorry, but we cannot take the chance the next time in the Benz will be more than your fender bender in the bank parking lot a few months ago.*

You're saying, Walter replies, *that I'm the most lucrative candidate in the community to be sued. Heaven forbid I cause a spinal paralysis, let alone a death, and you can kiss the family fortune goodbye. You're absolutely right.*

But the interesting result for Walter is the opposite of losing independence. He felt free in the oddest way at the time of Paula's declaration. Not driving will spare him meaningless errands, like hand-carrying deposits versus switching to online. Picking up the next prescription, queuing up in long lines at the pharmacy. Enough of retired life as a robot. More time for discovering the life of the mind…as when submerged in a good book, as Polly would preach, to shed one's shell and inhabit another's…as a child swallowed whole in a fairytale, to permissibly taste evil, to imagine possibilities so far beyond the known world.

And so goes his rationalization as an ex-driver before the next likely item of selfhood to go on the chopping block. *So what if such considerations are reverting to the denial stage I was supposed to have advanced beyond?* he thinks. *Because being in the throes of letting go still means grappling with it all. Sitting down to pee, indeed! That was a toughie.* Whatever, he is accommodating the spaciousness, a newfound pleasure of solitude. He can feel at times like he's landed on the moon or a new planet altogether, heretofore unphotographed and still a mystery. He finds it stimulating, what to make of totally new environs. So. Welcome to the wheelchair, Walt! Walkers of every concoction—been there, done that. Waddle, waddle, like a lame duck. Now, he can slide into this latest contraption without Irma and dash to the john, slide again by grabbing the new bathroom bars, accomplish both Number One and Number Two on the cushioned, elevated (and warmed!) seat, unaided. He pictures himself in training to be a circus monkey or one of those Russian toddlers picked with potential as a gymnast. He's had no say in the reinvention of his life, but no reason not to let it be a springboard…

Oh, Walter, who are you kidding?

That naysayer still gets a word in now and then but strictly as foil to his mover and shaker in the lead. The wheelchair has a brake, with forward and reverse, letting him crash on occasion for the heck of it into Polly's rare English highboy. Rattle that china, good for nothing nowadays. He did like his speed with the Benz, and lord knows with the Bentley. He's sure Gavin and his gal are having a blast. Why not? If just for conveyance people can now have what amounts to an electric golf cart on the open road! But this sleek wheelchair, who would have thunk? Such fun. He can only imagine the versions to follow as one body system of his after another shuts down. Mechanical wizards—probably German again, they lost the wars but not this race—are ready to outdo themselves. Paula dutifully restrained herself from imploding when learning of his gift of the Bentley to Gavin. For the time being, his daughter has rewarded herself aplenty by driving her home-building business ahead by leaps and bounds. She could have a fleet of such vehicles but for now she's chosen to postpone any semblance of frivolity. He hopes the right guy comes along and takes her by surprise. He hopes she doesn't go the whole shooting match like he did until it was too late. Gavin has been her identical twin in reverse. All play but now a glimmer of flexing the apparatus of enterprise. He hopes, Walter can hope. Is it too late to make up for his practically ignoring his children to suit himself? Him relying on Polly for all of that, denying that she, too, was off in a world of her own…

Walter scoots to the toilet and back for a break, but that doesn't stop Polly from taking up where he left off, never missing a beat to intervene, that Polly. But abruptly, for a change, she's having to listen to him.

You were so dexterous, Polly, expressing our feelings and opinions to our kids, so I thought was happening. But did Paula and Gavin hear them as just so many obligatory parental utterances? Did your heart back up your words? What about opinions from me? As if I had any about myself, let alone affairs of the family. Well, now I do. If not to share with you, at least I can acknowledge these misgivings here and now. For example, you strained to resemble the rich. Who gives a shit about the lineage of this highboy or that Oriental? I might have toyed at the time to wonder what you were doing with my, okay, our, resources, but to question you? Certainly not. Maybe unbeknownst to me I was getting off on all these acquisitions. Maybe I just assumed they were the appropriate spoils and proof of what I was producing from those steaming bowels of the factory. But so much of this didn't and still doesn't sink in. Because I'd become rich, it apparently voided the subject. I was indifferent to wealth once it was in place. I didn't so much want to stockpile more of it for me personally but to balloon the business, a separate entity altogether. Just how the script reads. It actually made it easier for me to have others dependent upon me. The reverse, unthinkable. My universe began and ended with the bridge of my nose, Walter continues, viewing himself not as Polly's ex-partner now but as a character in a film, at first neither likable, forgivable, nasty, neutral, or otherwise: a stranger whose acquaintance he has yet to make. Although he paid his people handsomely, he could never envision himself in their shoes. The grasping lives of his parents, Walter as boy witness, happened in another time and place altogether. He saw life as problematic enough without worrying about the burden of others. This became his mantra. (Another word from his Sufi books! Maybe it is sinking in?) But in time he proudly played his self-assigned role as the leader, and there can only be one of those, for good or ill. Walt for good, Will for ill, as it evolved. For thirty or forty-some years this was never in doubt. He cared more about the welfare of "his people," his own well-being no longer a concern. To him, not fretting over his flock would be like a driver with a carload of passengers suddenly turning around, taking his eye off the road, and letting them all crash into oblivion. Just because his parents survived at the brink of poverty didn't mean his own ultimate station in life was to be a carbon copy. They had no options, nor did he at first, the boy-knight, donning his initial suit of armor, which took ages to outgrow. Walter's first summer job at fifteen, lying about his age since it was then illegal, was to scour sunup to sundown blackened pots and pans caked with crud in a stinking hellhole of a greasy spoon kitchen. Complain? Unheard of, for him. That kid was delirious, he recalls, with the measly paycheck. It was real money he could save and have earn interest. For what? For more of the same. The following summer's job was in a proper hotel kitchen and, yes, scrubbing pots and pans, for a start. And then he got noticed, the boy wonder-worker, soon elevated to assist one of the sixteen sub-chefs, the garniche, who made swans of ice spewing champagne at cocktail hour for the guests, ladies bejeweled and gents in tuxedos. By midsummer he was rosing the radishes, sculpting lemons into waterlilies, finally charged with making the vichyssoise from scratch. *Yes,* muses Walter, ever reflecting on the various stages of his path, the path of this person who constructed the components that aggregated into the man he must acknowledge wound up as him. *From washing dishes to rosing radishes, there was no stopping young Walt…*

~

"A FUCKING MILLION DOLLARS! Excuse my French, Dad, but this is outrageous." Paula is livid, so unlike her ordinary tact with, above all, her benefactor. And with such an outburst, it does pack a punch.

"Paula, it's only one million not ten. What does it amount to as far as you and I are concerned?"

"But Adam is such a slouch!" Her arms are akimbo. She's in no mood to sit down. She glares at him, no unconscious, hesitant gestures or fussing with her hair.

"You know, it could be in your case, near same age as Will's son, it's like—sibling rivalry. You never could tolerate him. And you never felt threatened by your brother, of course, Gavin forever fumbling. Adam was somebody you could butt heads with."

"You couldn't tolerate Adam either! Nor could his father, your equal partner!"

Walter sighs. "So, Adam was the bad seed, his older brother Eli the good. Sound like you and Gavin, my dear?" He takes a deep breath. *Breathe*, counsel the yogis. "But that's all in the past. Adam is making amends. His new trucking business is taking off."

Now she sits, the ponytail having whipped around like a weapon quiets down. She will try a different approach. "This is guilt money, pure and simple. He's guilt-tripping you."

He nods no. “Maybe I’m the one wising up. Will was brilliant. So much is due to his ideas, his crazy imagination when we expanded into machinery. A power chipper-shredder for five grand that does exactly what a municipal professional rig can do but costs ten times as much. Every one of our power tools is a fantastic innovation, never heard of nor seen in stores. A string trimmer on wheels! The ads worked like magic. Catnip, as Will would say, to rough-country do-it-yourselfers.”

“Okay, Dad. I get that. But ideas are a dime a dozen. It takes the kind of bull-headed perseverance you brought to the business from the start. Dealing with vendors, customers, employees, payroll, HR and IT departments, the banks and lawsuits. Endless. Will got his fair share back then. When he could no longer function.” She is winding down, now gaping at the floor. Bottom line, she knows her father is bullheaded, where she got it from.

“Forget Adam,” he says softly, slyly. “Forget Will. We’ve got plenty to spare, Paulie. Think of it as an investment, all right, a long shot. It may end up as a gift or a tax write-off. But I’ve had Stanley, the young attorney at Horace’s, build in payback, a percentage, all that. Besides, our portfolio is half in bonds, so conservative, no harm in loosening risk.”

At some point Irma, whose job description is also apparently to overhear, offers vegetarian salad and iced mint tea, which Paula never declines, she being a Green obsessive, rail-thin and on the run.

“I do have power of attorney,” says Paula, manning the wheelchair to the sunny breakfast room. He can tell there’s a teasing tone to her voice, although as with everything having to do with his daughter, humor is low on the priority list. “But I am truly happy, Dad, that you’ve retained every ounce of your smarts. No chance of questioning your competence. You’re still the boss.”

Instantly Walter reacts: she means the exact opposite. And he doesn’t doubt her appetite, eventually, for claiming every iota of control.

~

Amazing how the wheelchair has increased Walter's mobility about the estate. He was creeping inch by inch with the darn walker. Now, he greets the groundskeepers and is likely to encounter the UPS or FedEx drivers. Often, he faces his visitors before they're escorted into his makeshift headquarters in the dining room. Invisible, he always thought of the disabled upon seeing them in public. The average bloke like himself, he figures, does not want to identify let alone empathize with the poor sot missing a leg or quarantined to a wheelchair. A blatant reminder of where one could end up with a breakable body. All of us issued the same at birth but then, oh no, things can go awry. We do not want to go there. We, superior beings, are in full throttle. We do not slow down to give it a thought. And now, here he is. The embodiment of decay. The precursor of death. But hell, far as he's concerned, despite these trappings his thoughts can be elsewhere. Tressie, God love her, the next session of PT… ideas for more of the wild watercolors with Alexander, maybe, if he can return…the interchange with his father Adam who Irma said called to visit the day after next…

~

He can barely see the child, the dust kicked up by the tank or truck is blinding him, how can he possibly get there in time? He is not behind the wheel, he is not speeding too fast or under the influence, he is not at fault the kid or the tricycle or both are smack in the middle of the road, he is not to blame…

He leaps up in bed, not of trace of infirmity there. Pitch dark, middle of the night, he longs for the solace of daylight, not sleep. Even his daydreams are never this noxious. The same ferocious nightmare with implanted fangs that he cannot release, heedless of reason…He knows, yes, he knows, it's what makes us human.

~

"You're looking very well, Adam," says Walter. "Don't mean to insult, but you've shed a few pounds." Goodness, never before in his right mind would he have made such a comment let alone have noticed.

"Thanks, Walt. No time to exercise but I am eating less junk. I look at the drivers. Used to be one! At the mercy of truck stops."

"So, tell me how it's going, Adam. You really don't have to on any regular basis like this. Good of you, but not necessary."

"The least I can do, Walt. I've hired six new men, actually, one is a gal. We've expanded into Barton County."

"And you're leasing the trucks. Still a better deal?"

And so they catch up, mostly for Adam's sake. Walter knows full well the one million is one-hundred-percent crapshoot. And he doesn't care. It is doing this man good. Walter himself has had his turn. It's up to others now. And what else is he going to do? Loan or give to total strangers? Maybe. Oh, the charities forever nip at his heels like raving hyenas. He's tired of feeling guilty about the next-to-nothing donations he's doled out all his life. Major contributions are in order, if he can hoodwink Paula somehow, although little chance of that. But Adam here, Walter has known him since he was a boy. So unlike his older brother, Adam went astray like his dad Will. Drink, but it was mostly indifference that did them in. It feels good to toss a lifesaver. Walter's own lot is over, the battle won or lost depending upon his mood of the moment. But Adam has a gleam in his eyes. He's still in the game.

"You have that look, Adam, that reminds me of your father when he came up with a brainstorm. More often than not it was a dud, but the important thing was the wheels did not stop churning."

"I can bullshit like Dad." He blushes, having to accept this as praise, not a fault.

"Don't dismiss it that way. I call it salesmanship, and you've got it in your blood like he did. Your brother owns a big insurance agency. But you—charm the widow out of her life savings!"

"That's why you made Dad so successful, Walt. You put a harness on that ox." Adam is still ruddy of cheek indicating more the outdoors than alcohol. He shakes his head, as if to clear it and make room for what follows. "I'm so sorry, Walt. I came in here months ago, no restraint, I just outright asked."

Walter grins. "That took balls, Adam. Brash and all. That gene missed me completely. At least at the beginning of my career. Your father supplied that. I learned from him. And eventually I had to do it on my own."

Adam takes this in, agrees with a slight smile. "What Paula tells me, even here flat on your back, well, propped up for now, I'd say you still have a pair, Walt."

Walter lifts and turns his head to face his visitor more squarely. "You've spoken to Paula?"

"She's emailed me a couple of times. Wished me well with the new venture. I thought she hated my guts."

"You were kids. Probably that was a reflection anyway of Will and me with our slings and arrows. It's never too late to start over."

Adam leaves, and Walter rushes to the bathroom. He's hell-bent to stay off the diapers now with his racecar on big wheels.

Paula nice and sweet with Adam? Surely she's trying to outfox me, he thinks on the heated toilet seat, once he's duly relieved with his mind again free to meander.

Too much of the world. Back to the books.

Midway means nothing to infinity.

Chapter 13

I deserve nothing.
Today I recognize that I am the guest the mystics talk about.
I play this living music for my host.

ANA, THE CLEANING LADY, looks unusually burdened hauling her mop, a roll of paper towels, and her pail filled with rags and more, shuffling from the bathroom across the broad expanse of his chamber without making eye contact. With her head slightly bowed, her disposition of deference is the norm.

"I'm sorry about the mess, Ana. Again."

She casts a faint smile his way and bustles on.

"Things were great for a while, me getting to the toilet on time, but—" He composes a pained, apologetic expression even though he realizes it's beyond her view.

She nods quickly and is gone. Now he wishes he hadn't said so much. It interrupted her preference for moving smoothly about, unnoticed all the better, the hallmark of the pride she clearly takes in her work.

So, I am back on the pad, Walter announces the verdict to himself, this subsidiary voice impartial and uncontestable. "On the pad" he recalls from high school, boys referring to their menstruating girlfriends shoving them off. So much for his mad dashes to the john. He can do it all right here. Irma checks and changes the nappies with dispatch, no different from her brewing him a pot of tea. He can't even tell when he is soaked. For his poops—hardly worth the effort twice a day—there is no urgency. He and Irma have all the time in the world. He can no longer stand and slip off and onto the wheelchair. Even for those wheeled occasions she must lift him into place. Often in a drugged stupor, Walter cannot distinguish where he ends and Irma begins. Hands down, she occupies the lion's share of the energy field; he is just along for the ride, like the passenger on a motorbike, arms encircling and clasping the driver. In his case with arms so weak, he can't compose a grip nor does he need to.

He shuts his eyes. Urinary function is kaput, another pronouncement from the judge as his latest sentence. He has told Irma to tell the doctor not to catheterize him. Dealing with a bag—one more thing for her, not that she would blink at the extra task. Later it may be necessary, the doctor has said, echoed by the visiting nurse. He hasn't pursued their reasons, imagining all too well the likelihood of his being comatose or the difficulty without such a procedure of hoisting him about in order to change the soiled pads. Despite his increasing tremor, he can reach the button to elevate his upper half. He does so now. Next, he presses the tab on the circular gizmo around his neck and buzzes Irma.

She speaks into the bedside intercom. "Yes, Walter?"

"Please ask Ana to come to me. I have a question for her."

Within sixty seconds Ana is front and center.

"Ana, you're still taking the piano lessons, like your granddaughter?"

She beams and shakes her head, seems incapable of something intelligible to say, let alone her tentative grasp of English.

"Actually, I wanted to ask about your husband. If I recall correctly, he's a custodian at the medical center?"

This question appears to take her breath away, likely from surprise. "Yes, Mr. Walt. One time when you hospitalized…I deliver mail to you from Irma, Carlos he is collecting the trash in your room." She seizes one wrist with her other hand, to hold steady, the very conversation unsettling.

"Forgive me for getting personal, Ana, but I assume he earns minimum wage."

She barely nods yes, while swallowing with difficulty is the more obvious gesture.

"I have an idea. I understand there's an opening in the yard crew. It pays well. Perhaps your Carlos would be interested? You two could save on commuting costs, as well."

Ana grins ear to ear, is speechless but he gathers this might work out. "I'll talk to Irma, and she'll make it happen."

Ana cannot control a fat tear rolling down one of her chunky cheeks as she lays both hands atop his and then hurries out.

Walter prefers that Irma guide the wheelchair outdoors to one of the terraces facing the sun. He can still operate the motorized unit, but it's become too much of an exertion for his trembling hands. If the sun ducks in and out, he'll simply buzz her to switch locations. Plus, he can offer a fluttering wave to yet another workman tending the trees, the gravel drive, collecting twigs littering the grounds from a recent wind. What an enormous spread, thinks Walter, surveying the scene. The rippling brook twisting to the pond, the benches artistically angled to enjoy the finest views. Whatever was it all for? He's presided here for so many years after Polly and Gavin have gone. There must be a rationale, and don't dump it all on Polly, which he's done from the start. Despite the scale and sweep of the place—the million acres of cerulean sky a canopy all his own—in truth he is but a single man squatting on a mere slip of a desert island, not even a passing ship in sight. At least he thinks of himself not as the owner but more as the current steward. This fiefdom has a life of its own and will go on long after him. *But for whom?* he reflects. *That is still up to me…*

~

"It must be Wednesday!" Walter exclaims. "It took forever for you to get here from Monday, Tressie."

"Don't be greedy, Walter. Three times a week, I see you more than anybody else." He had asked her to address him as Walt, but she keeps reverting to Walter, more formal but, as he was known to his family, more intimate as well. Today she is in yellow, a polo shirt and matching toreador pants, are they called? She reaches to level his bed, but he has beaten her to that, shaking hand or not.

"I like the chartreuse headband, Tressie. Alexander taught me that's complementary to the yellow—oh, but there's already green added to yellow to get chartreuse—forget it. Watercolors are something else. Anyway, you keep me guessing with your glad rags of the day." Her dark springy hair does indeed need the headband like a rambunctious kid does a car seat.

She winks and lifts off the sheets. Tenderly she taps his legs from knees to feet, taking stock.

"When are you moving in?" he asks.

She frowns. "Maybe next month. Don't be in such a rush, Walter. You're not going anywhere."

"You're telling me."

"Quiet now. Let me concentrate." Her bulbous lips burst into a big smile. Painted a glossy bright apple red, the soft yellow outfit pales by comparison.

"I will have you at least for a little bit every single day, my dear," says Walter. "What bliss."

"Shush. You already pay me over and above what I earn from the salon and doing my PT." She holds his ankles and pauses. "I will do all I can for you, Walter. But it's taking time to ease off from working with others. Some I've seen for years. I am getting a few of the newer salon girls to help."

She begins by lifting his left knee and flexing.

"Tressie, I must tell you. That doesn't hurt."

"When it did, it meant you still had active nerves in there for me to work with. We'll get you standing again even if you have to hold on to something for support."

"I'll hold on to you any day, Tressie."

"Don't be fresh. But yes, of course, I will be your crutch."

"The balance is gone," he says, sounding glum even to himself.

"The muscles are being stimulated. You've been too long a couch potato. Now with me here, no excuse."

"Even if I'm dying?"

"You're not dead yet. Now do shut up." She fails at keeping a straight face by winking.

Finally, he does her bidding. He loves taking orders from this lady. Irma, she's in charge and doesn't need his complicity. Polly, he probably never truly listened to. Paula, the itch, has an iron will but it's always forced him in dealing with her to adopt the same, often resisting. Of anybody ever in his life, his Paula is a spitting image, now that he's able to see from this distance. But Tressie here, this light chocolate Latina-Black, must encapsulate as a hybrid both yin and yang, according to the Buddhist teaching: sunshine mellow sweetness coating a backbone of steel. Like a woodpecker among the inhabitants of the aviary he views out his picture window, she's a bird of soft feathers like any other but she can fire up that beak.

"Relax, Walter. Let go. This calf is still tight as a knot. There. That's better."

Stroking, stretching those muscles in his lower legs: he knows this is invigorating, this is keeping them alive. For the time being. Massaging his feet and toes and ankles, this must consume the better part of an hour. He fights to stay awake, to not miss a single sensation.

"Now that I'm back in nappies," he says at some point, "I'll be less shy about your working the upper legs more often."

Tressie shrugs, as if he's a lunatic. "You think I've not seen it all? Bodies are bodies, God-given, each beautiful in its way."

"Actually, there's not much of me left to be embarrassed about."

"I'll probably be changing your diaper sometime when Irma's taking a break. Big deal. Every big or little part of you, Walter, needs maneuvering. Next time we do the neck, scalp, ears. You realize there are hundreds, maybe thousands, of muscles just in the face? The jaw, on and on. Oh, by the way. I'm convinced I can flip you over on your tummy in another week or two. There's all of your back! Hamstrings! I told Irma to make sure you get plenty of beef broth and miso soup to keep up the protein." She refolds his sheets and tucks him in. By way of signing off, she pats him on the crotch. "You ready for a change? We might as well take that plunge."

"No!" he near shouts but laughs.

"Just joking," she giggles, kisses him on the forehead, and dances off, another Latin beat or African, however would he know, weaned on Patti Page and *Your Hit Parade*?

~

IT IS EASY FOR Walter to lose track of time. One moment he's convinced that Tressie's ministrations are in fact waking a sleeping giant within. He wriggles his toes. He pinches open a jar of pills, if awkwardly. The next moment he sinks into the hollows of his head and thinks such optimism is a pipe dream. The effervescence of the woman has seeped into his system but does zilch for his bladder dysfunction, increasing imbalance, the bedeviled blood pressure, which fluctuates like the needle of a lie detector when fed nothing but falsehoods. One second, he's hot, the next, freezing, with no connection to the room's actual temperature. So many picayune irritants to keep track of, blessedly they cancel each other out. And he's back to whatever entertainments he can contrive—Rumi and Company, thank his lucky stars, and the gaggle of visitors either summoned or arriving unannounced to wish him well. In truth, an obligation, but with that he holds no grudge.

This new person, Stanley, presently sits upright as a cadet by Walter's bed. He is tall, lean, a short-cropped blond, his navy suit pinstriped, perfect creases just grazing the long, elegant polished shoes, the quintessential WASP, but Walter does not hold this against him. Until proven otherwise, there's no need to disparage Harvard, Princeton, and Yale.

"How long have you been working with Horace, Jim, and that lot? You must have the creds to join the area's top law firm," says Walter.

Stanley smiles, but readies his laptop. "I do have a specialty with trusts. Horace has filled me in completely, and I've reviewed it all."

Walter nudges his bed upward a trifle more. He doesn't want to miss a thing. "Stanley, you can see I've taken care of my family, my children, their children, well, Paula's. But I've had plenty of chance to think—about a range of other options. Oh, not instead! Nothing crazy here at the last minute. It's more—I'll get to the point—charitable... Well, yes and no." He takes as measured a breath as he can, deep breathing no longer readily at his disposal but he's gotten used to that. "I want to start a foundation. A foundation assigning various bequests but also administered by Horace, well, you specifically as trustee, and another person yet to be decided, not a family member, to oversee continuing gifts from the interest earned by principal."

Stanley nods, taps his laptop, and makes a few comments indicating this is all very doable.

"You would work closely with Charles. my investment counselor—he and his group you must realize know all of this backward and forward."

"Horace already introduced me to Charles. We've spoken several times prior to this meeting, Walter."

Walter sinks pleasurably from the effort of maintaining eye contact with this hyperalert young man. They chat further on. Walter manages another lingering breath, suddenly infused with extra oxygen, conviction, or a combination of the two.

"I'll start with my ex-wife Polly. Let's say one million for each of these, to simplify at this juncture. Hers is to be designated for

Planned Parenthood but with Polly as administrator, or sub-trustee? You'll figure that out. There's a million for my son Gavin but for an institution he and I have yet to decide on. More on this later. This is in addition to his piece of my estate already established in the primary trust. I'm getting ahead of myself, but I suppose this last item is not from the foundation but from a separate trust, which includes previously stipulated gifts. So in addition, I want to assign a half-million for the education of the son of Gavin's current partner Trudy—we'll get the surnames later—if and only if they are still partners, legal or otherwise at my demise. I don't care if they're married. She's been the best thing for my son. I want some other gifts in this category or from the foundation, we'll have to sort this out…"

He pauses, eyes stretched to ceiling.

"A million dollars to my physical therapist Tressie with the suggestion, not requirement, that she start and run her own business, along with a half-million to educate her son, Mo. We'll talk more about details. I know his name is Mohammed in deference to the supposed father with whom Tressie wants to assert some sort of linkage, even though the man, best she understands, has that name as a matter of popularity or convenience, not religious faith. We have to be absolutely specific with each of these gifts to preclude even the slightest of possible litigations from next-of-kin or any other parties. But that's why Horace and Co are the tops! Let's see. Oh, yes, I want this property in its entirety—now back to the primary trust—given to my caretaker Irma. Plus a million dollars—maybe two or three, I have to think this through—to establish it as a small hotel or B and B, I hope that's her wish."

Stanley has taken every jot of this down, the meticulous bright-eyed attorney that he so obviously is. He reminds Walter of one of those lovable brats who win the National Spelling Bee, not even blinking, so cocksure. I suppose if you've gotten through Harvard…

"Back to the charitable foundation. You and Horace and Charles, of course, can work through the tax consequences and advise me of those." Walter picks up his notes. "Okay. A half-million to each of these nonprofits: the Sierra Club, the Save the Children Fund or Feed the Children—whatever it's called, the Nature Conservancy. Greenpeace—hard to read my writing. Oh, yes. Environmental Defense Fund. Doctors Without Borders. Habitat for Humanity—that good soul Jimmy Carter. Animal Rescue Mission." He looks up. "I think that's enough for now, Stanley. Have to do more research. Thank goodness I can still operate my laptop. Oh, one more thing. For the trust, the new one for the purposes of my gifting right now, you will need to arrange with Charles that I have a checking account—online for me to manage although I can have Irma physically write checks for me. This may necessitate Charles to set up a totally new account not merged with the others. I'm determined to avoid squabbles after I'm gone. And who knows? Could be ages still. I'd like to do some good now so I can at least have a glimmer of that."

Stanley, still expressionless, nods.

"Here it gets a touch confidential. You see, my daughter, Paula, as you know, has access to it all. She's kind of a watchdog for my finances. She also, as you know, has power of attorney."

"This I'm very aware of, Walter. I'm sure, given your—decline, this can become contentious. Family and money matters, it's why many of my colleagues are in business, I'm afraid."

Now it's Walter's turn to nod. He's said plenty for today. And, good grief, there is so much more to follow. As they exchange a final chat, Walter takes nourishment, such as it is, from the likelihood that the brain remains unscathed in his otherwise lethal, irrefutable, damnable disease. *Mentally incompetent.* To hell with that phrase, Paula!

~

Walter is thrust once again into solitary confinement after Stanley takes his leave. No, his ailment is not damnable, he counters a while later. Thinking that way is a reaction to this young lawyer, him like a thoroughbred blasting forth from the starting gates. If all I'm left with are my wits, let them, too, surge ahead unencumbered.

~

"Damn it, Irma. This latest container of pills, I just can't do it."

She squeezes, twists, flips off the lid, then punctures and breaks the foil seal. She places the jar on his bedside stand and walks off. "Take just two, Walter, for now," she says over her broad shoulder, the fat braid confirming her authority.

Before he shakes out the pills, the dining room door quietly closed, he pauses for a moment and ponders: should I stash some more away, in case it gets unbearable? He does so into his sock-covered bottle shoved to the back of his drawer. Nevertheless, he is hopeful it will be mind over matter that serves as his escort to the end.

Chapter 14

Know yourself in the light of true ones,
as the ground sees its face in the garden.

HE STARES AT THE child in the dusty road retrieving a tricycle. Or is it a pet? A puppy as blind to its immediate surroundings and imminent danger as the child itself? The child, a little boy, has as his sole focus this object: a lovable possession that must be reclaimed. The thunder from the wheels of the roaring machinery—trucks? tanks? buses?—is deafening to Walter, who is spellbound and aghast at having to witness this, but helpless, choked up, unable even to scream. The vehicles are in a convoy, clearly military. Is this during the war? Is he, Walter, the child slowly turning his head toward the onrushing motorcade? The small boy is in a red-striped shirt and dead center on the roadway, his gaze now held by the ever closer rumble. Walter can see the men or soldiers at the wheel of the first vehicle, high up, way above the mass of gleaming steel, their sights straight ahead, their mission ever urgent. Dust and pebbles are being spit and sprayed in all directions. Slowly, as in a time-lapse movie, the boy raises one arm. He is smiling, he is saluting the powerful men who are winning the war. Walter can no longer watch. He presses shut his wet eyes but cannot prevent them from opening a crack. Finally, he warbles a low howl. *No!* he issues with all his might. But it is too late. The tanks or trucks have passed. There is only a tattered piece of red material flapping in the aftermath. Eventually it too is collapsed upon the crushed small mound in the road, dirt settling down and covering that as well.

Walter blinks and then closes his eyes. It is so vivid it could have happened yesterday, a scar that refuses to be forgotten, an ugly red ridge of near-calcified flesh as eternal reminder. Was it a war movie he saw as a kid? Why does it accuse him of doing nothing, forever after? Is it meant as a stand-in for some drunken hit-and-run, if in fact that ever occurred? *How would I know for sure?* he continues the assault. *Drunk, early twenties, navigating home by careening from the curb to the one opposite. Did I hit a bicycle? A person? A tricycle…a child? It all remains a blur. But it remains.*

~

Doctors and nurses come and go. He improves at this, declines at that. He listens and thanks them as they do their job. None of it matters, one minute to the next. Right now, he is sweating. He's on fire even though nothing has changed in the room or the weather outside. His comfort is all he can possibly consider. It's like an animal in the wild confronting its predator in that second of stillness before fleeing: one unalloyed goal, all others obliterated. He fumbles for the intercom, asking Irma in a rush to bring him the gelled vest. It's kept in an extra refrigerator, which she will allow to rest for a few moments before strapping it on. This she does to his instant relief. She refreshes his iced tea, checks his pad, takes his blood pressure and records it. *Does anyone really care?* thinks Walter but appreciates how useful it seems to make Irma. It also satisfies the doctors and particularly the visiting nurses whom she's supplanted. Irma, the recording secretary in addition to all else. *Have I ever seen her with her hair down,* he wonders, *glancing at her retreating backside, dramatized faithfully every day by the thick, dirty-blond braid. It's snug between her shoulder blades like a menacing snake, all business, tightly wound.*

He's left again to his daydreams, his own devices. He has recovered from the living nightmare of the innocent little boy flattened to death by the stampede of steel. He is amazed that reality is whatever the mind chooses to display, the screen embedded in one's brain being so much closer and etched with finer precision than any images fleeting before the open eyes. This is also true in reconstructing his relationships, like his reflections of his business partner Will. While they were together, Will was a royal pain in the butt. Now, Walter can acknowledge that but also embrace the good and grit of the man. *Is this the new, improved reality, the interior composition, or just a shallow bid to make me feel better, more well-rounded than my former, clueless self? I was not a very nice man,* Walter carries on. *Just because I didn't say much, people could fill in the blanks, assume the best…to flesh out their own agendas (I'm okay at slave labor, an employee might reason, since the boss must be brainier; I'll butter him up because he's great when it comes to bonus time), or, in the case of genuinely nice people, like Polly, to give him the benefit of the doubt.* Walt means well. So he doesn't pay attention to anybody else but he works so hard. And he's not evil, which goes a long way in this tawdry world.

Get me out of here. He reaches for a book of Rumi poems.

Figure how to be delivered from your own figuring.

~

"Irma, here's one that confounds me. Well, they all confound me but that's okay if I don't really understand them. They're a tease, and I almost get the joke, but, I don't know, usually these lines from Rumi satisfy me somehow. I feel like I'm swallowing a sugar-coated pill."

She nods, seated by his side on one of her breaks. "And you don't know what you're swallowing but you suspect it's doing some good."

"Yes. It's totally counter to the way the world or my world at least works. These poems, they stretch me."

"What about the one that's so confounding?"

"Weird, because this one makes sense. It doesn't even seem that profound." He recites: "'*No man has ever seen a part greater than the whole.*'"

"What's your problem, Walter?"

"Well, all right, I'm the measly part, if I'm able to grasp that much. But, given such obvious limitation, how the hell can I even know there's a whole to be a part of? How does one get beyond thinking of oneself as a whole being? Plus zillions of other wholes, and together, sure, there's this much bigger body."

"I think you're onto something but not quite there. In just acknowledging yourself as a part, you accept a whole that's composed of lots more than other replicas of yourself."

"But *no man has ever seen*?"

"Try this," says Irma. "Stop looking in the ordinary way. At least use the mind's eye. Imagine. Something else altogether. And maybe unknowable, that's the point."

~

"DAD! THEY'VE GOT YOU in a goose-down parka!"

"Freakin' freezing, Gavin. It's just the wild swings of my blood pressure. Part of the deal. Say, you're looking great." However did it happen, given Gavin's gene pool, to turn out this hunk from the pages of *Esquire*—listen to me, so darn dated, that magazine likely gone the way of *TV Guide*.

"I am one-hundred-percent drug-free, Dad." He paces the room, circles the bed slowly. "Yes, I'm an addict but it's totally centered on the gym. Or the weights and stretch bands I've set up at home. I love eating the way I do. I love feeling this fit."

"Wait a sec. What home, Gavin?"

He stands still, legs splayed, faces his father. "Trudy and I have split. She's been a terrific chapter for me, but enough racing boats up and down the East Coast. Got a condo, thanks to your helping me out. And the Bentley. I love to drive. I've started a private escort service—not in the Bentley!—for shut-ins, nursing homes and hospices without wheels of their own. I take folks to and from their medical appointments, carry them in my arms if necessary. Often easier than a wheelchair. Oh, sorry, Dad." He taps his father's trusty device. "Anyway, I love it. It pays well enough, but I don't need much anyway."

Walter is astounded. "Wonderful," he says.

"And my place is near a couple of neat bars and night spots, great crowds. Now wait! I'm sitting there sipping my Pellegrino, all relaxed, and some really cool women have picked me up. Fed up with their abusive boyfriends. What more can I ask for, Dad?"

"What about Trudy? And her boy? You'd said how bright he is… and you were both concerned about getting him into a decent but affordable school, no?" Here he was just spouting off those tentative gifts to Stanley the young attorney—didn't it include something about Gavin's formidable Trudy and her son? Serves me right for meddling…

Gavin tilts his head aside, a reflective pose. Despite the loose sweatshirt, Walter can't help but notice the raised, rounded outline of his powerful upper chest. "Time for me to get myself squared away, Dad. I have lost time to make up for. I'll never be like Paula. Or Mom's dreams for me, forever the fuck-up. But I'm on the right track. It's all good. And I'm an hour closer to you now and can help, help however you like. While still holding this new job."

"You're a people-person, Gavin. I used to say that about Will. I can picture these feeble elders thinking you're a marvel."

"I accept tips. I'm no saint. There are a couple of rich old birds in the mix who make up for most." His smile alone could get him the combination to a bank vault.

Walter cranks up his bed. "I have an idea, son." He sees furrows scatter across Gavin's brow. Is the old man about to intrude upon his newfound equilibrium? And so Walter hastens to say: "There are lots of smart kids, like Trudy's, like my therapist Tressie's boy, who belong in top prep schools and colleges but those are way too far a reach. Financially, for sure. And these kids and their families, usually a single parent, probably don't even know of these places. Exeter,

Choate, all that lot in the woods. They would regard the Ivy League like getting into Buckingham Palace to meet the Queen. Besides, despite good grades and SATs and so forth they likely don't have the sports, the extracurricular brownnose gems, internships with a Congressman, whatever, to qualify for a scholarship." He takes a breath.

"Where is this going, Dad?"

"I think we, meaning you, could embark upon an enterprise—office, staffers, computers—to scout our region for starters, finding youngsters who should get financial aid. Help them make a case on applications you provide after their interviewing with your counselors to select schools with the right fit. Tutor them for their essays, knock-out essays, blood-and-guts life stories to pound the heart. Total opposite of the privileged and pampered. Find the boys and girls who have the—balls to better themselves."

"Wait a minute. Who pays for this?"

"I will."

Gavin's mouth drops.

"Look," Walter fills in the gap. "You well know I've provided Paula with enormous funding. She's not done it all by herself. Why shouldn't I give you an opportunity—you're still early forties—to taste the thrill of being an entrepreneur—"

"Like you. Like Paula." He sounds grim.

"No, unlike your sister and me, making a real impact on the lives of others. Sure, it'll be my money that gets it going, but there will be a for-profit part, too. Parents and teens are overwhelmed by navigating all this business nowadays. I know this. I've read all about this. That blasted *New York Times* online. People are happy to pay serious fees for the service and advice you will be arranging for deserving kids. And wouldn't it be nifty, Gavin, for you as well as your mother, to rewrite the book of your being busted on peddling dope and kicked out of Deerfield all those forlorn decades ago! I can picture the bright glow on Polly's kisser when this venture takes her by surprise. Now wouldn't that feel just dandy, for me—'the absent father,' and for you?"

Gavin is rubbing his eyes. Walter sees he has delivered a punch to his son, a positive one for sure. And yet. As they chat, Walter must acknowledge Gavin's edge of hesitation, the lion's share of his life having been shackled with self-sabotage. Back off, Walter. Let the idea, for now, sink in. Or possibly not. You've delivered a vote of confidence. If that's all it amounts to, to your son, given your history, it's an avalanche.

Maybe it's Parkinson's. Same symptoms. They don't really know for sure. Meanwhile, damned if that Tressie doesn't have him standing again, easing around to the back of the bed, holding on for dear life but lifting the chest, squeezing the shoulder blades, pulling the make-believe string attached to the top of his crown, and lifting the whole bloody carcass up, up, up. It's not him hurling the orders like a drill sergeant albeit in his noggin, it's her, every inch of her Imperial Majesty running this show, installed now she is in the very room no less above his. The boy, too, with a room of his own. Still, the upstairs must be deserted as a ghost town. Thank heaven she doesn't threaten Irma. Irma has more than enough on her hands just in the kitchen and managing the staff outdoors and paying the small bills. Tressie is manipulating his face, jaw, neck as if they are pliable as Play-Doh. She is getting him back on more solid foods—salads, turkey burgers, sweet potatoes…plus salsa, chicken burritos, beef fajitas…Good grief, this reincarnated Carmen Miranda hustles to her calypso beat, reverberating beyond his limbs into his very gut. Go for it, girl, as he's heard it said on TV.

"Thanks for coming, Polly. Yet again. I know you've got so much going on. As ever." Walter is sitting in a new wheelchair that tilts, swivels, vibrates, rocks, and rolls. Not the Bentley nor the Benz but he's having a good time of it, Paula's latest find.

"Imagine, Jack is a trifle jealous!" says Polly. "He thinks I'm taking it too literally with you—'till death do us part.'" Her coils of now-gray hair have always fascinated Walter, springing about as if underscoring her every remark in italics.

"Jack is joking, Walt," she reassures, reaching to graze his forearm.

"It's no joke, Polly. How many people do we say those words to? So we're divorced. The court of law. What's that to do with—"

"Of course," she interrupts, deflecting inappropriate intimacy, or maybe the opposite, reaffirming the obvious and very valid measure of their continuing connection. "Well, Walt. You're sitting up. You must have the durability of heavy metal. A year flat on your back, I guess it's been."

"In spite of my whole life as a slug. Maybe all that ordinary energy was conserved in my case, not squandered."

"But Irma tells Paula and Paula tells me some things have gotten worse. The periodic dizziness, the difficulty swallowing." She screws up her forehead, clearly concerned.

"Even so, we are waking up whatever's left of my muscles. Not just Tressie doing her thing, but she's got me flexing and stretching on my own. Kegel exercise, for the sphincter! Bottom line, pardon the pun, maybe down there is not a lost cause."

"Oh, Walt. You've become a very funny man."

"Anything's more fun than that factory."

"No, really. I can see hints of that young guy I fell for, way before you took yourself so seriously. Or the work consumed you."

"I think when you don't have a clue about yourself, usually looking to others, unbeknownst there's a kind of free spirit crashing around."

"You would compose that Alfred E. Neuman look and ask the stupidest question—Are we home yet?—one block off on our trip. It made me giggle every time. You could be fun."

Polly crosses the legs of her pantsuit, checkered up close but mostly a muted gray. She's always dressed smartly without calling attention to her clothes. Intentional or otherwise, any flash is saved for the force of her words, her unflinching eyes.

Walter is now operating on low octane. The bravura of his ex-wife, with no ill intent, reverberates, rendering him comatose by contrast. Even silent, she's the fuselage of a fighter jet, waiting for takeoff. But, here and now, it is his place to lead the conversation.

"Polly, I'm deadly serious why I asked you to visit. Apparently with my leave-taking taking all the time in the world, I have all day to find amusements as well as to think hard about—about what to do with my good fortune."

Polly sits stone-faced. To him it's as if she's confronting someone entirely different from the Walt who shared the first half of her life. She appears both perplexed and intrigued.

"Paula says you're still up to your ears with Planned Parenthood. Goodness knows it's under siege more than ever."

"This is true."

"I don't read every item in the paper, but enough to know some current facts of life. Anyway, I've had to start outlining gifts in my will. I should say, further specify. There's already so much for our children and grandchildren. And I want to include Gavin's someday if he ever becomes a parent. But here's the point, Polly. There is so darn much. Money sitting still and making more money. Borderline immoral. What have I ever spent it on, really? Whatever did we spend it on that actually amounted to so much? This place, the crewel-work curtains, a few antiques? A pittance."

"You provided so handsomely for me, Walt. You know how thankful I was, and am. And it was me who ended our marriage."

He sighs. "Okay, I don't still love you. That way. But I've always been crazy about your stamina. Your genuine interest in helping others. You did this also on my behalf, I suppose, letting me go about my business. Well, now it's my turn."

Polly swallows visibly, strains to let Walter continue without interfering.

"A while ago I began thinking: what's the point of giving it all away once I'm gone? Why not now, at least some of it, now where it can really help? And so I've been researching all the stuff Planned Parenthood does with its donations. Beyond the clinics. The nitty-gritty. Organizing people to elect the leaders and politicians in the first place who will defend this work. And women's rights. Flood key members of Congress with mail. Attend rallies. Host voter registration drives. Drive people to the polls. Golly, it's a crusade. And it's led by women like you, my dear."

Polly slumps. She is not used to praise, least of all from her ex-husband. Their boundary lines from each other have been well established and long respected. But she is absorbing this like surrendering one's aching body to a hot bath.

"The gag rule! I had no idea what that meant, bandied about in the press. Incredible! Preventing women, especially on the low end of things, from how and where to access abortion. Makes me embarrassed to be a man!"

Polly hears him out. She was never one to hold her tongue. They have flip-flopped.

"I want to give you a million dollars right now, Polly. It's from a new foundation I'm setting up. Not for you personally but for you to manage its distribution. You can create a modest board of directors to oversee or advise, but that's up to you. You'll be the boss."

Polly takes both of his hands in hers. His are trembling but that's the disease, not him. She squeezes his hands gently and licks her lips. Her thick rolls of gray hair are oscillating as if what's inside her head, in spite of her silence, has shifted into overdrive.

"What do you say, Polly? Would this be okay?"

"Walt. I do love you, still. No!" she adds, addressing his grin. "Not in that way!"

"A new way," he says. "I can live with that."

They chat for a while about her ideas. She is soft-spoken, measured, clearly taken aback.

"I wouldn't mind serving on the board, Polly. I promise not to obstruct, just eavesdrop. Paula could set up the teleconference or Skype or whatever it's called."

Polly leaves a pause, looks up, aside, and then directly at him. "If you really believe you want to make such a major gift to Planned Parenthood, Walt, now or later, that's incredible. But leave me out. Your gesture seems more about me than the organization. If I accepted your proposal, it just feels like you're making a final bid for—my affection—or releasing you from any lingering heartbreak at my leaving you—or releasing me from any guilt for that. None of this is valid."

She stands. "Thank you, Walt. You're a wonderful man. I'll visit again soon." She taps a lower leg and takes her leave.

Chapter 15

You have locked yourself inside disappointment.
No actual hunter would trap himself.

WHAT WAS I DOING all day before this? Walter wonders wheeling about the downstairs at random. The wheelchair is motorized, battery electric. He is no longer capable of pushing a simpler version of the wheelchair as before. This latest rig is absolutely silent, tricking him into sensing at times that he is fully mobile and that nothing has changed. At this moment he's looking out a narrow window, which delights him with a view he's never experienced: the isolated corrugations of bark on a massive locust tree. Beautiful. The rugged peaks and valleys strike him like an aerial shot of the Rocky Mountains, no civilization in sight. This window in the living room is oddly spliced into a cranny next to the towering fireplace, which is faced with elaborate dark paneling, which next entices his gaze. All hand-crafted. He stares point-blank at the intricate cobwebs of grain, Walter overwhelmed by the rich umber wood. The happenstance of patterns like the locust bark is likely not an accident; nature knows what it's doing. Forget the furniture. He's seen all that more than enough. How about these floorboards, talk about grain, allowed to peek out along the baseboards, the room otherwise exhibiting the flashy, endless prized Orientals, as if it's home to a sheik, not himself…

For the past few weeks Walter has been liberated from "his room," a far cry from its pretending for a few decades to be the dining room at Monticello. White House? No. Williamsburg? Not that overly elegant, Polly reassured at the time. More Jefferson and slightly rough homespun around the edges. French fabrics but stained with the master's appetite for tobacco and wine. *Where was I?* he ponders, idling before a watery, woodsy oil landscape in the hallway, the painting an imitation Impressionist. *I like it, I don't care,* he recalls justifying it to Polly, who claimed it was so obviously not Monet. He rolls down the hall to admire a piece of crockery, not refined and glossy and significant but clearly old and simple and cracked like himself. He negotiates a few doorsills to get outside. Enough of the manor house as stillborn replica. He parks on the south porch. The swaying trees and shifting clouds welcome him to their cathedral. The lone parishioner, he feels dwarfed by the grandeur…

Before all the doctors and the testing and third opinions, Walter was as frustrated with time on his hands as he was by his increasing inability to split open a ziplock bag…his having to ask Irma to crack the combination of the lock to open a bottle of Advil. How could they make so much misery for oldsters who were the very souls who need painkillers and acid relief and stool softeners and such? After a while, bored with the willows sashaying like hula skirts, he rolls back inside to the library, love it, lined with leather-bound volumes of classics even Polly admitted was for show. *Well, maybe you'll read someday, Walt, when you're retired. Bodice-ripping spy thrillers if any,* he laughed, as did she. Retirement meant going into his office three times a week, to "consult" with the new owners whom he knew darn well counted the days until the golden handcuffs of the contract expired. Too bloody dark in the library. Maybe he can maneuver over the higher doorsill to the front terrace without asking Irma. Irma. Changing his pads. *What will I do all day,* he asked her, *when I don't have to get myself to the john every hour? That's my chief occupation! I'll miss it.* But he does not miss the restless leg syndrome, finally under control. He does not miss prior to the diagnosis getting up to pee in middle of the night and falling flat on his face. At times after that, falling backward, thank bejesus for Polly's thick wool pile, wall-to-wall carpeting for the private bedroom, not permissible for the downstairs museum. This falling must have gone on for over two years, three? *It will pass,* he thought. *Why bother a doctor just because I tripped and fell? Deal with it!* Isn't that what he's done all his life, practically half his life solo after Polly for sure? You get on in years and stuff happens. A crybaby he is not. So he can no longer run up the stairs. So, descending, he grabs hold of a railing. What a railing is for. Who doesn't get dizzy, certainly winded, after dashing from here to there? Getting up from sitting hours at his desk and becoming light-headed, okay, that began to bug him. But all these dots and dashes, they never amounted to much on their own. Until the time Paula caught his leg twitching like a cat's tail, and then the third time when she laid down the law. You don't argue with these women, not the ones in his scene. Paula grilled him on the funny movements of one eye only, kind of swiveling when there was no reason. One thing led to another, Walter summarizes, finally letting sink in the sheer beauty of his lawn, the sculpted evergreens, the pearly blue of the sky on this fine day. And so Irma gets hired part-time and then full. He's losing track of the sequence, not that it matters. He can hardly remember the gap between his official departure from the factory and a sort of numbness that set in, all day home and alone. Maybe there's a connection. All that inaction and laziness and poking about his estate—never having to lift a hand, paved the way for these tremors, an open invitation to compensate for his sitting still. Nothing far-fetched when Walter allows his mind to wander, to percolate with all sorts of absurdities, his crippling disease for which there is no cure being the craziest if cruelest idea of them all.

~

"How old were you, Irma, when you came to the States?"

She halts abruptly in collecting his tray from the little table she's set up in his room, the table a British antique gaming board beautifully inlaid with hexagrams and curlicues, dark woods to rosewood to pale yellow curly maples that Polly thought would be perfect for the parlor. Not too informal but proper still. Irma sets the tray back down. She is not used to him inquiring of her past let alone traipsing beyond the unspoken but firm no-trespass zone of their privacy, long agreeable to them both.

"I was nineteen. A young adult but adult enough to know what I was doing." She arches back her broad shoulders to stand even more erect, if that were possible.

"May I ask what were you doing? Only vaguely do I know that you, like all immigrants, want to have a better life."

She strains to smile but does not expose teeth. He feels reckless, putting her on the spot. But these days he can be reckless if he wants. "Yes. A better life. There was no opportunity—" She stops.

"Yes, yes," he says, almost impatient. "They all must say that. But you weren't in the country. The city. Budapest. What was your family like? What did you parents do?"

She moves not a muscle. She adopts the stance of her original preference, to serve and be silent. But she's become more relaxed so long as the focus is him, not her. "My father was—a professor, of chemistry, at the university. She was a teacher. What you call high school. But a private school."

"Did you go there?"

She nods in the affirmative.

"Really, Irma! That you're well-bred, this doesn't surprise me. Just your manners. Yours is not the bearing of, well, a person of lower rank. So. What happened? I know the Communists, the upheaval, but when I do the math, you came here after all that."

Her hands are twisting the apron. He tells himself to cease. This is wrong, even hurtful. Suddenly Irma walks to one of the upholstered, armless, former dining room chairs set up for his guests, picks it up, and places it by Walter's side like when they chat about his books.

"It's so very long ago. And it's all so commonplace. I had a child out of wedlock. It was given up. I was disgraced. My family was disgraced. I just left without telling a soul. Except for a friend of my cousin who lived in Milwaukee and helped me arrange it all, moving to their community. Of course, I spoke English. And French, Latin, German, and so on. My mother's school was for the elite of Budapest." Irma's hands are now folded on her lap. Walter sees that she is settled into this, the latest requirement of her job, the request of her boss. "I've been quite content on my own. As you know I love to cook and bake. In fact, I was raised by the household cook as much as the nanny. Did my schoolwork in the kitchen much to Mother's dismay. But she was never there to object." Irma offers him a faint smile. Positioned at this range by his side, her hair seems more blond, her eyes a deeper blue.

Walter is without words. "Extraordinary," he finally says. "All this time, and I've never known."

"You've been too wrapped up in your affairs. And then the illness. It's been my privilege to care for you, the whole staff, all the vendors. A cottage industry, though in this case it's a mansion!" She chuckles. For the very first time Walter sees this large-boned, fair-skinned woman for the enigma that she is, she with the clear azure eyes, finely carved cheekbones, the beautiful teeth, if anything elements of aristocracy more than servitude if he'd taken the trouble to notice.

"Irma, I'm indebted to you for sharing this much. You know you are invaluable to me. To Paula. To everyone helping in various ways. I just hope—I hope I haven't taken advantage of you. Restricted you somehow." He is tightening his hold of the wheelchair armrests. He is knocked over by his next thought without the discipline to edit or reconsider.

"What about your child? Did you ever have misgivings? Does it haunt you? Are you all right, Irma?" And he leans toward her but cannot manage the effort to reach her large, soft shoulder.

"Oh, Walter, ages ago we found each other. Through an extensive network of relatives both here and over there. My son, Hendrik, is an accountant, long-married, father of three grown daughters, my granddaughters, two of whom are hoping to visit next year. One of them, Sophia, is determined to live in America and study at one of the culinary institutes. I send her recipes, all the things I learned as a girl."

"Marvelous! Oh, Irma, this is fantastic. You've kept this from me."

"I haven't wanted to burden you, Walter."

"Why burden?"

"My son is struggling. I send him half my pay. What do I need, living here in this luxury? And Walter, you have enough on your mind. Why add my issues as well? This is my job, and I love what I do."

"Have you seen Hendrik?"

"He's come over on some holidays, we've met in the city. It's all very well."

"No wonder I love your goulash."

She shakes her head. "The exception. You are for typical American comfort food."

"Next time, more paprika." He slouches, exhausted, but his eyes are open wide. "Yes, Irma, I have much on my mind. For months it's been one brainstorm after another. I'm channeling Will, my old business partner! But listen to me, Irma. This is as serious as I can get. Already broached the idea with the attorneys. I'm glad you're sitting down, but this time we're not talking about Rumi. Anyway, Irma, I want to change my will. Adjust it, really. I want you to have this place, the house, outbuildings, the several acres, the whole shebang. I think you may, emphasize may, no obligation, you may want to turn it into a small hotel. Or a bed-and-breakfast. Obviously, it would be perfect for that, close to the concerts, summer theater, near to the colleges, all that stuff."

Irma's sharp features, ladylike maintaining her position in the household, have collapsed into the soft folds of a cherubic child. She doesn't speak but her eyes do not waver from his.

"You could embark upon this after I die, or not. You can sell the place and do whatever. But I will arrange starter funds and a cash bequest sufficient for you to pull off such a venture in case you do want to keep open the option of running a hostelry. Or perhaps just a restaurant. With all your management skill. And with your love of cooking! It could feature your ethnic specialties, nothing like it for miles around. Cabbage rolls! Whatever. Just think about it, Irma. If you cotton up to it, we can noodle—sorry for the pun—ideas here and now before I kick the bucket. It could be fun. More than just changing nappies and your serving me bland carrot soup and rehashing old Persian poetry."

At this Irma allows herself another chuckle, hoists her solid frame up from the chair, and shakes her head side to side. Ordinarily that would signal the negative, and so it does now.

"Walter, I don't need to think about it. I already have, in a way. When you pass on, I will return to my family in Hungary, my grandchildren, my son. That is where I next belong." She heaves a sigh, as if it's all settled. "Your estate is for the young and ambitious. Or another good soul like you've been, as caretaker. Yes, Walter, you've had that role same as myself. All those employees over the years, and now your children and others, concerned for their welfare. Me included."

~

First Polly, now Irma. There is no gift if it benefits the giver. There must be hundreds of Persian sayings that by now should have been drilled into his brain. If it were possible for Walter to feel any further diminished, that has taken place.

~

"Alexander, wonderful to see you. It's been so many weeks." The boy looks taller, still a teen but he must be shaving. There is the slightest soft brown fringe above his lips.

"I'm afraid it's been several months, Walter. I wanted to drop by and see your artwork. Last time you were experimenting with those watercolor pencils." He prances some about the room, a polo pony eager to get started, not to linger with Walter but to leave.

"Look in the drawer, Alexander, the second from the top. The entire dresser is one big reject pile. My wardrobe's so limited, I decided to keep all the trials and errors of my efforts. Proof I'm still alive."

The young fellow does so, but in haste. To Walter, it's so clearly a courtesy call.

"Tell me about your artwork, Alexander. That's what is interesting. How's it going?"

"You know I'm working at Dad's, Adam's trucking office. I go there right after school and on weekends. The pay is fantastic! I wanted to thank you for helping him, us, out. It's going great." He makes fists and pulses them.

"We talked about college, didn't we? Soon you'll be having to deal with that." It hits Walter that here, right here with bright young Alexander, who is a prime prospect for the college aid scheme he's thought of for Gavin to undertake!

"I got my license, Walter! And a used VW. Saves so much time, more time at the office. I'm saving up—"

Walter dismisses the hitting-up-moneybags he's been trapped with forever, despite his smelling an unmistakable whiff of the same flavor as when Alexander's father Adam, Will's neglected son, tried to guilt-trip him into a payoff, prompting such a furious reaction. *Get out of here!* And now the boy…

"Yes," Walter says, "you've got the car and saving up for college."

"I'm not sure full-time school is right for me now." He punches a fist into the free palm. "I really like making the bucks. Mom and Dad never could."

"But arts school?" This slips out and then Walter shuts up. Here is the lad a year or so ago who came to his bedside loaded down with drawings and paintings and supplies to share his boyhood passion with the likes of this invalid.

"I—I wondered, Walter, maybe if your offer of help last year could apply to night school? I really need accounting and statistics and employee management. Let's face it. Dad is a trucker."

"And a salesman," adds Walter, swallowing multiple thoughts at once.

"I could take his business someday in a much bigger direction. I'm still a kid. But you know, broken family and all that, Mom barely above the poverty line, I've had to—grow up."

"I can see," says Walter, forgetting all else. *It's about this boy. His lot in life, his fresh start. My life has run its course. Isn't that now what I'm all about? The end?*

Alexander takes off after exchanging some pleasantries, leaving Walter utterly crushed. Must everyone on earth be enslaved by the dollar? As for himself, Walter well knows his parents slogged through the aftermath of the Great Depression. Not an iota of enlightenment in his background and long career let alone any place for art… appreciating it let alone making it. And then he thinks: *How stupid of me! Setting up expectations. It's a matter of fulfillment for this young man. Fulfillment for me at this point has long since been passed. Forget all your bloody, feel-good schemes!* Walter accosts himself. Still, he's devastated.

~

IT'S A CHILD! MAYBE it's a man, but does that make it any better? Careening drunk and hitting something in the road. An abandoned bicycle? Maybe it's abandoned because, he, Walter, slammed into the rider. What road? He's searched all night long, every conceivable road he ever traversed in his young life, paved or otherwise. Dirt and debris spitting up from the road, from whatever he hit, fogging his view and his memory all the more. He must find the road! He must find the parents of the child…the family of whoever would now be a man…the town where such a man had lived…*or died.* There is so little time left. He can still use his laptop, his feeble hands and his eyes. It's been his burden for as long as he has dreamed. His waking reality, anyone's, is malleable. And so he has fashioned his reality to be his factory business, which he nurtured with help from no one else. This is conscious. This is what he has chosen to do and built from scratch. But he has learned about the other kind of business during sleep, to dig into the shadows, unearth the evil lurking in him, in everyone, sealed for sanity's sake with a concrete lid in the light of day. However do we stay alive and on the straight and narrow? Denying the devil within. Isn't that better than going berserk and slaughtering people, becoming savage as we were in the beginning? Isn't savagery still the path for the bulk of people on this planet, whether those who inflict it or those who suffer its inhumanity? I am but one man, one part savage, who has wrought havoc only the gods know how or where or when. But you, Walter, crouching before the gates of reconciliation if not heaven and hell must confront at long last your self-imposed judge and jury comprised as no other person but yourself. No punishment, no sentence, but simply the bald truth. You hit something and/or someone and drove on. If not, you left the scene of some accident. How else could the fluttering remains of a boy's red shirt in a roadway spewed with dust, an image as calm and transparent as a diaphanous watercolor, whether a dream or for real, suck the lifeblood of your soul like a parasite at work without pause?

Chapter 16

A candle is made to become entirely flame.
In that annihilating moment
it has no shadow.

FUNNY," SAYS IRMA, EXAMINING the lineup of bedside pills. "This one shouldn't be ready for a refill." She squints. "This one either, for the tremors. Have you been taking these two more than twice a day?"

Walter shrugs, no eye contact.

"I'll count them out in a dish, a.m. and p.m., just to be sure."

~

"IS THIS GOING TO be like the BOSU ball, Tressie? That was such a disaster, it was laughable." Walter steps onto the metal disc supported by Tressie recalling the rubbery half-globe gizmo geared to promote balance they tried ages ago. He couldn't even step onto it, clutching Tressie's solid set of shoulders.

"No, this is a swivel disc, just step here on top. That's good, Walter. Right on the floor next to your bed, if you can slide to the edge of the bed, and then stand, yes! Now keep one hand on the bed edge, good, and turn ninety degrees. Yes! Now you can plop your fanny into the wheelchair. See how easy?"

He gets the idea but without clinging to her it's hopeless.

"Okay, let's get you to stand again from sitting, hold onto the bed, the disc won't move, up, up, yes. Now swivel again, aim your butt to the bed, and sit down. You did it!"

"Cripes. You really mean it—use it or lose it. More exercise than I had when I was supposedly functional."

"Catch your breath, then we'll do it once more."

He figures it must be scorching out. Today she's in short-shorts—no way would he know the current terminology—the hot-pink shorts, perfectly matched by the boisterous flowers of her tropical-themed halter. Not a smidgeon of fat. Of course, she's doing all the work, although his own efforts at physical therapy since Tressie's moving in are nothing to scoff at. Parts of him, at least, are in working order with the constant bending, twisting, flexing, even some routines with one- and-two-pound weights. Bladder and colon control have gotten worse. Sphincter exercises are a thing of the past. The dizziness and spastic eyes, no getting any of that back to normal. Meanwhile, it seems that Tressie has merged with his very own body. A mother's nipple, the baby's lips, seamless they are as one. With Tressie stroking up and down and around his limbs, Walter can be lost in a plume of passing clouds so far above his niggling, petulant concerns of the day. Is she not the one wonderful consequence of this otherwise heinous disease?

He is sitting once again on the edge of the bed…unsupported, almost upright, anticipating her next command. Here he sits void and senseless like the dummy of a ventriloquist. What a blissful, irresponsible state of being. Soon Tressie snaps again into action and settles him onto his back.

"Each single action we do involves the core," she instructs in the clipped notes of a castanet. "You've got to clench your gut with every rep. Not much left in there but we're not going to lose it, Walter. Keep your leg straight, now when I lift it, clench! Relax and lower. Clench and lift. Relax and lower."

To him, everything she says, every move she makes, is in response to the music inextricably bound to her very heartbeat. Buried treasure from her otherwise impoverished background. *Who says I'm so rich?* thinks Walter, hollow as a bell missing a ringer.

Tressie places her free hand flat on his belly. "Again," she says, and so they continue, each rep Tressie pressing gently below his navel. "There's a little flicker in there. Not much, but something to work with."

They take a break. Living upstairs, she now sees him most every day. Tressie sips her sports drink and hands Walter his plastic cup and straw, having cranked the bed up a few notches.

"How's your Mo handling this?"

"He's never here! Irma saves his meals since he eats on the fly."

"He gets up at four a.m. for his paper route? Gosh, what determination."

"His route has tripled even on his bike, this neighborhood with everybody subscribing. Customers like him. He got a summer job offer from the publisher of the local paper, distributing inserts…as well as collecting payments! How about that?"

"Your Mo is a good boy. I've seen him chatting with the grounds crew. I think my stock has risen, employing and now housing what do you say—a person of color?"

"He certainly is black next to my mocha. I guess he's no threat in a white hood doing something servile."

To Walter this stings, but he refrains from saying what he thinks. Instead: "He's thirteen, Tressie, and already making his way in the world. With your inspiration and support. Wish I could last long enough to watch him leap along the next steps."

"I don't think Mo will become entitled here. This is so beyond where we come from. It's just filling a role, doing a job. But he's such a hard worker. He can already see how that can get him to—be nothing like the father he'll never know. Nor want to, he says."

Walter stares at this woman residing within the splashy color of her fun clothes and the tight, firm body of a manual laborer all day on her feet. "Tressie, you speak as well as any peer I've ever encountered from, please excuse me, my station in life, my privilege."

"Think of my clientele, Walter. From the start. The women are just as polished as their nails I do for them."

"You've been so ambitious."

"I've had no choice. A mother on my own. I had Mo when I was seventeen."

"But lots of people—"

"Walter, I'm nothing special. Just an All-American girl." She continues working his calves. "There are millions like me. More like me than like you, my friend! But when you come from the rubble, I'll admit in my case, I grabbed for one glimmer of hope, a grandmother with guts. Scrubbed her kids. Made them go to school, took no shit from drug lords, she ruled her roost. My own mother didn't make it, but you only need a single life raft to stay afloat."

"Tressie, we have to discuss more about setting up your own salon. I've talked to the attorneys—"

"Oh, do shut up, Walter. Talk we know you can do. Now let's lie you flat on your back and tackle the quads. Missed last week."

She shoves down the bed lever, hip-hops to the end of the bed, and whips completely away the lower sheet. "The quads are the biggest muscles. So you can't run around, but there's life in there from all the attention we've been paying. Plus your effort. Even standing with assistance you fire those babies."

He wishes they could chat all day. At least she has set up music for him with help from the techie Irma hired. Endless dull days are no longer. All kinds of music he's never heard of—her music. Pink Martini! Salsa! Merengue, Rumba, Cha Cha Cha! A far cry from the classics Ana's granddaughter played at her recital for him. Minuets. Dainty piano taplings composed for palace swells. Now solos of harp and classical guitar that he found on his laptop have been much to his delight. Such simple strummings banish any thoughts whatsoever. They strike him as lullabies served up with the pedigree of concertos; to his ear they are rhythms to soothe aging, overwrought, addled adults at which he qualifies.

Shut up, Walter. Follow the leader. *Breathe.*

~

HE IS AWARE OF her supple fingertips reaching up to and touching the lower edges of the pad. His thoughts shouldn't be going in that direction since such sensations have long been shelved. His private parts have bypassed this outmoded designation for them. She, Irma, and others have dealt with all that for so many months. And yet he is somewhat relieved as her smooth hands glide back to the kneecaps, hardly an erogenous zone. And yet…Her very touch, up and over his thighs, stretching and releasing the muscles and whatever tissues underneath—every movement is relabeling itself as lovemaking, not therapeutic massage. He attempts to breathe more deeply, withdraw from the drift of this thinking. He must cast her solely as masseuse, not—call girl. *Walter!* he nears giggles to himself. *Whatever would you know of those shenanigans?* Maybe each touch is now reverberating as he once recalled Polly at their most playful doing nothing more than nibble his ear. And she would continue with that although his erection was on the brim of bursting but no, she carried on with the other lobe to tease him further, temper him ideally, someday, to her purposes as proper lover rather than a fire hydrant drenching himself instead of igniting her.

"This is silly. I'm not getting the inner thighs." Off come the nappies. And there he is, his former glory a landed, wrinkled parachute collapsed and plastered on the ground.

"It's true, this area up to the groin, it's ordinarily out-of-bounds. Not the muscles themselves. They too need working. But it's the proximity to the sex. For women, too, you have to keep this part covered. You okay, Walter?"

"Mmm," he mumbles.

She increases her reach up the side of his thigh to where it meets the crease of the butt and the sitting bone. "I'll just lift these out of the way," she says, referring to his squishy penis and ball sack, and massages the perineum, the space between scrotum and anus. "Now, this area is untouched, unseen, ignored by even the person him- or herself, and yet it's engorged with nerve endings. This is about stimulation today, Walter. Tapping these sections for whatever reactions. Do you feel any of this?"

"Ahhh," he attempts to answer.

"You look content, so I'll keep on. You know, my dearest man, we must acknowledge every ounce of you physically that can respond. Each fiber of you is connected to the next connected to the next. Why should anything be overlooked? You are telling me with that smile to proceed, so I will. Yours is just a body, Walter, like each of us has. Women and men react very similarly to erotic sensation. The parts are constructed or labelled as if they belong to entirely different animals. But no. The penis head and clitoris are first cousins. Hey, I like that! Now keep on with full, deep breathing. That's it. Sink into whatever you are feeling, my good man. You are fully alive. Let go. Let go." And she circles his flaccid genitals and eventually cups them, cradles them. And yes, he is ever-so-slightly swollen. Enough for her to tug along the limited length, twirl fingers around the head, pull some this way and then that.

"Umm," he moans, barely audible.

She is whispering now, not so much with discernible words as simplistic lyrics to a Latin love song. She is crooning, humming, and breathing through what must be almost closed lips. He is surrendering. He is beyond an inkling of control. She assumes all of that. He is nothing but on the verge of a miracle. Even this thought he must suppress and is able to do so.

"You are almost there, sweet man. You are going, going, keep going—"

Eventually he arrives. Under an avalanche of shudders, the whole of him, head to foot. He sluices deep within the earth that has buried him. He lies there, thinking: *It should be over, I should be gone now. What more?*

Tressie covers him with a sheet. Slowly she goes about collecting her things. She takes her time before exposing him and administering a fresh pad. He hoists his upper self to confront her, unaware of any facial expression he is capable of composing. Tressie settles onto a stool.

"You know women do this, too," she says. "It's simply pleasurable manipulation. Just because you're impotent…well, I guess you've got a thing or two to learn while you're still alive if not kicking."

"Tressie. I can't remember an orgasm like that. Ever. And without an erection."

"There are thousands of men with prostate cancer and other erectile issues. No need to give up sexuality. Receiving pleasure. Nobody talks about this. It's not covered in the US Department of Health Guidelines for Loving Couples Post Prostatectomy. Wives have shown me. Nope. All they feature are penile implants, injections to stiffen the penis, all this business to keep it up! Reassure him he can still perform. *Penetrate.* No loss of manhood, oh, my God, never that."

"Maybe you should run for office. Quite a platform."

She tickles his toes.

"But I can't—service you," says Walter.

She guffaws and slaps his leg. "You men."

"I feel I've moved beyond gender."

"Good! In our case, Walter, it's not only PT, physical therapy. It's also making love. We can love others! Not just our spouse or lover, sexuality can be elevated this way, and rightly so. But why on earth should simple, God-given touch be hamstrung by the Church and laws and all that crap? The Pope and priests, it's ridiculous. Look what perversion they've had to endure. So silly they're not married, to men as well as to women. Oh, don't get me going."

Walter folds his arms across his chest. “Tressie. Getting you going and keeping you going is my new mission in life.”

“No way. Don’t you dare forget your children! Irma and all these good people you care for. While you’re here, they need you. Me included! We give and we take. We are not here to be isolated from our fellow beings. Is that understood?” She zips off the stool, stands soldier-straight, and jostles her tight jaw as if scolding him. But this she cannot maintain and beams those bright red lips into her broadest grin. “Now I do have my other clients, Mr. Walt.”

He holds up a hand, makes the most pleading look he can contrive. “Oh, Tressie. When can I see you again?”

She smirks. “Tonight. On the sly. I’ll bring a popsicle to cool you off.”

Chapter 17

Not until it turns into gold
does copper realize
what it had been before.

BARS, BARS, EVERYWHERE I'M clinging onto bars. The bars each side of the toilet, the toilet seat raised as if that wasn't enough of an assist. Bars in the shower. New bars, lower, because now I have to sit there instead of stand." He blows out a sigh but Tressie appears occupied otherwise. "Now these bars up and over the bed."

"They're adjustable," she says and does so, focused on her work.

"It's like I'm a kid on a jungle gym."

"But you can grab and swing the horizonal one here and use the pole to stand without me helping you. Pretty cool, you have to admit, Walter."

"I admit to nothing except my total dependence on you, with or without these contraptions." He practices standing and sitting, amazed he has the strength to elevate and lower himself. "Of course, you're right, Tressie. This is pretty cool. However has Paula come up with all of this?"

"You're not the first person on earth to lose mobility. She had shipped that tilting wheelchair, whatever she thinks might help."

"Irma donated that to the veteran's hospital, yes?"

Tressie nods and rolls up the sleeves of her floppy white jumpsuit with variously sized black polka dots. It whipped about like a flag in wind just before when she did the rumba to Trini Lopez. Walter begged her to keep dancing the way he never did nor ever would.

"Okay, down to business," she says.

"My pole dancing was just a warm-up?" He reclines back at her signal. "Thank goodness you, like me, are too old for Mo's rap music. This stuff you're playing, I presume you're humoring me. I mean, Xavier Cugat? Even before my time, although the name rings a vague bell from my youth."

"Brown music for white people. If it makes you happy, I'm all for it. Now. Let's talk about bladder control."

"Oh, Tressie, that's a lost cause."

"You told the doctor no way would you go for surgery, the—suprapubic catheter," she pronounces by the book.

"I will not have all of you emptying bags. Changing nappies since I rarely make it to the john is bad enough."

"Fine. We're going to try pelvic massage. The Kegels isolated the sphincter. There's more we can do. And for this we can leave the pad in place." She winks. Her headband of the day—black with white polka dots—matches the jumpsuit but in reverse. He can't imagine the heaps she must cram into her dressing area. She claims her every stitch is from the thrift shop.

Walter submits and lies still. His only option with Tressie. Funny, he doesn't miss the few other times in the past months that he asked for a repeat of that thrilling encounter. Once he came close, and the journey was a joyride if not coupled with a destination. But the memory of that initial wallop was enough to give him a gift that keeps on giving. It had been all her doing, nothing that he could subsequently shift from his singular role as recipient to abruptly calling the shots. She often asked if he was interested in more pleasure that way, but he demurred. And it was impossible, he told her, attempting that on his own. With these hands?

"I could give you a vibrator, Walter," she says.

"A what?"

"You know, what women use. Men, too, I suppose. My gay friends who are the bottoms. They say it gets a bad press. Hugely sensitive in there, the final gut lining. We should consider—"

"No way! Are you kidding?"

"Oh, relax. You never took it up the ass?"

He smolders, speechless.

"Of course not, just joking," she answers herself and him. "But they say it's double the ecstasy, all those nerve endings inside and out. It doesn't have to be a dildo, a fake penis. It can be a butt plug. There are a zillion toys I know. For gents as well as the ladies."

"Stop!" he pleads when he can manage a word after laughing himself breathless.

In any event, Walter muses, now flat on his back for today's session, it is Tressie's touch, her loving energy that infuses every stroke, blurring the line between therapeutic and sensuous. What truly is the difference? The orgasm was great, he thinks as Tressie works the ridge of his pubic bone, but so is a good sneeze. He remembers how Polly sparked arousal in his earlobe. Tressie, day in and day out, is enlivening every particle of him, from his temple to his toes.

"Walter, I want you to breathe into this area, think of nothing else. You are empowering these pelvic tissues with new blood, more circulation. Close your eyes. Stop looking at me."

He tries his best to do as she says, although he'd rather not picture his pelvic tissues. He knows full well this effort is all in his mind, that it may or may not result in moving a microfiber let alone a muscle. *Where is my willpower?* he asks himself. *If it's mind over matter, well, the mind is the very last thing at my disposal. What has willpower ever been for me as a white man compared to her brown? What landed in my lap—forget how hard I supposedly applied myself—was because of the luck of the draw. My time and place. No foreign competition. A welcome mat for folks of my ilk and color of skin. But hers? A force of nature she needed just to exit the hovel and not look back. Or around, at all the wreckage of her kin. In junior high they were teaching us the foxtrot, partners a foot apart, while Tressie was bopping to the beat of conga and bongo drums…*

"You aren't concentrating, Walter."

"I was, in my way." He reaches for her hand and taps it. He can initiate that much.

~

He knows the city. The blocks are even-odd in a perfect square, how could one possibly get lost? He's completely familiar with the theater marquees, department stores, the pavement bustle of the affluent crowd, shoppers but mostly businessmen like himself. He, too, is striding to an appointment, he presumes. Across town and not too far down, the pedestrian traffic is thinning. The blocks are gradually composed of fewer commercial high-rises, the odd tenement wedged between otherwise faceless, purposeless buildings. Laundry is hanging out on lines strung here and there, limp, smudged with the ever-present soot, at least in this part of the city. The crosstown avenue, typically streaming with buses and taxis, narrows into just another street. He attempts to keep up his pace but must avoid the sidewalk clutter, debris from the curb spilling up and over into his path. Women are draped out of windows, screaming at kids. The crosstown street abruptly ends. He is forced to zigzag over and down ever-darker blocks to make his way. Eventually, there is not one other soul rushing or even strolling on the street. He hears shouts, laughter, anger, no way can he tell, but it is not polite. There are no buildings on either side, just caverns of dirt and rubble left from entire demolished blocks. The graffiti-splashed fencing becomes periodic and then ends. There is a clutch of boys, black boys, punching each other, kicking an abandoned car with their heavy boots. What is left of the windshield is smashed by one of the boys with a metal bar. They get bored with the car and are coming toward him. *He must cross to the other side of the street!* Some of them are swinging baseball bats. He cannot cross the street. He is doomed, utterly done for, either way…

Walter awakes, shuddering. Another one of those. So many times before. He lacks the will to think it through. Can only take the path of least resistance. Leaving the maelstrom of nighttime horrors and returning to the light of day where he simply exists, nothing required of him otherwise. A willing slab for Tressie. A mouth for Irma to feed. A listener for any who visit, their words hopefully unbeknownst to them like a swarm of sparrows fluttering across the picture window and then forgotten on the spot.

SINCE HE CANNOT ENVISION a future, Walter often revisits a moment he has long since ignored, an occasion he considers contrary at the least. He drops a skillet of scrambled eggs. His hand is suddenly without power, like a vehicle stalled for no rhyme or reason. He picks up the skillet, cursing himself, angry at the hurt on the top of his foot. He bemoans the loss of good eggs. But he does not connect it to the time his briefcase slips from the grip of his fingers onto the floor of his office. Out of the blue. Never before, and so it is easily dismissed. There is that scene at the supermarket, his holding open the door for a woman exiting and hugging two overstuffed brown paper bags. The heavy door slides from his clasping it and rams into her face, groceries scattered to the ground, blood gushing from her nose. He will not go to the doctor, does not want to be bothered. He thinks of buying a grip device to strengthen his hands but forgets. It takes a visit with Paula, his eaglet, who is shocked when he cannot twist open a bottle of water. He is reduced to her helping him, but soon after sipping from the bottle it lands in his lap.

What is going on, Dad? she demands and makes him promise to check it out at least with a therapist if not a physician.

Did I do that? he wonders. *When did the doctors intervene?* It takes several years, he cannot string together the eventual sequence of events. Presently it's all a muddle, even though his mind is supposed to be the last thing to go. *Well, it's going. Good. The less of this malarkey I can remember, the better.* And there is a future. He just hopes it arrives sooner than later. He is trying his darnedest to live day by day, moment by moment as the mystics advise. But the better, or worst, part of him knows full well: he is waiting, he is biding his time.

~

His room is electrified as if he's lived through a long-standing power failure and suddenly the lights are ablaze. Paula enters as was prearranged the day before, but he's totally forgotten. Before saying a word, she exudes the presence of her mother Polly. There is a purpose to her life that never is in question. Whatever personal wars she's engaged in are conducted within the confines of her solid skull. There should be more of this, of her sort, in the world, he thinks. Wishy-washy types like I've been go with the flow, as it was glorified, but we just add to the bewildered surface about which everyone has to crash and careen. For good or ill, right or wrong, she takes a stand. Paula strips off her dressy taupe jacket and shakes out the sleeves of the silky blouse before sitting comfortably in the bedside armchair. Immediately he had noticed the tailored suit and high heels. Her usual ponytail is pinned back into a tight roll-up in some fashion. So formal. Shiny earrings like gold coins.

"Have you been to the banks up here?" he asks when Paula is finished surveying the bed linens, the various equipment, the orderliness of jars on his bedside stand.

"No, I've been meeting with Horace. And smart young Stanley, his associate. At your suggestion."

"Oh, did I? Slipping my mind."

She recrosses her long, elegant legs, ordinarily draped in trim workaday slacks. "Dad, you have told me over the last several visits of some gifts, fairly modest ones, you were thinking of adding to our arrangements. I didn't know about the new foundation."

She is so cool, his grown-up girl. She doesn't reveal a flicker of resentment. No wonder she's master, mistress of her universe. "Oh, yes, Paula. I did do that. You know I had a steady wind of ideas over this past year. I didn't want to bother you. It's all kind of petty compared to your worth in my will."

"Petty? Please, Dad. A million dollars to Mom all of a sudden from the goodness of your heart. She declined to be involved but was flabbergasted. As I was."

"Well. It's like my brain has been in overdrive as my body has wasted away. I never thought about the good some of my money could do, apart from your and Gavin's well-being. For that there's plenty."

Paula nods but with a shade of reluctance, not a listless tilt of the head but one more held in check by neck muscles contracted.

Maybe I've been a keener observer than I ever realized, Walter thinks in a flash. *Maybe holding my tongue and letting others spout off left me no choice but to look folks hard in the eye, revealing even more than their words. Paula's very silence suggests restraining a jump to the defensive.*

Both Paula and her father take deep breaths, as if steeling themselves for what promises to be unpleasant.

"A charitable foundation, of course," Paula states, not inquires. "Nonprofits."

Do I have the wherewithal for this conversation? Find it, he hears in Tressie's voice. "To be honest, Paula dear, I'm thinking beyond charities. Until I've been virtually bedridden I never thought about the characters buzzing around me, doing this and that. Doing everything I no longer can. Caring for me."

"Their jobs."

"Not the highest paying." Score. Leave it at that.

"Did it occur to you to ask me whether I would like this estate? That I might not want to work like a dog—as you did, Dad—until some bitter end? Offering to Irma—wonderful Irma—but for God's sake! Have you lost your mind?"

"I did think that Gavin might—"

"Gavin!"

"He is back on his feet. He might make a go of the college counseling/financial aid assistance business."

"It's not a business," she says softly, swallowing her edge, shuffling to a more secure spot for her next volley.

"It could be a business, Paula. You started from nothing, really, except for my financial backing. Why not for your brother? Polly has always been a wonderful role model for you both. Well, we can now see I had something or other in my guts that somehow or other landed us with all this. Gavin could be capable of wielding clout. He just did so in the wrong direction. There was a fury to his addiction, but perhaps it's possible to harness that. Unlike you and me, for him it's not the money. Like your mother, there's a passion to help others. Even though he wouldn't speak to her all those years, he had to listen. You cannot shut Polly up." This triggers Paula to crack a smile. "Or tell your mother no it can't be done."

He's said enough. Or run out of steam. Or both. They each look aside, retrenching, not done, certainly in her case.

Walter jolts up as if from a stupor. "Paulie, I'm so sorry! It honestly didn't occur to me that you, someday, might want this retreat. You were off and running by the time Polly and I really dug in here. And Irma…" Where this is coming from, he has no idea. "It was just on the drawing board…"

"Dad." Paula shakes her head, her habit, even though there's no ponytail today to clear the air. "I know you are beholden to these fine helpers. Irma. Now Tressie. Adam and Alexander, Will's family, another story. But, how can I say this without feeling ungrateful? Dad, you are dipping, no, digging, into my inheritance, about which you've always assured me."

"And Gavin's."

"We're your flesh and blood. Isn't that most important? Even in a court of law?"

"I've made you and Gavin equal, Paula. Now he also has power of attorney. You've got to consult with each other about—the end stage for me. And of course after that."

Her lips, obviously painted for earlier in the day, are pinched and oddly pale. "Dad. Your doctors have told me that we cannot expect you to be as sharp mentally as you've been. As the end draws near. Nothing to do with your disease, just a natural part of your decline. There is the issue of mental competence. You and I have always spoken frankly to each other."

"And that won't change. But I am still on the ball, Paula. Believe it or not, I manage to learn something each day. For example, Tressie's Mo is helping her do some of the heavy lifting when Irma's not available. That boy is going to go somewhere. So what that he's black as the ace of spades? So self-reliant. Reminds me of me at that age."

"Dad!" Paula explodes. "You've already set aside a fortune for her, a fortune by her standards."

"I like having this extra checkbook. I like making small presents here and there. And they are small, Paulie, to you and to me. And yes, a few hundred or a few thousand is indeed a gold mine for somebody less fortunate."

This seems to silence her. Thankfully she doesn't know about his recent contributions to good-minded political candidates, a floodgate of appeals launched because of that.

She unhooks whatever is pinning back her hair and shakes out her long straight mane. She yanks the gold earrings apart, deals with the pieces, thrusts them into her bag. Finally, she tucks toes into her high heels, which she had cast aside. She sits erect once again. She is finished, for the time being.

She glances at the pill bottles atop this bedside stand. "Oh, yes, something else." She fingers the various pills, inspects them. "Irma mentioned—" She stands and opens the drawer, pokes through more bottles, uncaps a few and peers in, as if counting. She reaches and touches the hardened sock with a quizzical expression. She uncovers its contents. Uncaps the big bottle, filled to the brim. Replaces it in the drawer but not in the sock. Ever so slowly, she swivels her gaze to her father.

Barely moving, Paula nods. Her lips and facial muscles relax. She knows.

She swallows and says: "Where were we? Okay, Dad. It's true you were always very generous. It was just with your employees. They revered you, and you didn't know it. Not of a mind for that. The best possible health-care benefits and largest bonuses anywhere in sight. In the beginning it was Will this, Will that, the star of it all, you just the balding, beady-eyed guy in the back office, calling the shots. Yes, you were driven as the devil but it wasn't for you. It was for the good of the business, its foundation, the community's dependence upon its thriving. You didn't budge from your obsession with very limited debt if you were forced that way, temporarily. Do you realize there will be thousands coming to your memorial service?"

"No memorial service! Toss my ashes in the pond. May they sink quickly. I'm serious, Paula. Said the same to Gavin. And Irma. Lots of luck twisting her around. Hopefully you'll be scouting new suppliers in China when it happens."

Paula uncrosses her legs. Hands flop in her lap. This meeting is about to be adjourned. She will have to devise Plan B to deal with her dad. Or maybe not…

"One more thing I'm going to ask for," says Walter, "when they scatter, no toss the ashes over the pond. Tressie will have Ritchie Valens belting out 'La Bamba.' Blaring over loudspeakers. From here to kingdom come."

~

"Walter, I want to introduce you to Rufus, a new member of the household," says Irma, louder than usual from the doorway. Meanwhile, an animal has bounded into and around the room, madly circling the bed, and then abruptly thrusting its upper legs and paws atop the bedding, almost reaching Walter's lap.

Walter stares at Irma who is stone-faced, as he must be as well.

"It was Gavin's idea, but Paula approved. A rescue dog. From the network you've gifted. Rufus they think is about a year old. Abandoned somewhere in Arkansas. The vet said he's full of buckshot but it's of no health concern. Mostly Shepherd but a good helping of Lab..."

"Irma..."

"...the combination," she cuts him off, "to mean both highly intelligent—meaning well-behaved—and very affectionate."

"Irma," is as much he can manage. The dog has remained perfectly still, resting his head and jowls now squarely on the edge of the bed, looking imploringly at Walter, on cue.

"Black and brown and white and gray, with a smooth coat that won't much shed, and bright eyes, they say mutts are the best. Hybrid vigor." Irma stands tall, smug as a schoolkid acing the exam.

Two against one, Walter thinks. *Not fair.*

"So he's a puppy," she continues, "and is capable of learning every trick in the book. He already knows the basics. Down, Rufe." And he withdraws from the bedside and settles onto the rug.

"You'll be feeding and tending him and..." Walter looks from the dog to his caregiver. "Irma. If he brings you some welcomed joy..."

"He's for you, Walter. We've got his bed all set, to be right by your side. He's Rufus but Rufe for short. Good boy," she croons so uncharacteristically. "Sit, Rufe." And he does. "Up, Rufe. It's okay." The dog, slowly this time, climbs up the bedside and places his two forelegs and padded paws, outsized as typical for a pup, firmly on top, barely nudging Walter's waist. Once again, with the damnable, adorable kisser.

Walter composes a pleading look of his own, aimed at Rufe and then at Irma. Did his kids have pets? He can barely remember; not his scene.

"What if I trip on him, middle of the night?"

"He'll move. He's faster than you."

Gradually Walter releases the grip of his hands held tight over his tummy and places a palm on the nearest of the two fluffy paws.

Chapter 18

It is in hope of the fruit
that a farmer plants a tree.
The tree then is born of the fruit
rather than the fruit from the tree.

MONTHS HAVE PASSED, BEST Walter can tell. Rufe is allowed to snuggle close to his side, but during daytime only. Without complaint, after his last run of the day with Irma, dutifully and daintily he circles his large padded bed on the floor and collapses into a tight furry heap. It's with a groan, but Walter takes that as a sigh of pleasure at another fine day permitted to please his master.

Between being rapt by recordings of Mozart especially—such happy tunes!—Walter can be prone to reminisce about the good ole days. The Pisa Syndrome! That was a hoot. Leaning too far to one side, and then to the other. With his collapsible cane he would hobble around like Charlie Chaplin in a silent movie. At least I was standing, he thinks. To picture himself in retrospect appears almost comic. Flat as a corpse now most of the time, his head is supported and tilted upward to relieve the high blood pressure. The view of his surroundings is so devoid of interest at this point that images flickering across his mental screen sparkle by contrast. They can dangle, isolated, without competition from the big living picture, like studying a taxidermic rainbow trout instead of glimpsing it dash through the scene of a nature film.

Of course, he is always talking to Rufe—suggesting he's free to take a trot outdoors, for example, to frolic and entertain the yard troops. He's superb at Frisbee, and does his business discretely a few yards into the tree edge underbrush, never, ever the lawn, as if his chief purpose in life is to mind his manners and not impose. Little does he know, in terms of a love affair, he now rules the roost.

~

"Good morning, Walter. How are we doing?" says Eleanor, the latest visiting nurse. "Here for your daily vitals." Gracefully Rufe slips down from the bed and assumes the position of the calm, watchful Sphinx, several steps off and out of the way.

Walter rather likes being addressed in the plural. There's the Walter who is dying of this disease, and there is the Walter every bit as cognizant of the world as he was from Day One. He recalls reading of a nonagenarian who expressed amazement at her decrepitude while in her mind's eye she hadn't aged a single day.

"I'm fine, Eleanor. How are you? You're the one who has to bustle about."

She smiles and straps the blood pressure band around what remains of his bicep. She is young and pretty, her brown hair long like most women these days, he gathers. Nice breasts and bottom suggesting not promoting her curves under the trim uniform. But she is sexless, compared to Tressie. Who isn't?

"Elevated. As usual," she says matter-of-factly as she pokes an ear for his temperature, reads his oxygen or pulse—he forgets—with the clip to his forefinger. She comments about the few pills he still takes, for what reasons he hasn't the foggiest. She is gone before he has the chance to utter the question he had formulated, an attempt to make of the encounter more than punching a clock as did the hordes in and out of his factory. *You said last time your little girl is in first grade, so you can work longer days. How's that going for you? Oh, well. Best left unsaid. She is making her rounds. She is not a shrink or paid companion…*

All of my human companions are paid, Walter quips to himself, scratching Rufe behind an ear upon his return. *Including my kids. Is this what I've done with my money? Too late for regrets.*

The picture window is an impenetrable gray. No entertainment there. Condensation. Must have rained. Oh, for those drugs at the beginning! They left him so stupidly light-headed. No wonder he could get lost for an entire hour in just a simple one of Rumi's poems. The shortest of paragraphs bespoke of the universe describing the humblest of events—arising too early or too late, and turning one's pea-brain perspective inside-out, as if someone had just been born and was looking at things first time ever, say, or if you'd been locked in a time capsule and were beholding an unfathomable, utterly exotic new world. With each poem Walter would experience if only for a few seconds a hair-raising revelation no less astounding than discovering the earth to be round. But alas, the dopamine restorers to redress the deterioration of his neurotransmitters failed as did the high. But it was something, Walter reflects. Even if they'd been including a placebo, a trial about which he would, of course, have known nothing, the initial, heavy dosages at least offered him ample helpings of hope…

"Time for your sponge bath, Walter," says Irma, lugging in the basin and cloths. "It's been two days."

"I know. No more showers." Rufe saunters off to the kitchen, would in no way compromise Irma's command.

"Showering was too much trouble for you, Walter. I didn't mind." She rolls him on his side and spreads the waterproof sheet.

"All that lifting and hauling into the shower, Irma, since I can no longer stand on my own. Although once you got me seated on the stool, it was like a gentle waterfall."

"It was either too hot or too cold."

"I thought I was dissolving. That was nice."

"It stung your eyes. It sharpened the pain in your hips, sitting that long."

Of course, Irma is right. She has to be. It is all her doing. Even if she is wrong, who cares? All he has to do, like now, is enjoy the total release. Off with the diapers. Over and around with delicious warm water for which she has mastered the perfect temperature. It's cradle to grave minus all of life in between. This pushes him to the edge of sleep, but he struggles to stay alert. As with Tressie's massage, he doesn't want to miss a moment. Tressie's rubbings for sure but Irma's are wonderful, too. *Am I her missing child?* he often thinks. Her son a grown man. How else can she be so devoted? Irma's sole concern seems to be maintaining his total comfort. Tressie's is working to extend his time on earth and enhancing his ability to enjoy it.

I don't believe these compression stockings that the nurse brought, Tressie declared to Irma bedside, *are good for him.*

But they will give more stability to his legs, said Irma. *He needs them for support.*

He's made progress in preventing the muscles and tendons around the joints from going completely stiff, asserted Tressie, a decibel higher.

The stockings were ordered by the doctor, replied Irma, a tad more forcibly herself.

I know his body better than the doctors, the nurses for sure, Tressie shot back.

Fine, submitted Irma. *If he falls, whose fault will that be?*

I gladly take the responsibility, said Tressie, with lower volume, having won. *This is all that I do here, Irma. You handle everything else, for heaven's sake. I'm focused on stretching these legs so they don't go totally slack.*

The stockings are dispatched to an idle drawer. Walter revels in that he was not consulted in the matter. Any outcome involving Tressie is preordained to go in her favor. Of course, he does have to alternate grunts of pleasure at each of Tressie's releasing strokes with his grunts of pain at the stretching ones. No pain, no gain is the one truly detestable utterance from that otherwise lyrical Latina songbird.

"There we are, Walter. Nice and dry," says Irma. "How about more of my chicken noodle soup that you asked for seconds of yesterday?"

"I'm sorry you have to shred the chicken so I can swallow. And the noodles have to be mush."

Irma needn't say a word but warmly smile. He understands she takes for granted his bedrock appreciation, including his constant apologies for her extra effort. Even though he knows readying his soup requires mere seconds, he hopes it sinks into her stalwart Hungarian self that, to him, she's truly a saint. He needn't discuss any further how he's provided for her in his will. Paula let that one go. But not his continued dealing with his bankers and attorneys…

Momentarily Irma spoon-feeds Walter the soup. He can no longer wield a utensil without shaking.

"I love picking up the bread," he says. "Ripping it with my teeth. Finger food! It's like a continuous picnic, Irma. I feel like a kid. Too bad pizza is too tough for me. But grabbing that greasy hotdog last night, jamming it into the mustard then the ketchup, don't tell me that's not fun."

Irma expertly presses another spoonful of soup to his lips, if only to shut him up, fair enough.

~

It is for Irma never Tressie, if Walter has anything to say about it, to get him to the toilet for his infrequent bowel movements. Presently, she is lifting him up from the wheelchair and setting him onto the elevated, heat-adjustable cushioned seat. The cushion is necessary because the plain seat is either too hot or too cold. It's also because he basically no longer has a butt. She undoes and slips off his pad, promptly removing herself from the scene. At this stage it hardly matters to him, but he respects Irma's need for privacy and decorum, this business being about the last such opportunity. He's content to sit here apart from any action in his alimentary canal. Just to be installed here is a last vestige of independence. But, truth be told, he sheds no tears at loss of independence. *Totally on my own; isn't that what I did nothing but for endless decades? I can look at it this way: completely dependent now upon others, I'm a new man! How ironic.* His breaths are slow and steady. At least here on the toilet he is sitting up, more so than configured in his pliable bed. However, prone and passive is his position of choice. Yes, dependent on others for the basics but, except with Tressie, he is becoming increasingly alone even with faithful Rufe plus various people poking about, Irma included. This is good, he is thinking. I'm getting ready. It's getting close. Soon I'll have had all the rehearsal one could hope for. And then the show must go on.

You say you are about ready, he addresses himself, but meanwhile you manage to concoct one amusement after another. Teaching Rufe to toss one of his own toys to retrieve. Mastication of a hunk of beautiful bread. Anticipation of a repeated sublime Mozart theme. At what point does one irrevocably sever an endless string of perfectly gratifying moments? For someone immobile but in bearable pain, here in his well-appointed waiting room, these moments assume an enormity, like drops of water sustaining a man stranded in the desert.

If he could just shutter his eyes, once and for all…

~

"How long has it been since the last spasm in your calf?" Tressie asks aloud, running her fingers like a rake down the length of his legs. Walter is on his belly, face crushed to one side, unable to speak, but Tressie was addressing herself at any rate. "It was all of last week. And you see, we keep working this way. No more spasms!" She carries on, her magic fingers darting with the grace of a gazelle, all instinct, no decision. He has come to prefer her performing in silence, except when she hums, in spite of herself. Wordless humming is always soothing.

On his own, he loves the CD of mumbo jumbo mariachi, whatever-the-heck music of her blood. It has spiced his afternoons for the better part of a year, but he's growing evermore fond of the piano and harp and classical guitar recitals he's found online. Today he is reacting to the perpetual patter of her narration a trifle like chirping. It reaches the one ear spared of impaling on the bed not as the serenade of a nightingale but the caws of a crow. Usually, he's bemused by the colorful flash of her costume, but at this moment, his eyes clamped shut to withstand the borderline discomfort of her fingers digging into his flesh, her cheerful clothes are beside the point. What even is the point of keeping lubricated these otherwise obsolete limbs? *Enough,* he wants to say but doesn't dare. His body is all for her to deal with, but for him it's the setting sun. It's had its use for the world, to procreate, to keep his carcass intact while he played the hand he was dealt. Why run a gas-guzzler with a broken muffler no less when now you can sit pretty in an all-electric that drives itself while you sleep or play games? *Even though I'm relatively young or early senior by most standards these days,* Walter goes on, *I have lived too long with my handicap. It's a drag on all concerned, except for Tressie, who in any event is following the beat of her own drummer.* What will become of her when he's gone? He didn't dare mention again his idea of her own salon. His idea, not hers. Hopefully just the money will do, another item conceded by his daughter. Paula, chomping at the bit to claim her full share—well, good for her.

Tressie rolls him onto his back tenderly as a lady wrestler, implying his physical bearing thanks to her ministrations is more functional now than not. He winces but has to laugh at the Spandex number painted onto her lithe body, the outfit to his mind apropos of an ironwoman in the Olympics. "Now we do the reverse side. All muscles work in opposition."

"You're telling me," Walter whispers, the crack for his benefit, not hers.

~

"SHOULD YOU BE LUGGING that by yourself?" Walter calls to the young boy attempting to hoist a huge trash can onto his extremely slight shoulder, which the can misses, whereupon he grabs it to his belly and waddles forth.

It's Mo, Tressie's son, who has volunteered to help Irma with some chores when he's free. A whippet, Walter supposes, can be unnaturally strong for its compact scale, but this skinny black kid, according to Irma, tackles jobs with the yard crewmen thrice his size. Rufe greets him with a furiously wagging tail, obviously relieved after sitting guard by his motionless master.

"Son, come over here for a sec," says Walter as Mo gently rests the burden on the floor.

"Your mother is very proud of you, earning those fancy new sneakers she said just from your paper route."

Mo seems perfectly comfortable living upstairs and venturing into Walter's room as now when the task requires, but has never been spoken to by the boss. He stands arrow-straight by the bed.

"Are you saving any of your earnings, Mo?"

"Mom lets me pay for the jeans and stuff I want." Beaming, the sudden whites of his teeth cause Walter to flinch, the adjacent dark skin all the more shockingly foreign to a fellow, from his era, confined to the executive suites of supposedly superior white men...

"I know you're volunteering, but...I think you should be compensated. You're out there on your bike, crack of dawn, delivering papers, to have cash in your pocket. Impressive. Bear with me while I get my checkbook here."

Now it's the bold whites of Mo's eyes that widen in wonder. Walter scribbles what can pass for his signature. "Take the pen, Mo. Here. Use this book to write on. Print your name and then two hundred dollars—the numbers and then you have to spell it out. There's one more thing I ask—that you start a savings account."

He tells the boy the location of the nearest bank, to explain to the teller where he and his mother live and for whom she works, while

Mo carefully wields the pen, obviously not for the first time, also not unfamiliar with a check.

"This is just to get your account started. I'd like to make occasional contributions when Irma briefs me on your extra work for us. Will this be okay?"

Mo nods, no smile, solemn as a judge.

"For now, let's just keep this between you and me. Don't tell Tressie. Maybe someday you can surprise her with a gift. A new dress! Or a nifty outfit where you got your sneakers and jeans. Make sure it's not something from the secondhand store!"

They both nod now to seal the deal.

~

"Where are we going? Why am I all bundled up?" he asks of Tressie, wheeling him to the south terrace.

"You'll see," she says, indifferent as a parent understandably weary of answering a tedious child.

It's a gorgeous day. Bright blue cloudless sky, crisp nostril-tingling air. He used to miss this until one day months after his diagnosis he turned a corner, turned his back on outdoor excursions and sightings, simply preferring the isolation and tranquility of his newfound inner sanctum. Rufe, meantime, is ecstatic to gambol outside, which his young limbs must ache for, being cramped side by side with Walter, both of them stiff as boards.

"Apparently Paula shipped this to us ages ago," says Tressie, standing beside the odd-wheeled contraption.

"I think I remember, there were so many gadgets and roll-abouts in the beginning. Didn't I try this?"

"Before my time, perhaps. It's been in the storage barn. It's a recumbent bike."

"You must be joking, Tressie."

"Do I joke? I admit, I'm fun. But no joke." She picks him up as if he's nothing but a feathered pillow. She pulls the baseball cap snug to his ears. Tightens the scarf and then the shoulder harness followed by the seat belt. He is tilted back at a forty-five-degree angle.

"What about my feet? Where do they go?"

"On the pedals, dummy. It's a bike."

"There's no motor?"

Tressie frowns, places his gloved hands atop the handlebars. "You pedal and you steer. Remember when you were a boy, that far back? Look, the driveway is totally flat. This thing is geared so a toddler could do it."

"And squeeze the handles for braking?"

This she doesn't respond to as she shoves him along the broad path toward the driveway, Rufe, of course, in the lead. Walter's knees flow up and down with the pedals engaged. Instinctively he guides the bike, that's no effort. Nor is it any to heed the headmistress and go for a spin.

"Cycle out to the orchard and then circle around!" Tressie shouts. "Attaboy, Walter. Go for it. Isn't it easy? Don't forget to breathe! Suck in all this fresh air!"

She is scooting alongside but soon he outpaces her. He narrows his eyes to deflect the breeze. It's stinging his eyes but it's watering them, sharpening his vision. This is unbelievable. Suddenly it's no longer Walter the referee of his quixotic, wandering mind but Walter a body, pure and simple. Within seconds his body is no longer the albatross, the burden, but the web-footed bird that is attempting to fly. Is he awkward as heck, but who cares? He is soaring, he is sailing, he supposes it's his limbs and lungs, but no, it is mostly in his mind. His face is wind-whipped, his eyes are tearing, his feeble legs are pumping away, but it's his brain that overtakes him, begging for this marathon to please not end.

Chapter 19

The day is coming when I fly off,
but who is it now in my ear, who hears my voice?
Who says words with my mouth?

EVER SO GRADUALLY HE lifts and shifts his knees toward his chest while rolling onto his side to face the edge of the bed. This requires what remains of his core muscle strength. Without the months of Tressie's physical therapy, his middle would be no more than a punctured tire. No way could he maneuver as now, slide lower legs over the bed and sit, albeit slumped, and reach for the urinal. Urinal! Wishful thinking. The version they dignify with that title for the bedridden resembles a wine decanter—tall but with a wider neck. Not that there's any difficulty in inserting the shriveled stub of his appendage into the container to relieve himself. He does so. At least this saves the diaper, leaving it dry for Number Two. Not that he's aware any longer of the comings and goings in that department. He holds the tubular device in place to make sure he's good to the last drop, as went the old Maxwell House coffee commercial. But still he lingers, savoring one of the rare moments in the day when he is more or less upright. He doubts it serves to clarify his mind, the brain-blood drained for a change versus its usual prone disposition, the whole of his head lolling about like a bloated dead fish in a wetland swamp. He sighs, replaces the urinal on the bedside stand, and eases himself back down as if he's a sleeping infant, not to be disturbed.

He folds his hands atop his chest and thinks: *I miss going to the bathroom.* He chuckles. *No, not that phrase concocted for civil society instead of uttering poop, shit, pee, piss. I truly miss my helpers getting me to and from the loo, water closet, toilet, john, restroom, lavatory, gents.* For the past few years, these undertakings were the highlights of his day. An excursion, practically a party. Trading barbs with Tressie, expressing niceties with Irma and nurses as thanks for their assistance. At such a burst of attention he'd become light-headed, like an astronaut alone in an orb for a year suddenly the center of a ticker-tape parade. For the most part he stares out the big picture window for hours on end point-blank, enlivened to catch the near blossoming of forsythia, in that season, or a worker shoveling snow in the season just before. Rufe has long since become the mascot of the groundskeepers, and good for them all. That marvelous dog can snare a Frisbee sailing six feet overhead with the ease of an acrobat. Even better, his bottomless well of affection enriches myriad souls rather than a single, somnolent slab.

So here Walter lies, nearing the finish line. No complaints. There's his journal of Rumi poems to revisit, now that he can no longer write legibly enough to record more of his favorites.

Do you think I know what I'm doing?
That for one breath or half-breath I belong to myself?
As much as a pen knows what it's writing,
or the ball can guess where it's going next.

~

Today I'm out wandering, and turn my skull into a cup for others to drink wine from.

~

Ana the housekeeper is sweeping the floor. Ordinarily he pays her no notice. She never looks him in the eye. To her, it would seem her job is to be invisible. He respects that. Now and then he has enquired of her granddaughter, who is mastering the piano. But he knows his any comment reaches her as a minor violation. Her command of English is minimal. He shouldn't force her to speak, which addressing her even with a statement let alone a question obviously does.

"Ana, excuse me, but do you enjoy wine?"

Dutifully she stops sweeping and aims her head at his.

"*Vino. Si?*"

She grins. Good woman.

"Please help yourself to the wine cellar. Irma is keeping track so the gardeners don't get more than their fair share. *Vino tinto…rioja*? Yes, of course!"

She does a little bow and carries on with her broom.

For others to drink wine…

How about that? Rumi, from the thirteenth century, relevant as ever.

~

ANOTHER DAY, ANOTHER TIME, Walter has shuttered his eyes but not these thoughts. Being "me," he decides, is overrated. If he visualizes himself, the result is just an amalgam of memories. Me as a child in this instance or that. Overhearing his parents verbalize distress over money, yes indeed that record got worn thin. There is me coping with my insignificance compared to the class movers and shakers. For the high school yearbook, it could have said of me: least likely to be remembered. There is me fretting over grades…me gloating over my swelling bank account…me vainly attempting to hold my own with Will…me shutting up with Polly for fear of whatever I said was in self-defense, not assertive…All these moments, all from so many years ago, was there ever a certifiable me standing there, participating even if passive, or was it me as a hollow Kewpie doll lined up on the shelf, a deaf-and-dumb target for whatever happened to get hurled my way? No pouting over that malarkey. Who needs a me if that's all it amounts to? How neat this Rumi fashioned himself into an observer, left himself mostly out of the picture. Walter supposes this is what poets do. Sidestep the whole shooting match. Sure, they can feel pain and pleasure, but that's universal, available to all, not just some bigwig starring in his own production, written and directed by his truly. *I like this,* Walter thinks. *Moving me or whatever I'm coming to call it in the right direction.*

~

His television set stands idle, forgotten and forlorn with its blank stare, but Walter cannot summon a shred of sympathy. Same for the cell phone, face down. It's like he's sitting in a bus slowly pulling away from the station, his hometown spelled out on the hanging sign with its faded lettering, his gaze fixed on the familiar surroundings, which recede moment by moment, becoming smaller and smaller, about which he has no remorse. In fact, he feels nothing. It's so long ago that he left. He drifts off.

~

A television set. He's on the floor, reading his book—age eight, nine? His grandfather, really Aunt Peg's dad, is watching a movie on the television they all share, but no one else in the family is around. There's a rumble, deafening noise for a film. Walter looks up. There's a child, a small boy in the road, riding his tricycle, completely unaware of the onrushing military vehicles. Walter is riveted by this shocking spectacle. No! Surely the tanks or trucks are going to stop, swerve, do something! The old man is smoking his pipe, seemingly unconcerned. A war movie, he had said. Not for kids. Walter can see the eyes of the soldiers who are driving. They are staring straight ahead, dust spraying everywhere from the huge, angry wheels. There's no chance they can see the little boy, or stop in time if they could. Walter is frozen in fear. *No!* he wants to scream but doesn't dare upset his morose grandfather. It's over in a flash. The camera holds on the remains of the boy's tattered shirt, a crumpled tricycle wheel, and then shifts to the next scene. Walter wants to shout at his grandfather who is sitting here as if it's just all part of war, war Walter is old enough to know is very bad, with so many people getting killed. He scrambles up from the floor and races with his book upstairs to his room. He tries to continue reading but he cannot stop thinking of the little child. If only he, Walter, a few years older, could have been there in that moment and yanked the boy to safety!

Walter sits bolt upright in bed. How could I have not remembered the origin of this nightmare? Watching just seconds of that movie horror-struck on the floor as a kid could not be more vivid. How has this been so buried yet twisted his entire life as wreckage all his own doing? If he cared so much for the fate of this innocent child about which he could do nothing, maybe it left an impenetrable scar over his ability to…to what…to feel for others…express compassion ever again. Surely this is a fluke. A chance assault on the psyche of a youth. Surely it didn't warp the whole of me, he hopes, rubbing his temples. Yes, I was sealed off, a solo act, Walter attempts to conclude this poisonous interlude. But there were so many other reasons for that…

Mysteries are not to be solved.

The eye goes blind when it only wants to see why.

~

"You're right, Irma. The wine should stay intact. It's for Paula and Gavin to deal with, fight over, whatever. Just tell the folks I changed my mind about the wine cellar."

It stings him to recall Ana the housekeeper's instant grin. "Help yourself," he had said. She with the sturdy if misshapen lower legs, the callused hands…It had nothing to do with the wine.

~

There should be no such word as "I," he is thinking. At least for me at this stage. He pictures himself like one of those miniature Russian dolls that keeps getting encased in ever-larger outer shells. I have saddled myself with so many layers. Early on, Poor Kid who makes it big. Daddy. Then Father, or Dad. Casper Milquetoast to Polly (once, according to his disgruntled wife). Level Head, to finally realize Polly was right to leave him. Silent then Equal Partner to Will. Next, The Boss. Land Baron, not knowing a maple from a fig. Close Friend but to whom? Horace the tax attorney and Charles his investment advisor and all that lot. However, one role prevailed over the others. For all these years he was a slave to his business. True, a rich, slave-owning slave, but, bottom line, what's the difference, one person to the next? Each character thinks he or she is so special. And this is true. But it's because of a unique portfolio of multiple, accumulated layers, one padding the next when the prior one goes out of fashion or simply wears out.

In the end, after all those supposed explosions out there, we are nothing but stardust, every single living soul. He should find this consoling, but he is squirming under the sheets. Breathing erratically. Put a stop to this.

All right, we each have a foundation, reduce it to that. A solid slab. Walter knows he has one, deep down, intact. But then look at all the building blocks at our disposal—shingles, stone, stucco, clapboards, bricks, and logs. Endless variations. And that is what we see. Never the bedrock foundation, out of sight, out of touch, taken for granted, forgotten but always there, even when they tear the place down.

~

"Remember to squeeze your sphincter! And clench your toes!" Tressie assails him with this day's admonitions.

Has she just been here, stroking his body and about to leave, him oblivious? Or is she greeting him before the next of their sessions? He hasn't a clue.

"Must rush to Mo's graduation, so I'll miss your late afternoon muscle-memory work."

He can barely recall her son let alone the offspring of the others. And her son lives upstairs. "Hmm," he mutters and slides back to wherever he's been.

Let the letter read you.
You've escaped, but still you sit there like a falcon
on the window ledge.

~

"Dad. Dad? Hi there, Dad."

Walter is shaken lightly but from a very deep sleep. "Am I dead yet?" he warbles.

Gavin laughs, and Walter does, too. "You were just sleeping," says his son, who arranges his own long limbs over and about the easy chair as if he owns the place. Which he more or less does.

Walter is struck by the handsomeness of his children, almost believing they couldn't possibly be from his loins. Polly's, yes, but his own? Maybe that's just been of late as I withdraw, our opposite realities so exaggerated.

"That's all I do, is sleep," says Walter. "How will I know the difference if I die?"

Gavin beams. "I don't think that's a problem, Dad. In fact, doesn't everybody say what a blessing, to die in your sleep?"

Walter is bored with this exchange, about which he'd attempted to make light. "You told me the other week that you got some things going with the college aid work. I think there are more important things to discuss. While my wits hold out."

"Dad, everything you ever said to me was important."

"That's because your mother did all the talking. Anything I managed to say probably carried more weight than it should."

"Stop it. When you spoke up it really hit home. And, of course, I never said a word. Guilty as I was of the latest disaster."

Walter pauses, elevates his head and neck best he can. "That was never fair to you, Gavin. Like it was all black and white, you're wrong, your parents are right. For my part, I just seconded Polly's pronouncements. It was as if you were nothing but our kid, a reflection of us and our competence. Paula our success, Gavin our failure."

Walter is forced to swallow, collect himself before continuing. Gavin looks totally relaxed, eyes alert, an active recipient of his father's need, he must figure, to clear the air.

"Did we ever ask you why you were seized with a compulsion to—steal, destroy, delve into the next illegal drug? Not in an accusatory tone but, I don't know, treating you as an equal? Okay, not equal, but complete individual apart from your parents, our house and town, our privilege, all that stuff that must have overwhelmed you? Eventually we did learn you were lucky of a fashion that addiction in your case was another act of defiance more than slipping irrevocably into disease. But that should have prompted us all the more into really partnering with you, tackling something curable, not writing you off."

"Thanks, Dad. That's kind of you to say, but—"

"It's a little late," Walter interrupts.

"No. I just can't imagine I could have said anything at all. You did give me plenty of chances to share whatever I could. However does a kid put rage into words?"

"It was my failing, not yours," Walter says. "This is not an apology. Just a reckoning, Gavin. I had no vocabulary for this. Now I do have a bit of one. I know you do, too, without my help, because look where you've gotten yourself to."

"Now it's you that's a little wrong, Dad, and I'm the one who's right. Yes, it was Mom who had a backbone and ever so slowly I came to realize that I had one, too. In my way. And you, you gave me the gift to take myself seriously, at something or other. Just like you. You were really good at your thing. And you obviously loved it. Hell of a role model, Dad. And you kept yourself squeaky-clean. A beer here and there, but you took care of yourself, whether you realize it or not."

"I had no passion."

"The Bentley? The Benz? Hunkering down with Charles over your stocks and bonds? Give me a break."

Walter's eyes are watering. He no longer has command over his emotions, forever engrained to make decisions without interference. "We almost lost you, Gavin. So many times."

Back fresh from some program, well-fed, happy, and newly employed, driver's license reissued, dating a nice girl, modest apartment kept neat as a pin—and then Walter gets a call, his son in an emergency room, overdosed and barely salvageable, shattering his father, isolating Walter in a fugue with no boundaries or definition, a pure blank, until he can collect himself and reenter his office, his world, what he can grab ahold of and how he can hopefully continue to be of use to his family, his employees, reinstating the steady figure he has apparently been to others if not to himself.

"Yes, the drugs were deadly," Gavin is saying, "but they did fill a void. I look at it this way. Addiction gave me something concrete to overcome. And it was not just Mom's but your strength of character, too, however silent you may think you were, that became my lifeline. You know the funding of my scholarship aid project now—well, no way could I have gotten that off the ground otherwise. It's terrific I get a piece of your hard-earned affluence—so long as I can do something good for others, especially for kids who need a lucky break. But your guts, Dad, eventually I had to acknowledge I've got some of those myself. Taken a while. But how cool, better late than never, I get to thank you for that gift."

He makes a fist and aims it at his father. Walter gathers together the fingers of his right hand, trembling as it is, and thrusts, well, levels it forward until it meets the solid, clenched hand of his son.

When a man makes up a story for his child,
he becomes a father and a child
together, listening.

Walter composes a haiku or homily or pithy saying himself, spending most of his time under the influence of his Middle Ages sage. *Every person is like a snowflake,* he recites to himself. *Distinct while frozen and falling but melting on the pavement into the very same puddle as all of the others.*

~

His days proceed at an ever slower pace. If not numbness, which describes him for the most part, there is pain. The pain is mollified by lack of motion. At this he has become expert. His immobility gives rise to the flow of random thoughts, although these too can often be reduced to a mere trickle from their former rushing stream. He is presently considering his genderless state of being. How hard-wired are boys like himself to grab identity outside themselves rather than heed a more personalized calling. Work, money, provide. Survive! The Neanderthal man victor at the slugfest, he ponders, claims an additional acre and a half. What difference for young Walter millennia later? And equally valid, what difference for girls as they too adopt the cook-clean-swaddle of their assignment? There is the primitive source of power outside oneself, some seat of assignments, as basic to being alive as the next breath. And so it goes and has always gone. But don't the sexes have much more in common than not? Still ensnared by something or other without, at least at the core there is the exact same beating heart. Damned sick and tired of having his hand at the helm, the man should rock the cradle for a change. Here, Hannah, take the reins. Ready for that much human evolution, despite role reversal will likely be just as witless…

"Walter, not to offend, but let's try this sippy cup for your juice instead of the straw," says Irma soothingly, handing him the next course to imbibe.

He accepts the baby-blue vessel without giving it a passing thought. No different from the spill-proof pee-pot for the other end, it later occurs, masquerading as a proper urinal when one's aim and coordination are taken for granted in the quotidian world.

Thinking of his genitals, and the outward difference of the sexes, it dawns on Walter why he does not fear death. *I never truly knew joy in the flesh,* he mulls over in putting to rest those mostly stilted moments of his sex life. *If that had been central to who I was and what I made of it, its loss could be devastating. But such is not the case. We cannot do it all. I've done enough.*

He closes his eyes as well as drawing a curtain over his thoughts of the day. Interesting how silent spaces are taking over the lapses of his mind. This he neither encourages nor resists. It is what is meant to be, for now. Hopefully, for good.

Chapter 20

Last night the moon came dropping its clothes in the street.
I took it as a sign to start singing,
falling up into the bowl of sky.
The bowl breaks. Everywhere is falling everywhere.
Nothing else to do.

It is perfectly still, everything surrounding him. If there is motion outside the picture window—clouds, birds, shimmering leaves—it is now beyond his field of vision or his capacity or desire to focus. His eyes are turned inward, as they have been for ages and will likely remain. So little, at last, for much of anything to register on that screen either. Nor does he give pause to a single sound. If a door opens or closes, it is very distant from connecting to a purpose or person, an action involving the present. He is too removed from an external event cloaked in something formerly meaningful. Interesting because the inner ears are intact. He recalls a visiting nurse saying when it comes to that, the likelihood of slipping into a coma, people gathered for farewells are urged to speak aloud, the nurse claiming their loved one can hear it all despite showing no other signs of life. And so he will hear it all. The neurologists were unanimous in that his mind would not be compromised though the billions of other bedeviled neurons would proceed unencumbered on their crash course. The voice box must be enough of a muscular apparatus that it, too, has finally succumbed. Paula, his ever-battle-ready Athena, refusing to relent even though he is within the one-yard line of losing the game, bristled in with the elegant, trim microphone that straps and anchors about his head during visits or other interactions. It amplifies his voice so he can be heard above his now-normal guttural whisper. But it's mechanical, no big deal. Not feeding tubes and oxygen masks, IVs and other insults that would make of his airy large room an IC unit for those hanging on by a thread. Such would force him to blink at the whirligig of digital dials and twinkling lights as if his final resting place was a sideshow at an amusement park for the benefit of onlookers, certainly not himself.

He can reach for the sippy cup, he can reach for the tankard of cool water with its straw. Trembling or not, he can still serve himself, thank you very much.

How did I get so lucky? Walter thinks. *I have not shortchanged death but have had these years and final months when most poor souls, poor in every respect that I am not, are long since gone. No encore for them. For many that could be a blessing. I hope they don't begrudge me this time of my life. Surely many of them have been consoled, even cheered, by the prospect of uniting with their maker. Since that doesn't apply to me is perhaps why Fate, I guess I'll call it, offered me this reprieve. Self-destruct, if I must, but keep the thought waves flowing. The body mass is solid but must ultimately deconstruct into all of its multifarious original elements. The carcass is compromised by design. Brain matter, however, or whatever bounces between it, if not liquid, must be electrical, resilient, dodging the vulnerabilities of organic tissue to the bitter end. Strike that. Not bitter. In a way, dying has been kind of enjoyable. I've become acquainted with myself. Not such a bad sort. Easy for me to say, the only member of this jury, but no question, for good or ill, mine is the final verdict. I get the last word…until I can say no more.*

But there are more words, of course, like when the judge delivers his or her sermonette at the conclusion. Walter's is a scolding tone now. People have been dying forever, says that voice. This should come as no surprise. There is only one certainty in life: it ends.

Walter feels dampness on his forehead. His armpits are soaked. *Why am I sweating?* His breathing is no longer tranquil. *I'm resisting,* he realizes. Ideas are sparks just when he's supposedly put out the fire. If anything, there should only be embers. It is human, he knows, to cling to life in spite of everything. He is human, not yet a vegetable. Vegetative state, time to pull the plug. *There will be no need for a plug, even though I will not take all those pills I have saved. If this is what it takes to endure until I'm ready, so be it. Fan the flames. See if I care.*

Ideas are good! They make us human. Not that animals, even insects, don't think. *I can't know that. But I do know, or have come to believe, that life and death are not two separate events. They are two halves of a whole. For me, at least. Must be. Must!* Before this moment Walter has acknowledged that human beings among animals are likely alone in the awareness of life preceding us and following us on this planet. He has worked, yes, labored, to convince himself, however, that he is not summarily insignificant. Taking up his few square feet on earth has been justified as for any other soul. But conversely, he is not insistent on leaving a legacy of importance, influence, anything. The trials and satisfactions of his life have been plentiful. Failures, accolades, the whole lot. Why should he litter the Earth with his remains and hog more than his fair share of physical space? Do Christians believe you die a saint but commit the sin of vanity and go to hell after you're gone…the massive ugly mausoleum yet to be built?

Back to those lovable Buddhists. Or Hindu? He gets them mixed up, too far away across the globe. Reincarnation sounds wonderfully serene to him, so long as you can come back as a bumblebee or a peony and not yourself with yet another stage to learn, reform, an endless school with never a degree. Why can't we all simply decompose and become nutrients to materialize as the next bodies or blossoms? Isn't that good enough when it's one's turn to bid farewell? Now as for the multi-headed Hindu sculptures he's seen in the books of Eastern religion: he likes that step away from humanness, close to a gargoyle, still with eyes and arms and whatnot but only a pinch or two in the galactic scheme apart from an octopus. Polly said the Greeks were onto something brilliant beyond philosophers with their female-empowering Medusa and her head of coiling serpents. Multiple heads and sets of eyes, one head watching the next that is watching the next that is watching the next. It is not a solo brain in that business, at least a nod to downsizing the almighty Western individual.

All right, maybe God is merely the collective mind of the cosmos. It all gets boiled down to that. Nothing required of Walter in this regard. Nothing he has to seek or dismiss. Every breath pegs him as a participant.

He sips. He swallows. Not easily, but it works. He knows the time is near. Can he will it? Reach for it, or rather let it happen? The contentment of his mind merging with the compliance of his body to graciously concede?

~

PEOPLE COME AND GO, along with his strap-on microphone so he can engage in a semblance of conversation.

The days slip by, some of them noisy with the mental confabulations of his own making. But mostly time passes silently, stealthily, as if the clock is ticking away but no longer with rotating hands. He has accepted increasing painkiller but, as yet, there is no talk of morphine. The pain is not so bad. It's a way of life, his only one.

~

"HI, DAD. HOW'RE YOU doing?"

"Gavin! My boy." Walter grapples with the mic. "No, I can do it. About all I can do. But, hey, you're looking swell." Gavin nods. "Golly, it gives me a boost. My son in his prime. Take the place of the old man, right?" Gavin glazes over his father's put-down.

They natter for a half hour, until it's obvious Walter is losing steam. "I'm just dozing between daydreams, son. Really, it's not so bad."

They exchange some small talk, small perhaps for Gavin but for Walter, although at just a whisper, the words hold the weight of the world.

"Take good care of yourself, Gavin. You're worth it."

~

THIS MAY VERGE ON the maudlin, but, considering, what the heck if I sound smarmy even to myself. He exhales ever so slowly. Walter acknowledges he's had plenty to say. To others, for sure to himself. Hopefully this has amounted to more than words. Hopefully words have seepages that trickle between even the tiniest of dendrites to salve the soul. Hopefully there has been more to him, to everyone, than the body parts, especially the personality just on the surface but with all of its tending and grabbing the spotlight like the Master of Ceremonies saturated by floodlight in the center of the circus, captivating the audience sitting in the dark as if they are of little consequence, in thrall to the ringleader, nothing else mattering until the next marvel stepping into the spotlight, a juggling monkey, a tap-dancing dog, a flame-swallowing, bikini-clad beauty with a bosom to die for, a bare-chested he-man hoisting aloft a dozen dwarfs, an elephant en pointe, a prancing this-or-that so very outside even the far-fetched dreams of the ordinary person, the patron agog at what is possible in this world as an embodiment of human ingenuity for these stupendous others but no way for oneself.

Forget his journal. Here's one he memorized.

It's reasonable to be afraid of dying, but love has more courage than reason. A stone is not as frightened of rain as a clod is.

Thank you, Master Rumi, for your seemingly silly, innocuous, often goofy comparisons, but they have so helped me see the light.

We're all in this together, he wants to shout at the stadium filled to standing room only. But his talking let alone shouting days are over. He has repeated all this to himself inspired by the Persian poet. There is nothing more to do, nothing more to say. *I am covered with bruises, plenty healed over or not way before this fatal disease. They're part of the roadmap only I had to follow in the long run. And a long run this has been. I can let it go. Sad if I felt otherwise and compelled to hang on.*

Already said goodbye. In the best way I could manage. Why oblige them to enter that halfway house of conversation like this if I could leave with the best of their everyday bluntness, and mine? He feels an extreme heaviness set in, head to toes.

He fumbles with the headset and the laptop, which he had Tressie arrange at this spot. It will blow out his brains, the first stuff. And him, with hearing good and sound as ever! Came to love classical music, not with Polly at a concert or museum gala for donors but Ana the housekeeper's adorable little granddaughter, her recital of tinkling Chopin or whatever right here by his bed. And then Tressie made sure he was ever alert with music making up for her absence, the excruciating hours, days at first, between her massages, okay, sessions of physical therapy. Resuscitation, eventually, in truth. He felt like it was cheating on her, keeping the Carmen Miranda rumbas at bay and selecting Brahms, Mozart, the mellifluous romantics. But here and now he is playing the blustery Bruch, the infamous violin concerto, maybe his one smash hit, and blast it does, racing up and down the scales with the zing of a xylophone, sharp, grating, a thrill ride to propel him into outer space. It hums, it soars, it retreats, soars again, reaching to an orgasmic end but no, never that, it begins again and again, sweeping him up and over oceanic swells, in one good ear and out the other, all between he's reduced to rubble. Walter forgets himself. He is now nothing but the ride, the rush, the recumbent bike pedaling crazily on with no destination but the speed of the music, its fury and madness, above all, a celebration, a fiery, crashing, joyous thunderclap of final chords.

He is beyond relaxation, ready for a wonderfully deep sleep. His breathing drops to a near standstill. In sync with the gentle but lightly peppery strains of the next piece he's chosen, the delectable Mozart flute concerto, somehow selecting itself as the perfect companion if he were still to be awake. He is. But as the familiar, happy melody wraps itself around his very soul, meant to sing him to sleep, his eyes wedge open, and he beholds the daintiest of spiders—indoors or out?—working feverishly on its web in the triangle of picture window nearest his view. He hears the gorgeous music but is transfixed by the workings of the diligent insect, yes, with a mind of its own! It scoots back and forth to weave its tapestry of fine lines, shifts this way not that, maybe to muse for a nanosecond on its next move, who knows? It intends to capture its prey, its sustenance. It intends to reproduce, to stay alive, to seek mobility unobstructed by Ana's dusting—it must be in the great outdoors, and good for it. It has desires, motivations, purpose in its life. How marvelous, how reassuring, like the music. Like Mozart. Like all the geniuses who would mean nothing without an audience to bring the transaction full circle. To hear the music, to read the poems, to gaze at the stars. To make life, which is beyond meaning. The twilight of impending sleep is inching like lava over the whole of him. He will make it to the flute's third and final movement, the rondo, and does, which is followed by total silence. He grapples for the laptop button and presses it closed. There is just enough to his sight out the window to see two birds winging along, streaking across this last screen he's been granted. Of all things it is a small bird chasing one much bigger. Robbing its nest or threatening to? How lovely. *I'm the big bird leaving the picture. The little one, it's all yours.*

Author's Note

A FEW WEEKS BEFORE my husband, Ray Repp, was diagnosed with a fatal cancer, I completed the first draft of this novel. "Keep working on your book!" he urged, and I did. Although dying and death have shaped my life the past few years, this story is entirely its own, not his and mine.

My heartfelt thanks, as always, go to my supportive and loving friends.